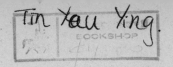

ELIZABETHAN LOVER

Rodney was looking at Phillida and did not at first notice Lizbeth's entrance; and then, as Sir Harry turned towards her, he glanced up and recognised instantly the girl he caught hiding in the lilac bushes and whom he had kissed light-heartedly for spoiling his hat.

She walked towards him and felt both embarrassed and amused.

'This is my daughter, Elizabeth,' Sir Harry announced, and two green eyes were raised to Rodney's face.

He had the strangest feeling that this moment was important to him, though why and how he had not the slightest idea.

Arrow Books by Barbara Cartland

Autobiography

I Search for Rainbows
We Danced All Night

Polly: the Story of My Wonderful Mother
Josephine Empress of France

Romantic Novels

Barbara Cartland

ELIZABETHAN LOVER

ARROW BOOKS

ARROW BOOKS LTD
3 Fitzroy Square, London W1

An imprint of the Hutchinson Publishing Group

London Melbourne Sydney Auckland
Wellington Johannesburg Cape Town
and agencies throughout the world

First published by Hutchinson & Co (*Publishers*) Ltd 1953
Arrow edition 1968
New Arrow edition 1970
Second impression 1972
This edition 1975

Made and printed in Great Britain
by The Anchor Press Ltd
Tiptree, Essex

ISBN 0 09 910590 X

To
MY WONDERFUL MOTHER
this my 50th novel,
with all my love

The author wishes to express her most grateful thanks to Mr. C. Christopher Lloyd of the Navy Records Society and Royal Naval College, Greenwich, for his valuable help and advice on ships and armaments of the Elizabethan era, and also to Mr. C. A. Lillingston of Harrow School for historical research.

1

The road was dusty and deep-rutted from the snow of the past winter. The horse had to pick its way warily, but his master raised his face to the green budding of the trees overhanging the road and drew a sudden deep breath as they came upon a wood carpeted with bluebells.

He had forgotten the miracle of spring in England, Rodney Hawkhurst thought. After months at sea it was breathtaking. It made him feel almost absurdly senti-mental and at the same time excited as he had been years ago when he first set out on a life of adventure. Now at twenty-nine he thought himself old and blasé only to find that the spring could arouse his emotions as easily as a woman might have done.

He drew his plumed hat from his head and felt the breeze upon his forehead. He had ridden hard and fast and had long since left behind his servants and the pack-horses carrying his luggage.

He felt the need to be alone. He wanted to think and to plan in his own mind what he was to say when he arrived at Camfield Place. He had heard many conflicting reports of Sir Harry Gillingham at Whitehall, but the majority had been reassuring. Sir Harry was rich and generous and there was no reason to doubt that, were a proposition put to him in a proper manner, he would agree to it.

It meant so much to Rodney, more than he dared allow himself to think; and if Sir Harry refused, where else could he turn for help? As he thought of failure, his lips set themselves in the hard line of obstinacy and his chin squared itself.

Failure was something he had not previously encountered in his life and he did not intend to anticipate it now. He must succeed, of course he must succeed, as he had done in so many other ways.

Deep in his thoughts he had almost reached a pair of high, imposing iron gates before he realised where he was. He had arrived—here was his destination and here was the beginning of his quest—a quest for gold!

The gates were open and the horse passed through them. The drive ahead was bordered by great trees and a profusion of flowering shrubs. There were lilac bushes heavy with purple and mauve blossom whose fragrance seemed to scent the air and made the traveller forget once again his anxiety as he glanced around him.

Laburnum trees were fountains of gold, chestnut blooms starred the trees like Christmas candles, pink and white. An early cuckoo called from the dark boughs of the cedars; there was a glimpse of lawns ahead, soft and lush as green velvet.

It was spring! and Rodney felt light-hearted and assured at the beauty of it.

Then, as his horse carried him forward slowly, something flew swiftly through the air, striking his hat and casting it violently from his head.

He turned startled, yet with that alertness to danger which comes to men who have lived close to it for many years. He looked not to where his hat had fallen in the dust, pierced by a fine arrow, but in the direction whence it had come. The lilac bushes were swaying as if someone moved behind their screening leaves.

With a swiftness that bespoke an athletic body, well-trained and utterly subject to the man, Rodney Hawkhurst leapt from his horse and in three strides reached the bushes; plunging into them he seized hold of someone who was hiding there.

He had moved so quickly that he himself had not expected that the fierce hardness of his hands would encounter anything so soft as a white shoulder. But before he had time to consider, he had gripped it fiercely and dragged its owner out on to the grass which bordered the drive.

He saw then that it was a woman he held captive, or rather, a girl. She was twisting and turning in his grasp and for a moment it took all his strength to hold her. Then, as his fingers tightened against her struggles, she was suddenly still.

'Let me go!'

She raised her face to his, throwing back as she did so a cloud of golden-red hair which hung loosely around her small oval face. Her eyes were strangely green, set beneath arched eyebrows which were drawn together now in an angry scowl.

'Did you loose that arrow at me?' Rodney asked.

Her lips pouted for a moment and then suddenly she smiled.

''Twas but a jest.'

Her smile was irresistible and Rodney found himself smiling back. She was a lovely, roguish child and he imagined she must be the daughter of some employee on the place; he could see that she wore a white apron and her loosened hair told him that she had no social position. But she was pretty—her breasts were round beneath the tightness of her gown, and at sea one had only dreams of fair women with which to relieve the loneliness of the long nights when one's arms ached to hold something warm and soft within them.

'If it were a jest,' Rodney said severely, ' 'twas a costly one, for my hat is ruined and I bought in it Cheapside but a week ago.'

'I could perhaps mend it for you,' the girl suggested.

There was no apology in her eyes and her mouth still curved in a smile which had grown mischievous, and strangely enticing.

'By Heaven you shall pay for it!' Rodney exclaimed.

'Pay for it?' She echoed the words in surprise as his arms tightened round her and he drew her closer to him.

11

His kiss was something she did not expect, for his lips found hers unprepared, unarmed, and for one long moment she was still beneath his strength. Her mouth was sweet and very soft. He could feel the beat of her heart against his, and then with a little cry and with a sudden violence which caught him unawares she had wrenched herself from his grasp.

Before he could stop her, before, indeed, he realised what she was about, she had run away from him through the thick leaves of the lilac bushes and was gone.

He knew it would be impossible to follow her and he felt, too, that it might prove a little undignified. Smiling, he returned to the drive and, picking up his hat, drew the sharp-pointed arrow from the crown.

For a moment he held the arrow in his hand, undecided whether to keep it or to throw it away; then he chucked it down on the grass and, mounting his horse, continued his journey down the drive.

The interlude had been unexpected and amusing. If Sir Harry's daughter was as attractive as the red-haired wench he had just kissed he would not regret the decision he had made before he left London. It was his god-father who had put the idea of marriage into his head.

'I have known Harry Gillingham since he was a boy,' he told Rodney. 'He is, if it pleases him, as generous as he is rich; but he expects value for his money, and as far as I know he has always obtained it. If you want him to finance you, you will have to offer something in return.'

'He will get paid a good dividend right enough,' Rodney replied.

The Queen's Secretary of State, Sir Francis Walsingham, smiled.

'Let us hope that you can give us the four thousand seven hundred per cent that Drake paid after his voyage round the world!'

'' Tis not as easy as it was,' Roger admitted. 'The Spaniards are growing wary, the gold ships are guarded; but if I can get my ship, I will bring home the booty even as Drake has done. I have not sailed with him for these

12

past ten years without learning something of the trade.'

'I would put up all the money myself if I had it,' Sir Francis sighed, his sallow, thoughtful face regretful. 'The last venture in which I invested brought me ten thousand pounds, but at the moment I cannot spare more than two. You can have that with my blessing, and an introduction to Harry Gillingham, asking him to supply the rest.'

'What will he expect of me?' Rodney asked.

'Yes, we must not forget that.' his god-father said, smiling. 'Harry has a daughter of marriageable age. There are rumours that he won't bring her to London because his new wife is jealous of her. Try your hand there, my boy. A man with a young wife is always ready to be rid of the tangles and burdens of family life.'

Rodney Hawkhurst had not been displeased with the idea. Most men, when they returned from the sea, wanted a home to be waiting for them. They were not concerned with the long, weary months that a wife must wait, lonely and anxious, when her husband was away. They thought only of the peace and comfort of their own homecoming.

"Besides," Rodney told himself, "when I am rich enough, I shall settle down."

He was shrewd enough to realise that a corsair's life was a precarious existence and though fortune might favour one for many years, sooner or later the tide would turn and one's luck would run out. He was far-seeing enough to plan not only for the present, but for the future. Like Drake, he wanted to buy a house and estates. Like Drake, he would take to himself a wife, but unlike that intrepid sailor, once he was rich, he would settle down and make a good husband and an indulgent father.

A turn in the drive brought Rodney in sight of a great home built of red brick and glowing in the sunlight of the afternoon. It was a house of gables with an exquisite oriel thrown out like a wing; a house of high mullioned windows, each of their diamond panes sparkling iridescent as a jewel.

Before the house were well-laid out flower-beds, edged

with rosemary, lavender, marjoram and thyme, while dark yew hedges were decorated with topiary work.

Someone must have been looking out for Rodney, for as he neared the front door servants came running out to take his horse and to assist him alight, and before he could enter the house, Sir Harry came out on the steps to welcome him.

Large and portly, Sir Harry cultivated his resemblance to King Henry VIII, not only in his appearance, but also in his private life.

He led Rodney through the rush-strewn Hall into the Great Chamber and introduced him to his Lady.

'This is my wife, Master Hawkhurst,' he beamed. 'My third wife, as it happens; and who knows how many more there will be before I die?'

It was a jest that must have been made often before, for while Sir Harry shook with laughter, Lady Gillingham showed not by so much as a flicker of an eyelash that she heard what he said. She was dark and pretty, Rodney noticed, and could not have been a day over twenty-one. She glanced at him from under her eyelashes and it seemed to him that her hand lingered a little longer than was necessary in his.

There was something in the expression in her eyes and the faint turn of her lips that was familiar. He had seen that look and that expression on a woman's face all too often these past months since he had been ashore.

He turned to look at Sir Harry again and saw that he was nearing sixty and knew that those at Whitehall who had called him an "old reprobate" were not mistaken.

'A glass of Charneco, my boy,' Sir Harry said. 'Do you find the journey from London wearisome?'

'Not in the least, Sir,' Rodney answered, taking a goblet of the dark red wine which a servant poured from a jug of Venice glass. 'My horse was fresh and it took a surprisingly short time. I am afraid my servants and the luggage are left far behind.'

'They will turn up,' Sir Harry said. 'My wife has made

14

every preparation for them, haven't you, Catherine, my love?'

'Of course, my Lord,' Lady Gillingham answered in a voice which purred like a well-fed cat. 'We only hope that Master Hawkhurst will be comfortable here, although after his exciting adventures with Sir Francis Drake, it is to be expected that he will find us country folk dull and staid.'

'On the contrary, Mistress,' Rodney replied. 'It is a joy to be on shore again and more than that to see the countryside at this moment. I had forgotten how lovely England—and all it contains—could be.'

He looked boldly at Catherine Gillingham as he spoke. She caught the innuendo, as he intended that she should. Her eyes dropped before his. Rodney realised all too well what she wanted of him. A young wife with an old husband—how banal and hackneyed a plot it was, and yet his instinct told him he must be careful. He must get Lady Gillingham on his side so that she would not influence Sir Harry against him, and yet at the same time he must not arouse Sir Harry's jealousy.

It was not going to be easy, he thought—and then the door at the end of the Great Chamber opened and a girl came in. At his first glance at her Rodney caught his breath. Surely this was the woman he had dreamed of all his life, the woman who would wait for him in that legendary house and estate which was to be his when he was rich.

Sir Harry bustled across the floor.

'Oh, here you are, Phillida, my dear!' he said, 'and here is Master Rodney Hawkhurst, whom we have been expecting.'

There was something in the way Sir Harry led his daughter forward, in the expression on his face, and the way his eyes were suddenly crafty and calculating, which told Rodney that Sir Harry already knew what proposition was to be put before him. His god-father must have hinted at it, Rodney thought, in his letter of introduction.

But now, as he looked at Phillida, everything that he

15

had come for, everything that he had planned, seemed for a moment unimportant. She was lovely—lovelier than he had ever imagined or anticipated that she might be. Very fair, with a creamy white skin, her hair beneath a cap of pearls lay like liquid gold against her head. She was tall for a woman, but her body was slim and delicately curved beneath a close-bodiced gown of satin, yellow-flowered. The sleeves were drawn close to the wrists and a lace wisp of a ruffle lifted above her shoulders to frame the round column of her neck.

Her eyes were the translucent blue of a thrush's egg, the nose between them was very straight, her lips drooping a little as if she were shy or afraid.

Rodney took her hand with an eagerness he was unable to repress and then felt rebuked because her fingers were cold and stiff in his, giving him no response and seeming rather to rebuff his impetuosity. Yet nothing mattered from that moment save that he could look at her.

He felt that his eyes must tell her all that his lips dare not say. That he wanted to take her into his arms, to feel the soft loveliness of her close against him, to find her mouth and hold her captive with his passion.

He was aware of a fire rising within himself at the thought of it. His veins were tingling and he knew the thrill of being the hunter with his prey in sight.

"I love you," his eyes told her. "I love you. You are mine. You shall not escape me."

But aloud he spoke conventionally even while there was a depth and a resonance in his voice that had not been there before.

Phillida said very little, uttering only monosyllables with downcast eyes while Sir Harry talked and Lady Gillingham strove to attract his attention.

How long they sat in the Great Chamber with its ornamental plasterwork ceiling and tall mantelpiece of mixed marble Rodney did not know. His thoughts and concentration were bemused by Phillida's beauty, and when finally Sir Harry drew him aside into another room where they could talk undisturbed, he asked first, not for the gold for which he had come from London, but for Phillida's hand in marriage.

'I thought it was for another reason you honoured my house with a visit,' Sir Harry boomed, his eyes twinkling.

'That is true, Sir. My god-father will, I think, have given you some idea why I sought an introduction to you.'

'There is a ship you wish to buy, I believe.'

'Yes, Sir. Sir Francis has advanced me two thousand pounds towards it. I can put up two thousand of my own money, and I need another two.'

'And your aim?'

'To do as I did with Sir Francis Drake on our voyage round the world—bring home the treasure of Spain for the glory of England and the discomfiture of our enemies.'

'You hope to find another *San Felipe*!' Sir Harry smiled.

'The cargo was valued at one hundred and fourteen thousand pounds sterling, Sir.'

'And you aim to be as successful?'

'If I am a quarter as successful, Sir, the shareholders in my ship will not complain.'

'God's life, no! You think you have enough experience for command?'

'I am sure of it, Sir. For two years I served in the Queen's ships. I bought myself free to sail with Drake on the *Golden Hind*. I was with him last year when he captured the *San Felipe*. Now I crave to be on my own. I wish to make a fortune—and to make it quickly.'

'Surely there is plenty of time? You are a young man.'

Rodney hesitated for a moment and then spoke the truth.

'I have a feeling, Sir, that things will not be as easy in the future as they are now. If the King of Spain sends an Armada against us, we shall be at war, and war is never conducive to great profits or indeed to the finding of a large treasure trove.'

'Yes, I see your point,' Sir Harry said, 'but do they really believe at Whitehall that the Armada will come?'

'From what I have heard, Sir, there is no doubt at all that the Spaniards are planning an invasion of this

17

country. Every seaman is convinced that sooner or later an attack will be made.'

'Why, truly, you may be right,' Sir Harry said. 'Yet, personally, I am optimistic enough to hope that the Queen's diplomacy will be able to prevent it, even at the last moment.'

Rodney did not answer. He was among those who thought that Elizabeth's desperate searchings for peace were completely useless. Spain intended war and the best thing England could do was to realise this and be ready to meet her.

'If I give you this money,' Sir Harry said, 'and, mind you, I have not made up my mind yet whether I shall or not, how soon could you put to sea?'

'In under a month, Sir. The ship I wish to buy belongs to some London merchants. They will sell it for five thousand pounds, and I require the other thousand for provisions and weapons.'

'I see." Sir Harry scratched his chin. 'You spoke of marriage. Was it your intention to be married before you sail?'

'No, Sir,' Rodney answered. 'I intend to return from this voyage rich. With my share of the treasure I shall buy an estate and it is then I need a wife to share it with me.'

'By St. George! You are a very determined young man. You seem to have made up your mind exactly how your life shall be planned. Suppose you are killed?'

'In which case, Sir, I would rather not leave a widow.' Sir Harry chuckled.

'That is what I have always thought myself—that I would rather not leave a widow, so instead I have been a widower twice. Phillida is the child of my first marriage. Her mother died a year after she was born, begetting another child. She was a lovely creature, but perhaps too young when I married her to know the duties of a wife. She was but fifteen when Phillida was born.'

'Indeed, Sir?'

'I married again the following year. I am not a man

18

to live alone, and that I gather is your feeling, too?'

'I think a man needs to be married after he has seen the world and sown his wild oats.'

Sir Harry laughed—a great, rich laugh that seemed to echo round the room.

'By King Hal, I'll wager your wild oats were sown thickly! What were the women like in the Azores and in the Indies? Were they pretty? One day you must tell me about them.'

Sir Harry rose from his chair, moving his bulky form with difficulty.

'I will agree to your request, Master Hawkhurst. I will lend you two thousand pounds to buy your ship and provision her, and I'll take a third of your prize money.'

'How can I thank you, Sir? . . . and, my other request?'

'You speak of Phillida? There I can also give you a favourable answer. You may be betrothed to her, my boy. Your god-father has been my friend for many years —we were boys together—and I have the greatest respect for him. He speaks highly of you and that, combined with my own instinct where you are concerned, is enough. You shall be betrothed and Phillida will await your return as anxiously as I shall do.'

'I thank you, Sir.' Rodney smiled, and there was a lightness and gladness in his heart such as he had never known before.

Phillida was his; that fair, golden beauty would belong to him. She was like a lily, he thought, a lily whose soft gentleness he could protect from the roughness and coarseness of the world.

Yet he would not be able to protect her from himself. He was afire for her, and his breath came quickly as he imagined making her his own. He would be kind to her —but, God's mercy, how he would love her!

It was her beauty that he worshipped—beauty for which he had been starved for so long. But he would make Phillida's cold, pale perfection glow with a new loveliness. Beneath his hands and in his arms she would come alive. Her lips would be warm and her eyes heavy with passion.

19

He would teach her to love him, to thrill to him, to desire him, Phillida! Phillida! He felt crazed with the need of her.

Sir Harry's voice interrupted his thoughts.

'There is time before supper for you to come and inspect my horses,' Sir Harry said. 'I have a mare which I consider the finest mount in the whole of Hertfordshire. Would you like to see her?'

'I would indeed, Sir.'

Sir Harry led the way from the house into the sunshine outside. As they walked through the gardens towards the stables, Rodney was aware that someone was watching him from the bushes. He turned his head quickly and saw a small face which was hastily withdrawn, and he thought in that fleeting second he recognised the red-haired girl he had kissed in the drive.

He considered asking Sir Harry who she was, and then decided against it. There might be some rule against the children on the estate playing in the pleasure grounds, in which case he might get the girl into trouble.

For the moment he could feel again her lips soft beneath his, and the springing youth of her slim immaturity. It had been like holding a fluttering bird within his arms. She had been still for an instant and then she had fought herself free and fled.

Strange that the memory of her kiss should linger on his lips. He had kissed so many women; but this had been different—the lips of a maid, unawakened, as yet, to love. He could swear that this was the first kiss she had ever known. There had been a freshness about it that he had never known before.

He had a sudden urge to see the child again, to find out if he were mistaken and she was just a merry wanton.

No—he was sure of one thing—she was pure, and still a virgin. He could feel the quiver of her mouth, hear the quick intake of her breath, smell the fragrance of lilac—the perfume of spring.

Sir Harry was talking about his horses, his voice booming out monotonously so that there was no need for Rodney

20

to answer him or even to follow what he was saying. As they reached the end of the path, he glanced back; but there was no one in sight and he wondered to himself if the girl with the red hair was still watching him.

Actually, she was waiting till the two men reached the end of the path and then, as they disappeared in the direction of the stables, she turned to the boy lying on the smooth grass of the bowling green which lay hidden behind the lilac bushes.

'They have gone now,' she said. 'Do you think I can get into the house without being seen?'

'You had best be careful. If m'lady Catherine sees you looking like that, there'll be the devil to pay.'

The boy spoke languidly, his eyes closed against the sun, his head supported on his crossed arms, while the girl stood hesitating.

It was obvious that they were brother and sister; they had the same red hair, the same fine bones and clear-cut features; but there the resemblance ended, for what was lovely and feminine in the girl was weak and effeminate in the boy.

'You might go ahead of me and see if there is anyone about,' the girl suggested.

'I might,' he agreed, 'but I am going to lie here and think about my new poem—you know visitors always bore me.'

'What has he come for anyway?' she asked.

She spoke almost fiercely, and then one small hand touched her mouth and her green eyes, looking straight ahead of her, were suddenly wide and apprehensive, as if she were remembering and savouring again that kiss, the first she had ever known.

The sun coming through the branches of the tree glinted on her hair and made it seem alive, a glory of riotous curls. It was red and yet it held in it the burning gold of the heart of a fire. She was not exactly beautiful but, although she did not know it yet, her face would torment and haunt a man so that he could not forget her.

Suddenly she sat down on the grass beside her brother.

21

'Francis,' she said in the imperative tone of one who wishes to be attended to, 'I am restless. If only we could go away, if only we could get to London.'

'You know Catherine won't allow that,' he answered.

'Catherine! Catherine! Everything revolves round Catherine.'

'You are jealous of her,' he said. 'She is not too unpleasant at times.'

'You say that because you are a man. She is always nice to men. Heaven knows why Father does not see through the way she makes eyes and postures at them. Not that I care, but when I remember how gentle and dignified our mother was and I see Catherine sitting in her chair, lying in her bed and running her house, it makes me sick.'

The girl's voice broke suddenly. She put up her hands to her eyes.

'Poor Lizbeth,' Francis commiserated. 'Do you still miss Mother so much? 'Tis four years now since she died.'

'Yes, four years, and Catherine has been with us for two of them,' Lizbeth answered in a bitter voice; then she took her fingers away from her eyes and wiped away the tears that hung on her long dark lashes.

'It is no use crying, I know that,' she said. 'What can't be cured must be endured. Wasn't it Nanna who used to say that when we were children? 'Tis true enough. One can fight and struggle for things which are obtainable, but it is no use doing any of those things when people are dead. Nothing we can do can bring them back.'

'Oh, Lizbeth, you torture yourself,' Francis said. 'You have always been the same. You feel things too much. Let life take its course. It is no use fighting Catherine and it is no use fighting Father. Not openly, anyway. Just take things as they come. That's what I try to do.'

He sighed as if he confessed his failure.

'Yes, I know,' Lizbeth exclaimed impatiently, 'but where does it get you? Mother always used to say you ought to have been a girl and I ought to have been a boy. That is why she asked me to look after you before she died. She didn't ask you to look after me.'

'She knew you could do it very well for yourself. I'm lazy, Lizbeth, and I hate rows. I do everything I can to avoid them. And at the moment I don't want to do anything except lie in the sun and enjoy myself.'

'Yes, dear Francis, you are lazy,' Lizbeth said fondly, 'and if you were not, I dare say I should not be so energetic. 'Tis your fault that I have shot an arrow through our guest's hat. If you had been practising your archery, as Father told you, instead of lying on the grass, I should not have put up your bow and been tempted by that bobbing red plume going down the drive.'

She paused for a moment.

'Do you think he will tell Father?'

'If he does, he's a babbling knave,' Francis replied; 'but then you can never tell with these rough, savage men who sail the sea.'

'A lot you know about them,' Lizbeth laughed scornfully. 'Why don't you take a ship and go out and plunder the Spanish Main? That is what I would do if I were a man!'

'And a bloodthirsty sailor you would be,' Francis retorted. 'Hadn't you better be getting back to the house?'

'Yes, I suppose I must,' Lizbeth said. 'It means a scolding anyway. Catherine told me not to wash my hair and I washed it. She told me I was to stay in the store cupboard and put away her saffrons and cinnamon, and of course I did not do so, and she is certain to be furious.'

'Well, don't let her see you with your hair all over the place,' Francis continued. 'Remember what a lecture she gave you last week for not looking ladylike.'

'The foul fiend seize all ladies!' Lizbeth exclaimed. 'I want to be a man and ride away from here. I want to sail with Drake and go to Court and fight in the Netherlands and kill the Spaniards.'

'A delightful programme for a young lady of quality,' Francis teased.

Lizbeth stamped her foot, but only for a moment, and then throwing herself on her knees beside him, she ruffled his hair.

'And I hate you at times,' she said, 'and yet I really love you. You are the nicest brother in the world when you are nice, but when you rile me I want to fight you.'

'Keep that for our guest,' Francis answered. 'If, as you say, you ruined his best hat, he has every reason to be annoyed with you.'

'And yet he was not annoyed with me,' Lizbeth replied; '. . . he kissed me!'

She spoke the last words so low that Francis did not hear them.

He had closed his eyes languidly and when he opened them again he was alone, and Lizbeth, creeping from bush to bush, was making her way towards the house.

She reached it without being observed and ran upstairs to her own bedchamber. She opened the door expecting an empty room, but instead, her nurse was there, laying out a dress and muttering to herself as she did so. Nanna was old and her once rosy cheeks were wrinkled now like a shrivelled apple.

'Oh, there you are, Mistress Mischief!' she exclaimed as Lizbeth entered. 'Where have you been, I should like to know? Her Ladyship was crying your name all over the house and exceedingly vexed she was when you could not be found. And a good thing for you she didn't find you like that. What have you done to yourself?'

'I ran out of the store cupboard, washed my hair and went outside. It was a lovely day. Why should I be kept indoors looking at ginger, cloves, raisins, almonds, spices and figs, and all the other dull things which Catherine keeps in the store cupboard?'

'Her Ladyship's a good housekeeper, I'll say that for her,' Nanna replied.

'Not as good as my mother,' Lizbeth said quickly.

'Now, dearie, you know as well as I do that your sainted mother was ill for three years before she died, and there was a lot to be seen to in the house when her Ladyship

24

came here. She's got her faults, I'm not saying she hasn't, but she's house-proud and that's a virtue in any woman, and well you know it.'

'I hate her,' Lizbeth said.

'Hush Hush!' Nanna looked over her shoulder as though she feared someone might be listening.

'I hate her and she hates me,' Lizbeth cried.

'Why you can't be more like your half-sister I don't know,' Nanna grumbled, unlacing Lizbeth's dress as she spoke. 'Now Mistress Phillida gets on happily with her Ladyship. Never a cross word between them.'

'Oh, Phillida! Phillida would get on with anyone,' Lizbeth said. 'You know that as well as I do. Why, she lives in a world of her own. And she doesn't care what happens to any of us. If the house fell down, I believe she would just walk quietly out and sit among the ruins. She doesn't like anything, she doesn't hate anything, she just exists. If I were like that, I would throw myself in the lake.'

' 'Tis a pity you are not a little more like it,' Nanna answered severely. 'But there, you were always the same as a baby—screamed yourself into a fit if you didn't get what you wanted the moment you wanted it. Many a time I have told your mother, "That child will take a lot of rearing, she will"; and sure enough, you were the difficult one. Master Francis was as placid and happy a baby as ever there was, Mistress Phillida as good as gold, and you a little limb of Satan himself.'

Lizbeth laughed.

'Oh, Nanna, you would have hated me to be any different. You know you would.'

'I'm not saying I don't love you as you are,' Nanna answered, 'but I'm not so old that I'm blind to your faults, and there's plenty of them for those who look for them. Now hurry or you will be late for supper. 'Tis ten minutes to six and you know what your father says if people are late.'

'I will not be late,' Lizbeth caid confidently. 'Why have you brought me my best dress? I thought that was to

25

be kept for very special occasions.'

'This is a special occasion,' Nanna replied. 'With Sir Francis Walsingham's god-son staying in the house and as fine set-up a young man as ever I did see, too. You should be thinking of your appearance instead of complaining about her Ladyship.'

'Thinking of my appearance?' Lizbeth asked. 'Why particularly?'

'Because there is a handsome young man to look at you. It's time you were thinking of such things and not ramping about like a veritable tomboy.'

'Handsome?' Lizbeth repeated. 'Yes, I suppose he is handsome, but strong and cruel I should think, if he wants to be.'

'You have seen him then?' Nanna enquired, and then gave a sudden cry. 'And you like you were just now, with your hair all over your shoulders and that dirty apron over your gown? Heavens, child, what must he have thought?'

'I care not what he thought,' Lizbeth answered.

But she did! He had kissed her! She could still feel the sense of shock, the surprise and indignation which she had felt as his arms enfolded her. She had known the strength of him and then, before she could cry out or, it seemed to her, even breath, his lips possessed hers.

Never before had she known the nearness of a man and suffered his touch. She would have had her mouth like iron to defy him, but her lips betrayed her. He was like a conqueror and she could not resist him.

His kiss was unlike anything she had imagined or dreamed. It seemed in some indefinable way to strip away all her pretences and leave her vulnerable and at his mercy. It was not only physically he conquered her, but spiritually, for he took something that had never been given before. She had been kissed! She was no longer an innocent, or as young as she had been this morning.

A kiss from a stranger and a veil was wrenched away from her eyes! She saw herself not as a wild, irresponsible girl, but as a woman—a woman with a depth of

26

feeling she had hitherto never even suspected.

Lizbeth was silent as Nanna finished arranging her hair so that it was drawn back from her forehead and set demurely under a small velvet cap. Her dress of green velvet seemed to echo the colour of her eyes and made her skin very white as it was revealed by the low-cut bodice.

She looked demure and not without dignity as she came slowly into the Great Chamber where her father, step-mother, Phillida and Rodney Hawkhurst were assembled before supper. Rodney was looking at Phillida and did not at first notice Lizbeth's entrance; and then, as Sir Harry turned towards her, he glanced up and recognised instantly the girl he caught hiding in the lilac bushes and whom he had kissed light-heartedly for spoiling his hat.

She walked towards him and he felt both embarrassed and amused.

'This is my daughter, Elizabeth,' Sir Harry announced, and two green eyes were raised to Rodney's face.

He had the strangest feeling that this moment was important to him, though why and how he had not the slightest idea.

2

The dew was still heavy on the grass as Rodney walked from the house through the formal gardens and down towards the lakes. The cows were busy grazing the fresh spring grass and the deer lay under the trees watching him with suspicious brown eyes as he strode past them, too intent on his thoughts even to notice their presence.

He had been awake long before the first pale fingers of the dawn crept between the curtains which shrouded his windows. He had, though he was ashamed to acknowledge it to himself, been too excited to sleep well last night. It was not the excellent wines at Sir Harry's table, nor the rich abundance of courses which had made him restless, but the knowledge that he had succeeded in his quest and what he had longed for so ardently and for so long was within his grasp.

A ship of his own! He could hardly believe that it was true. Tomorrow he would go posting to Plymouth and set down the money which was required for the purchase of the *Sea Hawk*. So thrilled was Rodney by the thought that he had with difficulty prevented himself from springing out of his bed then and there and leaving for the coast.

Already fears were beginning to torture him. Suppose the Merchants did not keep their word and sold the *Sea Hawk* to some richer and more influential purchaser? Suppose the reports on her were not as satisfactory as he believed them to be? Suppose she was not as swift or as easily navigable as he anticipated?

Such doubts and problems were enough to bring him from his bed to the open window. He drew back the curtains and looked out. For a moment he did not see the garden below him, the great trees bursting into bud and the birds twittering from bush to bush; but instead he saw a grey, empty horizon and fixed his eyes on that indefinable point where the sea meets the sky.

How often had he watched for hours, days and weeks, longing for the first sign of an approaching ship which might prove a prize. The lowing of a cow recalled him to the knowledge that he was not yet at sea but in a rich guest-chamber where the silk curtains were embroidered by hand and the furniture polished until it shone almost as brilliantly as the mirror of burnished metal.

He dressed then and, creeping silently from his room, let himself out of the house before there was any sign of anyone else stirring. As he walked across the park, his mind was already busy with calculations of what he would require to provision his ship and, what was more important still, how he should man her.

It was not going to be easy to find the right crew with Drake and a dozen other redoubtable commanders laying hands on all the best men, especially those with experience. But somehow, now that the night was past, Rodney could not be cast down for long by the thought of the difficulties which lay ahead.

It was in itself such a miracle that the most difficult part of his task was achieved—the raising of the money for the ship itself. He might have appeared confident enough of his success, but underneath there had always lain with him the fear of failure. His god-father, Sir Francis Walsingham, had been kinder than he had dared to hope. Rodney had not realised until he arrived at Whitehall that every adventurous sailor could count on the Secretary of State's backing and support. Ill-health kept Sir Francis at his desk; but there, tortured by recurring attacks of the stone, he had, as so often happens with sick people, an insatiable desire for war and violence. The prudence of Burleigh and the unceasing manoeuvres of the

Queen to keep peace with Spain troubled and distressed him.

He believed that the only way to deal with Spain was to fight and conquer her. He had helped Drake with all the influence that lay within his power and he was equally ready to help Rodney, although he had decided at that particular moment to do no more than put his hand in his pocket towards the cost of the ship.

Drake was in favour again with the Queen and although publicly she still held out the hand of peace towards Philip of Spain, she was giving to the man whom the Spanish Ambassador had called 'The Master Thief of the World' a fleet of ships with which he could challenge the growing might of the Armada.

It was not the moment, Sir Francis Walsingham knew, to introduce another interest in the shape of a good-looking, attractive young man. The Queen, however much she tried to close her eyes to the truth, had her hands full with the preparation for war.

There was time enough for Rodney to come to Court when things were not so tense or so turbulent as they were at the moment. Accordingly, Sir Francis gave his god-son two thousand pounds, his blessing, and an introduction to Sir Harry Gillingham.

Six thousand pounds in all—Rodney wondered with a sudden, piercing anxiety whether it would be enough. Had he under-estimated what he would require? And then swiftly the worry that had come to him disappeared again. What did anything matter—provisions, hardship, even hunger, so long as he could know that the ship was his and he could be at sea, sailing across the white-topped waves of the Atlantic Ocean?

'Are you dreaming of a woman or your ship?' a gay voice asked him.

He started violently as he turned to see behind him Lizbeth perched upon the saddle of a white horse. She was in the shadow of a chestnut tree and so intent had he been on his thoughts that he would have walked right past her had she not spoken to him.

'My ship!' he replied and found himself smiling in response to the smile on her lips.

'I thought so,' she answered. 'Poor Phillida!'

There was something mocking in her voice which made him flush almost angrily.

'The two are indivisible,' he said quickly, 'for on the success of my sailing depends the comfort and luxury of Phillida's future.'

Even as he spoke he cursed himself for being so weak as to explain himself to this girl. And as if she sensed his irritation, she laughed softly; then with a quickness he had not anticipated she dismounted from her horse's back.

She was dressed for riding like a boy, in a doublet, short breeches, and long brown boots fitting close to the legs and reaching up to her thighs. Her cheeks were flushed, her eyes sparkling, and her hair was like a fiery halo above her white forehead.

'Come, she said gaily, 'I will show you a wild duck's nest. The chicks have just hatched out. Everything is very early this year, but that is to be expected.'

'Why in particular?' Rodney asked.

'Surely you know the prophecies that this year of 1588 is to be a year of wonders! Old Amos, who will be ninety next birthday, says local people have talked of it since he was a boy, and Widow Bellew, who lives in a cottage on the other side of the wood and who everyone says is a witch, prophesies that great marvels will come to pass and England will prove herself the greatest country in the world.'

'Let us pray such tales come true,' Rodney said, and he was not laughing, for like all seafaring men he was incurably superstitious.

'They say, soo, that Her Majesty's astrologer, Dr. Dee, has told of these things to the Queen's Grace,' Lizbeth went on.

They had reached the edge of the lake by now and she pulled back some rushes to point to the wild duck's nest of which she had spoken. There were a dozen chicks, bright-eyed and open-beaked precariously near the water's edge.

'Are they not sweet?' Lizbeth asked.

But Rodney was thinking of something else. He was wondering how the prophecies of which Lizbeth had spoken would affect him personally. He had known, when he sailed with Drake, how tremendously luck, either good or bad, could affect a ship's company; how fanatically the men believed in good omens; how even the strongest of them shivered at the thought of witchcraft. He had half a mind to ask Elizabeth where this woman who was reported to be a witch lived, and then, as he thought of it, she turned from contemplation of the wild duck's nest to look straight into his face.

She was much smaller than he was so that she must look up to him, and yet as her eyes met his he had the impression that she was taller and stronger than he had imagined her to be. It was not a mischievous or teasing child who looked at him, but a woman who, in her glance, held some eternal wisdom at which he could only guess.

'You will succeed, she said quietly. 'Why are you so troubled?'

'I am not . . .' he began blusteringly, and then his voice died away beneath the honesty of her eyes.

'You will succeed,' she said again. 'I am sure of it. I have seen many men come here to talk to my father and somehow I have always known those who would return successful or empty-handed. Last year someone came who, I was sure, would not come again. I was right.'

'But how do you know this?', Rodney asked.

'I cannot answer that question,' Lizbeth replied, 'but I have always known things about people since I was a little child. I used to be whipped for telling lies until I learned to keep my mouth shut and say nothing. I only know that what I see about people comes true.'

'And you are sure I shall be successful?' Rodney asked earnestly.

'With your ship, yes,' Lizbeth answered, 'but perhaps not in other ways.'

'What do you mean by that?' he asked quickly, impressed despite himself.

But Lizbeth had turned away and was walking back to where she had left her horse cropping the grass. She walked quickly so that he had to hasten to catch her up. As he reached her, he put out his hand and taking her by the shoulder, swung her round to face him, and then, as he looked at her, the words died on his lips.

She was only a child. He was making himself ridiculous in taking her seriously. Her hat had fallen from her head and hung down her back, secured round her neck by a brown ribbon which should have been tied demurely under her chin. Her hair was curling rebelliously round her forehead and it had escaped the nape of her neck from the pins which secured it.

She was only a child—an untidy child who should be at home studying her lessons rather than roaming unattended through the woods at this early hour of the morning. Rodney released her shoulder and put his hand under her chin, tipping her face up to his.

'You almost deceived me into taking your predictions seriously,' he said. 'Come, it is time we went back to the house.'

Her chin was smooth and soft beneath his fingers. For one moment she looked at him and then her lashes veiled her green eyes and she twisted from his hold.

'Breakfast and Phillida will be waiting,' she said.

'Yes, of course, and I am hungry,' Rodney replied with a false heartiness.

Lizbeth turned to her horse and then, as she took the bridle reins between her fingers, Rodney set his hands on either side of her small waist and swung her up into the saddle.

'You are light enough,' he said, looking up at her. 'How old are you, Lizbeth?'

'I shall be eighteen next Christmas,' she replied, and he looked surprised, for he thought she was younger.

She wheeled her horse round and before Rodney had time to say more she galloped away across the park in what he knew to be the direction of the stables.

Slowly he walked back the way he had come. So Lizbeth was nearly eighteen, he thought, and her brother Francis was a year or two older. He remembered Sir Harry telling him that last night, which meant that Phillida was twenty-one or twenty-two. He did not know why, but the idea annoyed him. She was old for an unmarried girl and he wondered why, with her exquisite beauty, she had not been married before.

It was one of those questions to which he realised he would not get an answer because there was no one to whom he could put it; and yet it troubled him persistently, like the buzzing of a mosquito. A lovely girl, with a rich father, near enough to London to be assured of the company of many young men—it was extraordinary, whatever way one looked at it, that someone like Phillida had not been betrothed before.

Then he remembered the glances that Lady Gillingham had given him and the manner in which she had shown all too clearly that she was not particularly interested in either of her step-daughters. That, of course, was the explanation! Rodney felt the frown easing from between his eyes. Catherine Gillingham had kept both Phillida and Lizbeth in the background and had done nothing to help their chances of matrimony.

Something that had happened at supper came to Rodney's mind. He had turned to Lizbeth who was sitting silent at the other side of the table and asked.

'Why are you called Lizbeth?'

'I was christened Elizabeth,' she said, 'but found it a difficult name to pronounce as soon as I could talk. My mother had the same name and it was thought to be too complicated to have two of us answering when somebody called "Elizabeth". Now it does not matter, I am the only one left.'

As she spoke, she looked up the table at her stepmother

34

as if she challenged Catherine; and the older woman must answer her:

'One Lizbeth is, I assure you, quite enough to bear with.'

The words were spoken lightly, but there was a touch of steel behind them and Rodney saw that in response Lizbeth was smiling that mischievous, mocking smile which he knew had been directed at him when she came into the Great Chamber earlier in the evening.

It was as if she had known that he was embarrassed at finding her a daughter of the house rather than the lodge-keeper's daughter. At the same time she had made it a bond between them, a secret bond, so that instead of saying openly they had met before they greeted each other formally as if they were strangers.

Phillida's beauty delighted him, and yet, again and again during supper, he found himself watching Lizbeth. Her face was unexpected. It was pretty and yet there was so much more in it than mere prettiness. Her voice, too, was engaging. He found himself listening while she was talking with her brother, a languid youth to whom Rodney took an instantaneous dislike.

He was not alone in this, he discovered, for later Sir Harry spoke disparagingly and almost apologetically of his son.

'He likes writing poems! Poems! God's truth, at his age I was full-blooded—either chasing a woman or seeking an opportunity for a fight. I know not what the young men of to-day are coming to, but an ode to a bullfinch was never my idea of amusement!'

'Nor mine, Sir,' Rodney agreed.

He could detect anger and a sense of frustration behind Sir Harry's voice. He could understand what a bitter disappointment such a son must be to a man who had always lived rapaciously and to a great degree glutton-ously; yet there was a vitality and strength about Sir Harry which made Rodney understand why so many people compared him with the late monarch.

He had a vast sense of humour and when something amused him his laughter would seem to come from the very depths of his protruding stomach. He would stand with his legs apart, his hands resting where his hips had once been, and he would throw back his head and the roar of his laughter would go echoing round the room. One would understand then that he enjoyed life, that living was to him a continuous feast of experience and interest.

Little wonder then that he found it difficult to understand a son languid and effeminate, whose interest was in scribbling on parchment with a quill pen.

There was another side to Sir Harry too. He was shrewd where money was concerned and with regard to obtaining an advantage for himself. Just before they retired for the night Rodney had caught a gleam in his host's eye as he spoke of the marriage settlement which must be made upon Phillida before the actual ceremony took place.

It was then, for a fleeting second, that Rodney had regretted that he had been so precipitate. There had been no reluctance on Sir Harry's part to give his daughter's hand to a man of whom he knew nothing save that he was the god-son of an old friend. Rodney had a sense of disappointment that it had not been difficult. He would like to have fought for Phillida as he had fought all his life for something he desired; and while he told himself he had still to gain her love, he was conscious of feeling cheated and also of being suspicious of Sir Harry's motives, whereas before he had believed him to be overwhelmingly generous.

'Breakfast and Phillida!' he repeated Lizbeth's words to himself now as he skirted the lawn and came through the rose garden on to the terrace of the house. Why had Lizbeth said just those words? There had been a sting in them, he was well aware of that; and even as he wondered, the woman of whom he was thinking came through the open door of the house across the terrace to his side.

Phillida was looking almost lovelier this morning than she had looked the night before. Her ruff was starched stiffly behind her fair hair and even her farthingale detracted nothing from the grace of her movements.

36

'You are up early, Mister Hawkhurst,' she said softly as Rodney bowed before her. 'I saw you from my bedroom window and hurried so that we could speak together before the others appeared.'

'You wished to speak to me alone?' Roger asked, and his tone was caressing.

Her skin was flawless in the sunshine. She turned her blue eyes upon him.

'Yes,' she replied, 'there is something I would ask of you.'

'Tell me what it is,' Rodney enquired, 'and I promise to give you anything you ask of me—if it is within my power.'

Phillida looked away from him across the garden to the park.

'My father spoke of our marriage last night,' she said nervously. 'It is just that I beg of you that it should not be too precipitate.' Her tone was quite expressionless and yet Rodney felt chilled.

'There is no question of it being soon,' he replied. 'I thought you understood that first I am going to sea. Your father has interests in my ship and I believe that what he has entrusted to me I shall be able to return a thousand-fold. It is only when I return that we can be married.'

Phillida's face did not alter and yet he knew that some of the tenseness had left her body and she was relieved.

'I did not understand,' she said quietly.

Rodney took a step nearer to her.

'Phillida, you must not be afraid of me,' he said, 'I will teach you to love me. I will make you happy. I swear it.'

'Thank you.'

She did not move away from him and yet he felt as if she had withdrawn herself to where he could not touch her.

'God's light, but you are so exquisite,' he exclaimed. 'I never dreamed of such beauty. I long for you, Phillida. Will you think of me when I am away from you at sea?'

She looked at him then—a glance which told him

nothing, but which somehow managed to make his words sound empty.

'I shall think of you,' she answered, as if she were a child repeating parrot-wise a lesson.

Rodney stood looking at her. He felt suddenly helpless. He longed above all things to take her in his arms, to kiss her as he had kissed so many women before, to wake within her a passion equal to his own, to feel the flame flickering within himself ignite a flame within her. And yet her very beauty, the gold and white of her, made her seem inviolate. There was a purity about her that he had never met before and before which he stood abashed.

'I love you,' he said and felt the words were utterly meaningless and lacking in conviction.

'When are you going away?' Phillida asked.

'Tomorrow!' At the thought of parting from her Rodney laid his hand on her arm. 'I must see you alone,' he said. 'Where can we meet in the garden or the house where no one will see us, where I can tell you a little of my love and the happiness we shall find together?'

She moved away from him then, slowly and still with that grace which made nothing she did seem abrupt or ugly.

'We must go in,' she said. 'Breakfast will be waiting for you and my father will wonder where I am.'

'You have not answered me,' Rodney cried hoarsely. 'Where can we meet together, if only for a few moments?'

'I do not know; it is impossible,' Phillida replied. She did not seem frightened so much as repelled by the idea. 'We must go in,' she added firmly; and before Rodney could plead with her again, she had moved towards the house and disappeared through the door from which she had come on to the terrace.

He stared after her, frowning a little, his chin square set as it always was when he was opposed in anything he desired. He was not used to women refusing him. He told himself that was because he had had little to do in the past with virgins and maidens, and yet his pride told him this could not entirely account for Phillida's reluctance.

Moodily and in no good humour, he followed her into the house.

All through the day that followed Rodney strove and manœuvred to get his own way and be alone with Phillida. It seemed to him as if everyone was on his side and willing to help him save Phillida herself.

When others were present, she was there in the room, composed and lovely, if, as always, a little silent and apart from the general hubbub of the family. But when they were not there, she, too, had vanished into some fastness where Rodney could not find her.

Even Francis, usually obtuse where the family was concerned, realised that something was occurring and said to Lizbeth in a low voice:

'What is Phillida playing at? She has refused to show Hawkhurst both the Picture Gallery and the Maze.'

Lizbeth linked her arm through her brother's and led him into the garden so that they should be out of earshot of the others.

'If ever there was a reluctant sweetheart it is Phillida.'

'But why?' Francis asked. ' 'Tis time she was wed—she cannot wish to die an old maid.'

'I do not understand her,' Lizbeth answered, 'and never have. You would have thought she would have found Mister Hawkhurst attractive enough.'

'Personally I find him a bore,' Francis answered. 'I hate these hearty buccaneers, but women like such men and Phillida should be no exception.'

Lizbeth shrugged her shoulders. She was looking unusually tidy and demure. Nanna had scolded her for going riding so early in the morning and had made her change into one of her best dresses and had braided her hair so tightly that even her most rebellious curls could not fight themselves free.

She and Francis had reached the edge of the herb garden where the yew hedge divided it. They turned and looked back to where the rest of the family were seated around the sundial, Phillida busy with her embroidery, Catherine Gillingham watching Rodney's efforts with a spiteful look on her face, Sir Harry, quite unaware of what was happening, telling story after story and laughing heartily at his own jokes.

It was a pretty, domestic picture from where Lizbeth and Francis stood—if one was not aware of the undercurrents seething beneath the surface.

'Walk with me to the gate,' Francis said hurriedly.

'Why the gate?' Lizbeth asked.

'I am going for a walk,' Francis replied in a voice which told Lizbeth all too clearly that something else was intended.

'You are not,' she cried. 'I know exactly where you are going—to see Dr. Keen and his daughter. Oh, Francis! I thought you had given them up!'

'Why should I?' he asked sullenly. ' 'Tis no business of anyone else's who are my friends.'

'But Francis, Father has forbidden you to visit them. You know that Dr. Keen is suspected of having sympathies with Spain.'

' 'Tis a lie,' Francis said hotly. 'Just because he lived in Spain when he was a boy and was friendly with the Spanish Ambassador that is no reason to believe he is a traitor to his own country.'

'Dr. Keen never seems like an Englishman to me, and as for Elita, with her dark eyes and jet-black hair, she is a Spaniard if ever there was one.'

'Her grandmother was Spanish,' Francis said, 'but that does not make her a Spaniard.'

'Did she tell you that?' Lizbeth said interestedly. 'I thought they always denied having any Spanish blood.'

'They are not so stupid as not to tell the truth when there is nothing to hide,' Francis said. 'Elita's grandmother was Spanish. That was why Dr. Keen went out to stay in Spain after he had married Elita's mother. They came back about fifteen years ago and have lived in this country ever since. It is wicked the way people try to slander decent, patriotic citizens for no reason other than that their hair is dark.'

'All the same, Father has forbidden you to see them,' Lizbeth said.

'I am interested in Dr. Keen's experiments. He lets me watch him in his laboratory. I am no good at that sort of thing, but it interests me enormously.'

'Does Elita watch with you?' Lizbeth asked.

'What if she does?' Francis said sullenly. 'God's pity, Lizbeth, but I thought you would understand and stand by me, if no one else would.'

'I do understand, Francis. We cannot help where we love or whom, but be careful Father does not find you out. He is angry as it is, because you dislike all the things he cares for; and he is suspicious of Dr. Keen for all the Queen has been gracious enough to take an interest in his experiments. He is afraid you are falling in love with Elita and so am I.'

'And if I am in love with her, what can you do about it?' Francis said angrily.

'Nothing at all,' Lizbeth answered, "but oh! Francis, take care of yourself.'

'Pray do not be frightened for me,' Francis answered. 'Father will not find me out. And I am going to visit Dr. Keen and nobody in this world can stop me.'

He spoke so loudly and angrily that Lizbeth put her fingers to his lips.

'Hush,' she said 'your voice will carry and Father will be curious about what you are saying.'

'I am incensed with it all. Help me, little sister. When I go back to Oxford in a month's time, I shall not see Elita all the summer. Help me, there's no one else I can trust.'

His appeal melted away all Lizbeth's opposition, as he had known it would. He was weak and spineless and all his life he had relied on other people to cosset him and fight his battles for him and make life comfortable with the least exertion on his part.

His affection for the Keens was the most important thing that had ever happened in his life. For the first time he was making decisions for himself and even daring his father's anger in continuing a friendship that had been forbidden. And yet even in his new strength he must ease the burden of it upon his sister.

'Hasten your return, Francis,' Lizbeth said as they reached the gates. 'Promise me you will not be away for long.'

'I will be back before Father misses me,' Francis promised, and she watched him stride down the road towards the Keens' house, which was about half a mile distant.

She watched him go with a beating heart. She had no liking herself for the Keens, and yet she told herself it was not for her to thrust her opinions upon Francis—a new Francis, aggressive and defiant, whom she had never known before. Yet she was sure in her heart that her father was right. Dr. Keen, for all he was a brilliant chemist, was not the sort of man one would trust. He had been close friends with Don Bernardino de Mendoza, the Spanish Ambassador who had recently been drummed out of the country for complicity in the Throckmorton conspiracy.

Lizbeth did not trust Dr. Keen nor his daughter. She had never liked Elita though she had known her for many years, in fact, ever since the Keens had come to live near to Camfield Place. She had the dark hair, flashing dark eyes and olive complexion of a typical Spanish girl; she was bold and flirtatious in her manner and Lizbeth could see quite clearly how Francis, weak and inexperienced where women were concerned, could be flattered by her interest in him.

Lizbeth's face was worried as she walked slowly back up the garden to where the family was seated beside the sundial.

' 'Tis cold,' she heard Catherine say pettishly as she neared them. 'I shall return to the house. April sunshine is always deceptive and it is easy enough to catch a chill if one trusts it too far.'

'I will come with you,' Phillida said, rising to her feet.

'Will you not show me the dovecot?' Rodney asked almost desperately. 'Your father tells me you have over a thousand doves there. I would like to see them.'

'Father can show them to you so much better than I can,' Phillida answered, and Sir Harry, without realising what was occurring, agreed heartily with his daughter.

'I've made a study of the birds,' he said. 'Come, Hawkhurst, I would like you to see them. God's death, but I often wonder what we would do without doves in the winter, and our cook makes the best pie of them I have ever tasted. Is that not the truth, Catherine, my dear?'

But Catherine was not listening to him. She had turned to Lizbeth.

'Where is Francis?' she asked.

There was something in her voice and in her eyes which told Lizbeth all too surely that her stepmother guessed where Francis had gone. It was Catherine who had goaded Sir Harry into forbidding Francis the Keens' house in the first place. It was Catherine who would make trouble now, if she could be sure that Francis had disobeyed his father.

'Francis has gone to the stables,' Lizbeth lied. 'He wishes to mount the new grey which Father was talking about last night.'

She saw the suspicion in Catherine's eyes change to uncertainty, while Sir Harry roared out his approval.

'By my beard, I'll make a horseman of the boy yet,' he smiled. 'If he can ride the grey, I'll make him a present of it. How would that be for a birthday present?'

'Francis would be delighted, Father.'

Lizbeth felt miserable, even as she spoke. Francis was afraid of the grey horse, she knew that.

'We won't tell him yet,' Sir Harry said; 'we will keep it as a surprise. In the meantime, we will see how he manages the animal.'

He turned as if he would go to the stables.

'No, do not go and watch him, Father,' Lizbeth said quickly. 'You know how nervous Francis is. He would fall off for a certainty if you were there. Besides, Master Hawkhurst wants you to show him the dovecot.'

She looked towards Rodney as she spoke and he heard the appeal in her voice, and saw an expression of almost

43

pleading in her eyes. Instinctively he responded to it.

A woman in trouble or in need of his strength and protection was something he could never resist. It flattered his vanity, now, that Lizbeth should beg his help.

How pretty she was, he thought. He would like to put his arms round her and tell her that he would chase away her troubles, whatever they might me. Was her heart beating as quickly as when he had last felt it thudding against his breast?

He smiled at the thought, smiled also to Lizbeth and turned to her father.

'Yes, do show me the dovecot, Sir Harry,' he said.

'Well, of course, if you are really interested," Sir Harry conceded. 'Are you coming, Phillida?'

But Phillida had gathered her embroidery together and, rising to her feet, was following her stepmother up the path towards the house.

'If you will excuse me, Father,' she answered, 'I would rather go into the house. 'Tis cold, and I have no liking for the dovecot.'

3

Lizbeth lay in the dark and listened. There was only the silence of the great house, which had long been closed for the night. Outside she could hear the hoot of an owl and occasionally far away in the woods the bark of a fox and the high scream of a jay.

They were the usual sounds she heard at night when she was awake, sounds which were not only familiar, but dear so that often she deliberately lay awake to listen for them, feeling they were part of her life and being proud that she could identify each sound.

But to-night she was listening for other noises and she lay rigid in the softness of her bed, waiting for the soft creaking of a door and for footsteps coming up the broad oak stairs. She had heard footsteps descending those same stairs two or three hours earlier, and wondering who could be creeping about in the darkness of the night, she had opened her door and looked down the passage.

She had just a glimpse of a figure with a lighted taper in his hand disappearing round the bend of the staircase. That brief glimpse had been enough for her to recognise Francis wearing his cloak and hat. She had resisted an impulse to run after him and to ask him where he was going; for she knew the answer well enough.

It was the risk he took which horrified her; it was still early enough for her father to be awake and to hear, as she had done, the opening of Francis' bedroom door and the sound of his footsteps descending the stairs. But she knew that nothing she could say would deter her brother from his purpose and to argue would only increase the danger of his being discovered.

Softly she closed her door and forced herself to go back and lie down on her bed. Yet from that moment it was impossible for her to sleep. In her mind she followed Francis across the garden and out through the lodge gates. It would not take him long to walk to the Keens' house; and there her imagination ceased to guide her and she was beset by innumerable questions.

Was it a party that had drawn Francis from his home to-night on so late a visit to his friends, or was it something far more sinister? Lizbeth had heard her father's arguments against Dr. Keen too often for her to forget them. There was no doubt that the Doctor was a clever man. The results of his experiments had brought him both scientific and social recognition, and yet there had always been something strange and slightly suspicious about him.

He spoke very seldom of his life before he had settled in England, but it was understood that he had lived for many years in Spain. Local gossip related that he had friends who visited him late at night, cloaked and masked; and that, when visitors stayed with him, they were never seen even by the servants of the house and were waited on only by the master or his daughter.

There were those who swore that his visitors were Jesuits, members of the Mission which had come to England in 1580 and aroused great alarm. Their aim, the Jesuits said, was to save souls and they were forbidden to meddle in politics; but the Government had denounced them as traitors and had declared that they were working for the destruction of the Queen.

Despite stringent penalties if they were caught, the work of the priests went on with striking success. Moving about the country in disguise, hidden in gentlemen's houses, they inspired Catholics with their fanatical fervour; and the fact that they were spied upon, hunted and persecuted only resulted in their being venerated as martyrs.

Lizbeth knew it would be disastrous for her brother to

be discovered associating with Jesuits either at Dr. Keen's house or elsewhere. It was for Sir Harry Gillingham, as Lord Lieutenant of the County, not only to uphold the Queen's dignity, but also to ferret out and destroy her enemies.

He was, as he had said so often, deeply suspicious of Dr. Keen; but as yet nothing had been proved against him, and the Queen's interest in his work had, for the moment at any rate, lulled many people's suspicions into quiescence.

Lizbeth's dislike of Francis' being a visitor to Dr. Keen's house was also a feminine one. She distrusted Elita and believed that, if she was pretending an affection for her brother, it was not a sincere one. Elita would demand virility and passion from a man; and Francis' pale posturings would, Lizbeth was sure, be more likely to arouse amusement than any deeper emotion.

And yet there was no doubt that the girl was encouraging him, but for what reason Lizbeth could not guess. Elita was the first girl in whom Francis had ever been interested. Always when women came to the house he paid little attention to them, hardly speaking save out of the most ordinary politeness. When not at his studies, he seemed most content to be alone, reading or writing the poems which aroused his father's fury, but which seemed to give Francis, if no one else, a good deal of satisfaction.

There was a sudden sound outside on the stairs, which made Lizbeth sit up suddenly in her bed. Was it Francis returning? She hoped it was so, only to realise that what had aroused her was nothing more than the creaking of the panelling. All was silent again, but because she was restless and worried, Lizbeth rose once more from her bed, and crossed the room to the window.

It was chilly and cold outside. It had been raining earlier in the evening and the rain clouds were still heavy in the sky, partially obscuring the light of the moon. It was, however, possible to see the outline of the garden below, the great trees silhouetted high and dark around the house. There was no sign of anyone moving through

47

the garden or coming round the sweep of the drive.

Lizbeth sighed and then shivered a little from the night air. She could do no good standing there waiting for Francis, and yet she hated to turn away from the window with only that sense of anxiety and frustration for company. She wished now that she had run after him when she saw him descending the stairs, and pleaded with him not to go. Yet she knew he would not have listened to her. Like all weak people Francis could be incredibly obstinate on occasions.

There was another sound on the stairs and, thinking perhaps she had missed Francis' return, Lizbeth opened her door, hoping to see a flicker of light coming up the stairs. But there was only the darkness and the throbbing silence of the sleeping house; and then, as she stood there, Lizbeth heard something else—a strange, a different sound, but one that was continuous—from the room next door, the room where Phillida slept.

For a moment Lizbeth hesitated. She looked towards the Great Staircase with its carved balustrade and heraldic murals—if only she could see Francis! Instead of that the stairway was empty. She glanced in fear towards the oak door of the bedroom on the south side which housed her father and stepmother.

The sound from Phillida's room continued and now Lizbeth made up her mind. Closing her bedroom door behind her, she crept with bare feet over the polished boards. She lifted the latch of Phillida's door and entered. Phillida was kneeling at a *prie-dieu* by her bed. The candles on the table had spluttered low, but by their light Lizbeth could see Phillida's head bowed in her arms and her shoulders heaving with the storm of her weeping.

Quickly she closed the door behind her and sped across the room.

'Phillida, dear, what can be the matter?' she asked as she put her arms round her half-sister.

At the sound of her voice and the touch of her arms Phillida was suddenly still; her weeping ceased; but she did not move save to stiffen her shoulders and become, so

48

it seemed to Lizbeth, resentful of being interrupted.

'Go away!' Her voice was muffled but clear.

'No, I will not leave you,' Lizbeth replied in a low voice, 'not until you tell me what distressed you.'

Phillida raised her face at that. It was white and drawn and streaked with tears as though she had been weeping for a long time.

'I want to be alone. Why must you plague me?'

'You are unhappy,' Lizbeth answered. 'Is it for Rodney that you are crying?'

'You call him Rodney!' Phillida's lips seemed to twist as she spoke his name.

'Why not when he will be my brother-in-law?' Lizbeth asked. 'And do not weep for him. He will be a success. I know it as clearly as I know the sun will rise to-morrow morning. You know how I am always right about such things. I have seen it in his face—or is it some aura which lies about him? Whatever it is, I know for a certainty that he will return rich and successful, and then you can be married.'

Phillida had been staring at Lizbeth as she spoke, now she gave a muffled cry and put her hands to her face.

'Married!' She whispered the word and there was an intonation of horror about it which made Lizbeth pause and look at her in surprise.

She saw then that Phillida, still on her knees, was trembling. Her night robe was thin and the room was cold.

'You will catch a chill,' Lizbeth said. 'Get into bed, Phillida, and then we can talk. Come on now.'

She put out her arms as she spoke to help her sister, and Phillida, taking her hands from her face, allowed herself to be half-lifted into the big oak four-poster with its curtains of Chinese silk. Lizbeth tucked the sheets round her and then, pulling up the bed-spread, wrapped it round her own shoulders.

'Tell me what is the matter,' she said coaxingly, taking Phillida's hand in hers.

Phillida turned her head away wearily.

'I cannot tell you,' she said.

'But you must,' Lizbeth answered. 'There is no one else you can talk to. Catherine would not listen; and besides, I am sure you have no wish to tell her your secrets. Tell me, Phillida. It is easier to bear a sorrow if it is shared.'

'There is nothing to tell,' Phillida said stubbornly.

'Then why are you crying?' Lizbeth said.

Phillida tried to take her hand away from Lizbeth's warm grasp.

'You would not understand,' she said.

'Try me and see,' Lizbeth replied. ' 'Tis about Rodney, is it not? Can it be that you have no desire to wed him?'

She saw Phillida press her lips together and knew she had struck the right note.

'You do not love him, is that it?' she went on. 'Perhaps there is someone else you love—another man?'

'No, there is no one,' Phillida answered hastily.

'Then I cannot understand you,' Lizbeth said. 'If there is no one else, you should be happy to marry Rodney. I like him. He will be kind to you, I am sure of that, and he loves you.'

She shut her eyes for a moment. She could see Rodney's face as he watched Phillida intent on her embroidery; she saw the look in his eyes as he said goodbye to her. It was the look of a man who finds beauty a priceless treasure.

'I cannot marry him!' The words seemed to be wrung from Phillida's lips almost as if they tortured her.

'Why not?' Lizbeth asked. 'You will have to marry someone.'

'No! No! No!' Phillida answered; and then suddenly she was crying again, bitter tears which seemed to shake her tempestuously.

'Oh! poor Phillida!' Lizbeth's arms went out impulsively; then Phillida's head was against her shoulder and she cradled her in her arms, rocking her as one might rock a frightened child.

'You shall not marry him if you feel like that. You must tell Father and he must explain to Rodney. I

50

cannot believe he will force you against your will.'

Still Phillida wept.

'I cannot understand your disliking him so much,' Lizbeth went on; 'but you will find someone you like more. I thought that you might care for Sir Richard Sutton or Master Thomas Hunter who courted you last year. They came here often enough and yet they never asked Father for your hand.'

Phillida still said nothing. A sudden suspicion made Lizbeth ask:

'Phillida, did you send them away?'

'Yes.' Phillida's was muffled but clear.

'But how?' Lizbeth asked.

'I told them that I would never live with them as . . . as their wife.' Her voice was hardly above a whisper and yet Lizbeth heard the words.

'Phillida!' She was both shocked and astounded. Everything she felt seemed to explode in her voice as she cried her sister's name.

'They believed me and they went away,' Phillida said; 'but somehow I could not speak of such things to Master Hawkhurst. I felt he would not have listened to me. He wanted to be alone with me so that he could make love to me. He wanted to kiss me . . . he tried to . . . but . . . I managed to escape him.'

The words were whispered, but even so they seemed to quiver raw and trembling on the air. Lizbeth's arms tightened round her sister.

'But I do not understand,' she said. 'Why did you fear Rodney's kiss? 'Tis not unpleasant.'

'No man shall touch me.' Phillida moved now within Lizbeth's arms; in the light of the candles her face was very white, her eyes wide and dilated. 'Do you not understand? No man shall touch me.'

'Do you mean you hate them all?' Lizbeth asked.

'I hate them all,' Phillida repeated violently. 'No, hate is not the right word, for we must hate no one; but I will not be touched. My body shall be given to no one— it is . . . it is dedicated.'

'Phillida, you are not . . . a Catholic?' Lizbeth's voice was hoarse.

Phillida nodded.

For a moment Lizbeth was speechless.

'But how . . . how did you become one?' she stammered at last.

'You remember Mister Andrews?'

'Francis' tutor? But of course. . . . You mean that he . . . ?'

'He told me what I wanted to hear. I have always known that it was being kept from us. He took me several times, when we were supposed to go riding, to a friend's house where Mass was celebrated. I was received into the Church by a priest who lay there in hiding. I am a Catholic, Lizbeth, and I wish above all things to became a nun.'

For a moment Lizbeth was too aghast to speak and then she bent forward to kiss her sister's white face.

'You are braver than I ever guessed you could be.'

The gentleness of her words brought tears to Phillida's eyes.

'You understand!' she said, 'and I never dreamed I would find anyone in this house who would understand.'

'I cannot pretend to understand your feelings,' Lizbeth answered, 'but I admire you for doing what you wish to do. I thought that you had little interest in anything or anybody, which shows how mistaken one can be even in those one knows best.'

'I dare not confide in anyone,' Phillida said. 'Besides, it would be wrong to involve you in my secrets.'

'To think that Mister Andrews was a Catholic and we never guessed it!'

'He was desperately afraid of being discovered,' Phillida said. 'Just as I, too, am afraid that Father will find me out.'

'He will never guess unless you tell him,' Lizbeth said; 'but he will think it strange if you refuse to be betrothed to Rodney.'

'I know he will,' Phillida replied. 'With the others I was

able to speak to them first and send them away before they spoke to Father. Master Hawkhurst asked for my hand the very first night he came here.'

'He wanted Father to give him money for his ship and he decided to offer for you even before he saw you; but when he did see you, he fell in love with you—that was what happened.'

'It makes no difference how it happened. I cannot marry him. Jesus have mercy! I cannot. I have written to Mister Andrews asking him to help me.'

'When did you send the letter?' Lizbeth asked.

'Only to-day,' Phillida replied. 'I gave it to one of the servants to take into Hatfield. He was just leaving, so there was no chance of Father seeing it.'

'Or Catherine, I hope!' Lizbeth added. 'Catherine is far more dangerous than Father when it comes to being suspicious of or suspecting us of doing anything that is reprehensible.'

'Yes, I know that. She merely despises me. She thinks I am a fool—a fool who cannot get herself a husband; but she is afraid and jealous of you.'

'For no reason,' Lizbeth said.

Phillida's tired and miserable face suddenly lit with a smile.

'You are very attractive, little Lizbeth. I hope you will find someone who loves you and whom you can love in return.'

Lizbeth was silent, and Phillida went on:

'What looks God has given me have brought me nothing but unhappiness. If I had been born plain or deformed, no man would have wanted me. It would have been easy for me to slip away from the world and be forgotten; but as it is . . .'

She made a gesture with her hands.

'As it is, Father is proud of you,' Lizbeth said. 'He likes to see you admired, he wants you to be married.'

'Yes, I know that,' Phillida said, 'and he is ashamed to think I have remained single for so long. In some ways he thinks it is a reflection on himself. He is proud of his own charms and cannot credit that he has children who do not attract the opposite sex as readily as he does.'

'He has often talked about Sir Richard and Tom and wondered why they never came here any more. I wondered, too. Oh, Phillida! are you sure that you would like to be shut away in a Convent?'

'I want it more than anything else in the whole world,' Phillida answered.

Her face lit up, her eyes were shining and there was a look of spiritual ecstasy in her face which Lizbeth had never seen there before. She gave a little sigh. She realised that Phillida was asking for the moon.

Nunneries no longer existed in England. They had been abolished by Henry VIII, reinstated by Mary and abolished again by Elizabeth. The latter had made a clean sweep of her sister's efforts and the nuns had fled to Ireland and France, after which no one heard any more of them. If they communicated with their families it was kept a close secret.

Lizbeth knew there was not a chance of Phillida's attaining her desire, but she was kind enough not to say so. Instead, she put out her hand towards her half-sister and for the moment the two girls looked at each other, linked together in the dark shadows of the curtained four-poster.

'If Father should discover what you are he would kill you—I think,' Lizbeth said in a low voice.

'Yes, I know that,' Phillida replied.

She spoke steadfastly with a strength which Lizbeth had never known she possessed. Then, as they sat there silent, one of the candles spluttered in its wick and went out. Lizbeth remembered Francis.

'I must leave you now so that you will go to sleep,' she said to Phillida. 'Promise me that you will cry no more.'

'No more tonight. Thank you for comforting me, little Lizbeth. I somehow believe that things are not as hopeless as I thought they were earlier to-day. God will help me.'

'I pray that He will,' Lizbeth answered.

She bent to kiss Phillida, tucked her up and turned towards the door, blowing out the remaining candle.

'Good night,' she whispered, her hand on the latch.

'God bless you, Lizbeth,' Phillida replied.

Lizbeth crept back to her room. Her thoughts were chaotic and she wondered, as she slipped between the sheets, whether what she had learned was true or whether it had just been a strange dream which had come to her in the night. She could hardly credit that Phillida, the quiet, rather stupid sister of whom she had often felt slightly contemptuous, was really the same Phillida whom she had just left—a woman fraught with emotion, fighting a lone battle for the sake of her Faith.

Religious feelings ran high in the country and there was so much controversy that Lizbeth was content for it to mean little more to her than noisy, fiercely-contested arguments and lengthy, boring services every Sunday in the village church. There in the big family pew, with its high, oak sides screening them from the congregation, her father usually slept while her stepmother read from a book. Lizbeth could remember fidgeting endlessly as a child until, as the years passed, she managed to let her mind slip away to some imaginative place of her own so that she did not hear the long, laboured discourse which usually took the best part of two hours.

Yet now she wondered whether religion should have meant more to her. The prayers she had said as a child had seemed adequate enough; yet beside the flame which was driving Phillida into rebellion against her father and the life in which she had been brought up they seemed insignificant and paltry, like Francis' poetry.

Was Francis' interest in Elita love or the intrigue of religion? Lizbeth thought of her father's face if he should suspect that two of his children were caught up in the toils and tangles of Popery; and even as she tried to conceive his horror, she heard a step outside her window. It was Francis returning, she was sure of that; and when she hurried across the room and pulled back the curtains, she saw that her assumption was right.

The clouds had cleared a little from the sky and the moon, pale and watery, was shedding its rays over the garden. The shadows were thick and dark and the silver light gleamed on the wet paving stones and the puddles in the drive. Francis was just below her now. She could see the darkness of his cloak and hat pulled low over his forehead. He was trying the door, which he had left unlocked. Though he twisted and turned the heavy circular handle it would not open.

With a sudden fear which for the moment made it impossible for her to move, Lizbeth guessed what had happened. After Francis had gone from the house, someone had closed and locked the door behind him. She felt a sudden constriction in her throat and her heart began to beat very fast. Someone, then, knew that Francis had gone out!

She heard Francis turn the handle again, saw him push with all his strength against the door; and then, as he stepped back, surprised and alarmed, Lizbeth gave a low whistle. He looked up quickly at her window. She knew that he could see her face in the moonlight, and she set her finger against her lips. He understood and pointed to the door.

She nodded her head and moving from the window, snatched up a warm shawl which lay over the chair and wrapped it round her shoulders. She opened the door of her room—the passage was in darkness save for the moonlight coming through the high, diamond-paned window on the stairway.

Swiftly, on tiptoe, Lizbeth ran along the passage; then, with her hand on the broad oak banister, she started to descend the stairs. The rushes in the hall tickled her feet; they rustled, too, as she moved across them to the front door. As she anticipated, the heavy bolt had been drawn and the big iron key turned in the lock.

It took all her strength to move them, but when she had done so, the door was open and Francis stepped over the threshold, drawing his hat from his head.

'Thank you,' he whispered.

56

Even though the words were hardly breathed, Lizbeth shushed him into silence. She closed the door and strove to shoot the bolt, but it was too heavy for her. She beckoned to Francis and he moved it into place, making a faint sound which caused Lizbeth to say again:

'Hush!'

He smiled at her. It was as if he scorned her fears. He bent to kiss her cheek as if in gratitude for what she had done for him. His lips were warm and she smelt the fumes of wine upon his breath. He had been drinking, she thought, not heavily, but enough to make him careless and not so fearful as he might be at other times.

The most dangerous part of their journey now lay before them. As they walked across the hall, Lizbeth looked down at Francis' boots. Would it be best, she wondered, for him to remove them before he went up the stairs? And even as she considered whispering to him to do so, she saw Francis' eyes widen as he looked towards the head of the stairs.

The expression on his face made her look up with a sudden sense of horror and what she saw made her draw in her breath with a sudden, audible gasp. The door of her father's room was open and light was streaming forth from it on to the passage at the top of the stairs. For just one second Lizbeth watched it, fascinated. Then into the passage came first her stepmother holding a silver candlestick in her hand, and behind her Sir Harry with his night-cap on his head and also carrying a candle.

Catherine wore a *peignoir* of white silk over her night-gown and her hair was in two long plaits on either side of her face. Her eyes were dark and spiteful, her lips were smiling as if she was delighting in the scene that was about to take place. It was enough for Lizbeth to look at her to know who had bolted the door.

Sir Harry, despite the fact that he was wearing only a nightshirt, was awe-inspiring. He stood leaning against an heraldic newel at the head of the stairs, his candle in his hand, his face red with anger, his heavy eyebrows almost meeting across his forehead. He stared down into

57

the hall at Lizbeth and Francis and then his voice rang out in a sudden roar.

'Come here, both of you!'

It seemed to Lizbeth that the stairs ascended endlessly. She felt as if she and Francis would never reach the top. As they walked up step by step, Francis' boots making enough noise now to raise the whole house, Lizbeth could feel his courage and the elation and happiness of the mood in which he had returned home ebbing away from him slowly but surely.

He had never been able to stand up to his father. He had always been afraid of him since he was a little boy; and long before they reached the top Lizbeth knew that he was trembling and his lips were dry so that he must moisten them with his tongue, not once but continuously.

'Now, Sir, perhaps you will explain to me where you have been,' Sir Harry said as Francis reached the top step.

Lizbeth could see her brother's face in the light of the candles. He was pale now and his eyes were blinking as if they were dazzled and also as if he were ashamed. He looked stupid and insignificant and for a moment Lizbeth could understand what her father was feeling. Red-faced, pompous and overbearing, he was yet a man! In his youth he must have been good-looking, but that had not mattered beside the dash and courage he had shown, whether he was enjoying a fight or seducing a woman.

Lizbeth realised that, if Francis could say he had been to London to see some fair lady, or even avow he had been courting some village maiden, his father would forgive him and be proud of him. But it was not love which made him go to the Keens—it was something which she feared even as she knew their father was afraid of it.

'Well, speak up, where have you been?' Sir Harry asked again.

'To ... to ... to Dr. Keen's, Sir.'

'God's death! I knew it. I might have guessed that you would disobey my orders. I told you that I would not have you going there to listen to seditious talk, to be

58

involved in some Papist plot. I forbade you the house, did I not?'

'Yes, Sir.'

'And yet you have defied me. You creep out when I am asleep, leaving and entering the house like a thief or a servant rather than as a gentleman. Well, I must teach you a lesson, for I cannot trust you, it seems. You will not go back to Oxford next term, but you will sail with Master Rodney Hawkhurst in his ship for which I have just subscribed a substantial sum of money. We will see if the sea can make a man of you.'

'No, I won't go, I won't!' Francis spoke passionately, but his protest lacked conviction. His voice rose shrilly, the voice of a boy, not a man.

'You will obey my orders,' Sir Harry replied harshly. 'I shall send a letter to Master Hawkhurst to-morrow apprising him of your arrival. You will get your clothes together and start for Plymouth as soon as it can be arranged. In the meantime you are under orders not to leave this house. Do you understand, you are not to leave this house, nor will you have any communication with Dr. Keen or his daughter? That is my command. If you don't obey me, I will have you locked in your bedroom, and if necessary, chained to your bedpost.'

Sir Harry turned as he finished speaking and walking with a dignity which was surprising considering the circumstances, withdrew into his bedroom. Catherine followed him. When she reached the door, she looked back. Her smile was a triumph of maliciousness.

Francis made no effort to move when his father and stepmother had gone. He stood staring at the floor, his hands hanging helplessly at his side, his fingers clenched, but limply as if he had not even the energy to square them.

'I won't go, I won't!' he muttered.

Lizbeth pulled him by the sleeve.

'Come into your room,' she said urgently.

Shuffling his feet, Francis obeyed her; and when they entered the bedchamber and Lizbeth had closed the door behind them, he flung himself downwards on his bed, beating his fists against the pillow as a child might do.

'I won't go, I won't!' he said again.

Lizbeth felt for the tinder box and lit the candles on the dressing-table. She wondered what she could say to comfort Francis and as she walked across to the bed, she remembered her mother's words.

'You must look after Francis,' she had said as she was dying.

'Yes, Mother,' Lizbeth had answered.

'He cannot look after himself. You must remember that, always.'

Lizbeth was remembering it now. Francis could not look after himself. She sat down on the bed and started to stroke his hair.

'I won't go to sea,' Francis cried helplessly and miserably into his pillow; but he said it without conviction, for he was not strong enough to defy his father, and both he and Lizbeth knew it.

Lizbeth felt the tears gather in her eyes. She, too, was suffering.

'I hate them all. They are all against me, and I never have a chance to do what I want to do. It isn't fair. It isn't fair,' Francis sobbed.

It was not fair, Lizbeth thought, that there should be so much unhappiness under one roof.

4

Rodney Hawkhurst walked up and down the quarter-deck watching the last-minute turmoil of getting the ship ready for sea. Men were scurrying about the decks; the shrill whistle of the pipes, hoarse orders from the boatswain's mate and several round oaths told him they were heaving the pinnace up alongside.

On the quay were the usual crowd of weeping women and round-eyed children, their forlorn helplessness all the more pitiable because Rodney knew that many of the men to whom they said farewell were as excited as he was to know that the moment had come to leave the shore and take to the open sea.

He was impatient to the point of irritation with all the last-minute delays which invariably occurred and which, every time one sailed, were unexpected and unanticipated. Among the noises on the decks he could hear the baaing of the live sheep which had been brought on board at the last moment.

There was a litter of pigs, too, down below decks, and two or three dozen hens which he had purchased in the market that very morning, but which he thought now might have been an extravagance. Over and over again he had totalled up in his mind the provisions and stores he had sent aboard and had wondered if they would prove enough for the voyage that lay ahead. Among them were rice, peas, oil, candles, lanterns, lamps, sails ox-hides, hemp and sheet lead to stop shot holes.

He had spent every penny he could spare on the best

salt beef, bacon and pork available, besides six tons of ship's biscuit which the chandler swore had not been long in his possession.

Any man who went to sea expected incredible hardships, danger and bad food; but Roger was determined that as far as possible he would save his crew from unnecessary suffering. He knew how easily men got depressed and disgruntled on a long voyage and that the monotony and rottenness of their victuals had much to do with their ill-humour and petty spitefulness.

He had learned, when he sailed with Drake, to consider the well-being of the men as well as that of the officers. In most ships, the treatment meted out to seamen was unnecessarily brutal. Rodney was determined that on his own ship, while modelling his discipline on naval tradition and custom, he would temper justice with mercy and try, if possible, to lead his men rather than to drive them by sheer physical violence.

The *Sea Hawk* was not a pretty ship and Rodney had had no extra money to spend in decorating her, but she was sturdy and well-built, and his First Lieutenant, Master Barlow, had confirmed his opinion that she would be easy to manœuvre. She carried twenty-two guns, seven demi-cannon on each side of her lower deck, six falconets firing grape on the upper and two chasers of bronze on the poop near the helm.

Besides these more formidable pieces of artillery, Rodney had a number of arquebuses and an armoury of fire-bombs and javelins tipped with tar which had proved so effective when used by Drake.

The *Sea Hawk* carried a crew of eighty; fifty were good fighting men, seasoned and experienced, whom Rodney and Barlow both considered themselves extremely fortunate to have obtained. Nearly two dozen of them had served with them before and had been tempted to embark on this adventure by a promise of a larger share of the booty than was usual.

Rodney had indeed worried himself almost into a fever about his crew. It was not to be expected that he would get the pick of the best men when they had a chance of sailing under the leadership of acknowledged heroes like Drake and Raleigh. Men were also being taken up for the Queen's service for the ships which Her Majesty was preparing to put under Lord Howard's command.

It was Barlow who had relieved Rodney of his anxiety, and who had eventually collected a better crew than he had even dared to hope for. Ships' boys, volunteers and a number of craftsmen like the ship's carpenter and blacksmith made up the complement.

Then there were the officers: Barlow and three other lieutenants, Baxter, Gadstone and Walters by name; Hales, the Master; Simson, the Purser; and Dobson, the Surgeon—a reputedly good man although Rodney already had his doubts as to the wisdom of engaging him.

He was elderly for one thing, and had come aboard with bloodshot eyes and a thick, repulsive stomach cough which he attributed to a thick night ashore, but which Rodney suspected came from an undermined constitution. However, it was too late to do anything about it and Rodney hoped that, once they got to sea, this and many more problems would settle themselves.

The pinnace was aboard, the few remaining stores were being taken below. Rodney looked to see that the waterbutts were secure in the hold. They were one of the last things he had had filled. He knew only too well what the casks became like after a few months at sea—foul and alive with living things. It was always desirable to put off bringing them aboard till the last possible moment.

In a few minutes now they would cast off. A diversion was caused on the quay as a seaman, very unsteady on his legs, was half-dragged, half-supported to the ship by a painted prostitute whom Rodney remembered seeing around the docks on previous occasions. She steadied the man across the gangplank; then as he fell face downward on the deck, she shouted a cheery, if lewd farewell which raised a roar of laughter from the men working on the deck.

With her hands on her broad hips and her dress open

63

almost to the waist, the harlot exchanged a spirited badinage with those on board, which was listened to sourly and with disgust by the other women on the quay.

'Make sail, Master Barlow,' Rodney said sharply. He could delay no longer.

Everyone should be aboard by now; and as he thought of it, Rodney's expression darkened and he turned to walk impatiently up and down the quarter-deck.

He was remembering the moment when he must see Francis Gillingham and welcome him to the ship. He had particularly instructed Barlow to meet him when he arrived and to keep him out of sight at least until the turmoil of sailing had subsided a little.

'I swore I would have no damned gentlemen adventurers aboard my ship,' Rodney had cursed when Sir Harry's letter was brought to him. 'By my Faith, I have a good mind to refuse to take him.'

'But Sir Harry Gillingham is a chief venturer!' Barlow answered quietly. 'Suppose, Sir, he asked for the return of his gold?'

'I would tell him to go to the Devil,' Rodney replied; but he knew, as he spoke, that it was mere bravado and that he must do as Sir Harry asked, take his son on the voyage and try to make a man of him.

Sir Harry had not explained why he had come to this sudden decision regarding Francis, but from the tone of his letter Rodney guessed that something was amiss.

'The boy's got himself into trouble of some sort,' he growled to Barlow, 'but we've no time to play nursemaid to some puling brat.'

It was true that Rodney had long ago decided to have no gentlemen adventurers aboard the *Sea Hawk*. They were invariably a nuisance, for, impatient only for the treasure which the voyage would bring them, they were usually too sea-sick and undisciplined to be of any real use in the management of a ship.

Rodney was also well aware that this voyage was likely to prove both dangerous and precarious. One ship on its own was very vulnerable to attack; and though he had every hope and confidence that they would quickly capture a smaller ship or a pinnace, that was small comfort in the initial stages of their journey. There was also the other side of the picture—they might be sunk or taken prisoner and there would be no one to come to their rescue.

The ship, too, was full to capacity, and although there was a spare sleeping cabin alongside his own aft under the poop, Rodney had decided to keep it empty, thinking there was every likelihood of its being used by some important prisoner. If not, it always could be useful for storing part of the spoils.

However, it was no use complaining. There was nothing he could do about it save try and sail sooner than he planned and hope that Francis would reach Plymouth too late.

There was a shout to man the main topsail halliards; Rodney watched a rush up the rigging as the men scurried from the halliards to the braces while a roar forward told him that the moorings were slipped. He licked his finger and held it up to see if the wind was freshening—rounding Devil's Point was not going to be easy. Then with the yards braced round the *Sea Hawk* turned to starboard and slowly gathered way.

There was a sudden wail from the quayside, the children were fluttering their handkerchiefs excitedly, the wives holding them to their eyes. For a number of them it was the last time they would ever see their men alive.

'Keep your eyes inboard, there,' yelled a Petty Officer, for every man's attention was needed for the business in hand—that of trimming the sails to the wind.

Rodney felt the ship heel over; Barlow was directing her course as close to the wind as she would lie; and suddenly as he felt the heave and swell of the waves, heard the familiar slap of the sails and the rattling of the blocks and the creak of the timbers, he felt excitement sweep over him, so that he must swallow hard and press his lips together to prevent himself joining in the cheer that the men raised as Stonehouse Bill opened up before them.

They were off! Adventure lay ahead, England lay behind.

Rodney had a sudden vision of Phillida. For a moment she seemed to stand beside him, so beautiful that she dazzled him. As he said good-bye to England, so he wished now he could say good-bye to Phillida—not as he had done on leaving Camfield, touching her cold hand to his lips, but as his seamen said goodbye to their sweethearts and wives.

He should have kissed Phillida on the mouth; he should have infused her with his own fire. Now in retrospect he could hardly credit that he had been so foolish as to let her keep him at arms' length.

Despite every possible manœuvre and plea on his part, she had evaded being alone with him. Rodney cursed himself for a nitwit and a weakling. He should have forced himself upon her, even gone to her bedchamber if necessary—it would not have been the first time he had overpowered a woman's protests and her reluctance.

'Phillida! Phillida!' he whispered her name to the breeze; and then, uninvited, Lizbeth's face was before him, her eyes alight with mischief, her lips red, mocking. . . .

'Curse the wench!

Rodney forced himself to think again of Phillida, but the moment of her nearness was past and he forgot her a second later.

The sky had been grey and overcast all day, but now the sun broke through, seeming to bring a message of hope and cheer. It glittered on the waves, dazzling Rodney's eyes as he glanced aloft.

'Set the topsails, Master Barlow,' he said.

With the wind blowing fresher as they neared the open sea they headed into the Sound. The waves were under her bows and under the pressure of increased sail the *Sea Hawk* made her first big roll. The men were beginning to be seasick and Rodney congratulated himself that it was many years indeed since he had known the ignominy of staggering and lurching towards the rails. He had not, however, forgotten the misery of his first voyage when he had been so sick that he had prayed that death might take him. He had learned in the years that followed that many men, however experienced sailors they might be, were always sick in the first few hours of a voyage, before they got their sea-legs.

He must remember to tell Barlow a little later on, he thought, not to push the sea-sick men too hard. The Petty Officers were being very free with the rope's end he noticed, and he decided that he would speak to all those in authority and tell them that he would have no unnecessary cruelty on board.

The loyalty and affection which Drake inspired was, Rodney knew, to a great extent due to his innate kindliness. The men did not expect it, and it never ceased to surprise them that someone so successful and so fearless as Drake could show them personal consideration and have, what was more, an individual knowledge of every man under his command.

Rodney had sworn to model himself on the same lines; but now he felt almost a sense of helplessness as he watched the men hurrying about the deck and swarming up the rigging. To them he was a figurehead, the Captain of the ship and of their fate, someone who must be obeyed, hardly human, hardly of the same flesh and blood as themselves.

He had got to get to know them; he had got to teach them to trust him. They knew he was untried, they knew, even better than he did, the perils and pitfalls of his first command. And yet no fear, no anxiety could dim the elation in Rodney's heart. They were at sea, the sails were full-bellied.

He had never known such a thrill, such a sense of wild excitement as filled him at this moment. The *Sea Hawk* was his desire as surely as if she were a woman who had surrendered herself to him. He felt his whole being tingle with the triumphant joy of a man who has fought and conquered—a man who has proved his manhood.

He thought not of Phillida nor of any woman at that

moment; he was infatuated by a mistress more exacting, more temperamental and more unpredictable than any he had ever known and her name was the *Sea Hawk*.

For a long time he stood watching the sea ahead, feeling the wind on his face. Then at length he realised that the wind was still freshening and there was every chance of their running into bad weather before they reached the Bay of Biscay.

'Get the foresail in, Master Baxter,' he said to the Lieutenant on watch; then, turning, he found his way to the after cabin.

It was small but comfortable, furnished with an oak table and carved oak chairs. Fortunately the furniture had been included in the purchase price of the ship or Rodney would have been hard put to it to afford such luxury. He was glad, however, that the *Sea Hawk* was well fitted up. It was an important part of the Captain's dignity. Drake had insisted on both pomp and finery, and aboard his flagship trumpets announced his dinner and supper hour. He carried fiddlers to make him music and the vessels of his table, and even of his kitchen, were pure silver.

All those who served with Drake boasted, when they were ashore, of the silver service which their Captain used when he dined, and of the fine linen on which he wiped his hands after he had dipped them in the perfumed water which he said the Queen herself had given him. It was all a show of strength, Rodney knew.

He could not attempt to emulate the magnificence of his former Captain, but he gave a sigh of satisfaction as he sat down in the big armchair at the end of the table and rang the small hand-bell which lay on the polished surface. The man Hapley, whom he had appointed to be his personal servant, came running.

He was a tall, good-tempered-looking Cornishman who had been aboard the *Golden Hind* but who, when the voyage was ended, had offered himself to Rodney with an eagerness that he could not help but find flattering. Hapley had a big, muscular body and fists which would make

68

have been his to command. He pushed back his chair.

'Good evening, Master Gillingham,' he said. 'Allow me to welcome you to our company.'

It was growing dark in the cabin, the gleam of sunshine which had heralded their departure from Plymouth had vanished into low clouds, the waves breaking on the portholes obscured much of the daylight; for a moment Rodney had an impression that Francis was smaller than he had remembered; and then, as he touched the hand outstretched to him, as he felt the fingers warm and soft beneath his own, he felt a sudden startled suspicion which left him breathless, so that he could only stare wildly and incredulously at the small oval face looking up into his, at two green eyes which he remembered all too vividly.

It could not be true—it was impossible! Rodney told himself, and looked again. But there was no doubt of it. It was not Francis who had come into the cabin, but Lizbeth. Her red hair had been cut short and was drawn back from her forehead. Her elaborate doublet of dark blue velvet with its short, satin-lined cape, was exactly what Francis might have worn, the sword dangling at her side was undoubtedly his.

Disguised as her brother, taking her brother's place, she was yet undoubtedly herself, too. Rodney stood before her in silence striving vainly to find his voice, to collect his senses.

It was Lizbeth who spoke first.

'Thank you for your welcome, Master Hawkhurst,' she said in a low voice. 'I am delighted to be here and my father sends you his greetings and wishes you all possible success on the voyage which lies ahead of us.'

She turned from him as she spoke and, crossing the cabin, seated herself on the one chair left empty at the far end of the table. She made it clear to Rodney what course she expected him to take and for the moment, his brain in a whirl, he could think of nothing better to do than to return to his own seat.

Lizbeth was now speaking to the officers.

'May I introduce myself, Gentlemen?' she said. 'I am

71

Francis Gillingham, as Master Hawkhurst may have told you.'

They all bowed as was expected of them and then, the formalities dispensed with, they looked to Rodney and waited for him to finish his speech.

What was said after that he really had no idea. He supposed that almost automatically his voice spoke the thoughts which he had planned earlier in the day. He knew, though, that the fire and spirit with which he intended to deliver this oration was lacking, so that the attention of the officers wandered and the Surgeon's cough seemed, from time to time, to drown his voice.

In a daze he finished speaking, and those who listened waited, their faces impassive in the waning light, Rodney dismissed them sharply.

'That will be all, Gentlemen. There is, I know, much for you to do this evening.'

They rose automatically to their feet, Lizbeth with them. Then, as she reached the door, Rodney said:

'You will remain behind, Master Gillingham.'

She did not answer, but stood waiting till the officers had filed from the cabin and the door was closed behind them. It was then, as it seemed to Rodney, that the cabin grew even darker and he could see only the whiteness of her face against the darkness as he asked hoarsely:

'Why are you here? Where is your brother? What does this mean?'

Lizbeth came forward, moving until she reached his side. Then she faced him, her hands resting on the back of a chair.

'I am sorry,' she said softly, 'that I could not let you know of my presence when you were alone; but when your man came to fetch me, I debated whether it would be best to wait or to obey your orders. As you see, I obeyed.'

Rodney's clenched fist came down hard on the oak table.

'In God's name, this is intolerable! I must send you back, I must put you ashore.'

72

He looked around him a little wildly as if he expected some means to materialise by which he could fulfil his threat.

'I think that is impossible,' Lizbeth replied.

She spoke gently enough, but he suspected that she was laughing at him, knowing full well that it would be impossible for him to turn back now. They were at least three hours out from Plymouth, with the wind behind them. Besides which, nothing would be more unlucky or ill-omened to put back into harbour when once the voyage had begun.

'How dare you do this?' Rodney cried furiously. 'And where is your brother?'

'I owe you an explanation, I know,' Lizbeth replied. 'May I please sit down?'

Her plea did not inspire Rodney to any show of good manners.

'Yes, sit down and explain yourself if you can,' he said roughly.

Lizbeth glanced at him for a moment under her eyelashes, and then with her hands clasped in front of her on the table she began.

'Father was furious because Francis would visit a neighbour of ours, Dr. Keen, who is suspected of sympathy with Spain. He caught him coming into the house very late at night and told him he would be kept to his room until he sailed with you; and the next morning a messenger posted to Plymouth to bring you the news. Francis was desperate at the thought of what lay ahead of him. He has hated the sea all his life. He has a horror of it and he swore to me that he would rather kill himself than come on this voyage. We thought of every possible way of making Father change his mind.

'We planned that Francis should sham being sick or even make himself ill by eating something which would disagree with him; and then, while the preparations for the voyage went ahead, Father began to boast that Francis was setting out to fight the Spaniards.

'He has always been ashamed that Francis was not like

73

himself, brave and robust, and now he had the opportunity to prove to his friends and neighbours that his son was no different from any other boy. People came to call—they congratulated Francis, they wished him "God Speed," they even brought gifts for his comfort.

'We soon saw that it would be impossible without loss of honour and decency for Francis to draw back at the last moment. It was then, when he swore that nobody would make him go aboard, that I had an idea how to save him.'

'To come yourself!' Rodney ejaculated.

'Yes, exactly,' Lizbeth answered. 'Father had agreed that I should accompany Francis to Plymouth. I think he had an idea that Francis would run away, but if I were there, I would be able to prevent him. Four servants came with us and Father's instructions were that they were to see Francis aboard and then bring me back. He was taking no chances, you see.

'We started off from Canfield with a crowd of friends to say good-bye to us and Father as proud as a turkey cock because Francis was off to do what he would like to have done at his age—or now for that matter. All the way to Plymouth I tried to persuade Francis to change his mind, to sail with you, to see the world, to force himself to endure the punishment which Father had given him, no matter how hard it might be.

'But Francis would not listen; he drew his dagger and swore on the Bible that he would use it on himself if I didn't save him from what he believed to be a living hell on earth.

'Last night we put up at an inn and it was then I realised that there was no chance of turning Francis from his purpose or of changing his mind. He was determined not to come on this voyage, even if it should cost him his life, so I was forced to agree to his wishes.

'When morning came, we sat talking happily together in front of the servants until it was nearly time to go aboard; then in a last-minute flurry we sent them into town to buy various things we said we had forgotten. As soon as their backs were turned I cut my hair, changed into Francis' clothes, and came down to the docks by myself, while Francis lft the inn to hide until the ship had sailed.

'I gave the landlord a note to give to the servants as soon as they should return, telling them that we had received a letter from you saying the ship would sail half an hour sooner than was anticipated. We had therefore both gone aboard. They were to bring Francis' sea-chest and my baggage down to the ship as soon as they received the message, for I, Lizbeth, had accepted an invitation to sail with you as your guest.'

'You said that?' Rodney said incredulously.

'What else could I say? I had to make some explanation for my disappearance. It was not for the servants to argue.'

'But your father, what will he say?' Rodney asked.

'What can he say? The ship has sailed. He will swear and curse, but perhaps Catherine will persuade him that it is for the best. She will hope that the sharks will eat me or that you will throw me overboard in sheer exasperation.'

Lizbeth was laughing now and Rodney was glowering at her, his rage making him almost tremble with the violence of his feelings.

'God's death! You dare to laugh! Can you imagine what my reputation will be? Why, I shall be the laughing-stock of every ship that sails from Plymouth!'

'No! I thought of that,' Lizbeth replied, 'and in my letter I bound the servants to strict secrecy and told them to speak of it to no one until they returned home. I also wrote a letter to Father, saying that Francis will not sail without me and suggesting that he told no one where I had gone and merely said I was staying with friends. Few people at Camfield will worry whether I am there or not, I assure you.'

'And Francis?'

'He swears he can take care of himself,' Lizbeth answered. 'He will not go home until I return.'

'If you think I am going to lie to your father about his

75

precious son, you are mistaken. When we return, he shall know the truth.'

'When we return, it will not matter much,' Lizbeth said.

'In the meantime, what am I to do with you?' Rodney enquired. 'God's pity, was there ever such a situation?'

'I suggest there is very little you can do about it,' Lizbeth answered. 'I do not know whether you have told anyone about the age of Master Gillingham; but when I looked at myself in Francis' clothes with my hair done like a boy, I thought I looked a not unpleasant lad of say fourteen or fifteen.'

'You look what you are, a girl disguised as a boy.'

'Is not that because you know the truth?' Lizbeth asked. 'You will notice that your officers never took a second glance at me. I introduced myself as Master Gillingham and they accepted me as such. People believe what they are told, and who would believe that you brought a woman aboard?'

'Who indeed?' Rodney said grimly. 'There are captains who take women with them, but I am not one of them and I do not intend to sink to that level.'

'Then you had best throw me overboard,' Lizbeth said quietly.

Rodney brought both his clenched fists down on the table this time; and then he rose to his feet, striking his head against the beam as he forgot how low the cabin was. He let forth an oath and made no apology for it. He wanted to walked backwards and forwards across the cabin, but there was no room. He sat down again.

'You realise that you will doubtless die anyway on this voyage?' he began. 'Men suffer from many strange and divers illnesses at sea, provided that it is not fire from a Spaniard's gun that takes their lives from them.'

'I am not afraid,' Lizbeth said simply, 'and frankly, I think I am no more likely to die that Francis. I am far stronger than he has ever been.'

'It is intolerable,' Rodney said; 'and to think that I must lower myself to lie and prevaricate to my officers and to the men who trust me. If you should be discovered, what then?'

'You must swear that you had no idea of my sex,' Lizbeth said. 'I am sorry I have angered you and I apppreciate the difficulty in which you find yourself, but my brother's honour and his life were in the balance.'

'If your brother were here, I should like to give him what I ought to give you—a good beating,' Rodney said grimly.

Lizbeth's laugh, infectious and untrammelled, seemed to echo round the cabin; and now Rodney realised that darkness had come. He could no longer see her face. He could only hear her and hate her because she could laugh while he longed only to do her physical violence. He was defeated and he knew it.

Lizbeth had come aboard; and there was nothing he could do but accept her pretence to be her brother, and pray that no one would discover the trick which had been played on him. Too late he cursed himself for not having behaved as he should have done and met the son of his benefactor as he came aboard. If he had seen Lizbeth then, he could have sent her away and he realised too late how he had fallen into the trap of his own ill-humour.

He could see all too clearly how cleverly her plan had worked. When the servants had brought the luggage, they must have asked if Mister Gillingham was aboard, and on being told he was they had gone away contented that the task of getting Francis to sea had been completed.

He hated all the Gillingham family, Rodney thought suddenly—Sir Harry who had decided to send him his son Francis, a weakling and a coward; Lizbeth, who was clever and wily enough to place him in this predicament from which there was no possible escape; Catherine Gillingham with her hungry eyes and promiscuous body; and Phillida . . . no, she alone was different!

Rodney sat at the table in the darkness, feeling impotent and frustrated. He could hear Lizbeth's soft breathing and was conscious of her close beside him.

She had spoiled everything, the elation he felt at taking

command, the joy and sense of freedom that had been his as the *Sea Hawk* sailed out of harbour. All were gone, to be replaced by a feeling of apprehension, of fury and of utter incompetence to cope with it.

'Get out of here, damn you, get out of here!' he cried suddenly.

He heard Lizbeth rise from the table, heard her light footsteps as she walked across the heaving floor. He heard the door open and saw her silhouetted for a moment against the light outside; and then he was alone in the darkness, and his fingers drumming on the table made the only sound in the cabin.

5

Lizbeth, walking on deck in the sunshine, heard the look-out on the masthead hail the deck with a sudden excited cry which brought everyone to attention.

'Land ho!' he yelled. 'Deck there! Land three points on the larboard bow, Sir.'

Lizbeth stared out to sea. She could see nothing but the water, shading from emerald green to sapphire beneath an endless expanse of blue sky; but she knew that the information was what Rodney was waiting for and the mountains which would soon come into view should be of Dominica or Guadeloupe, while the Channel between these islands was the gateway of the pirates into the Caribbean Sea.

It was the thirty-seventh day since they had left Plymouth. On the twelfth day they had sited the Canary Islands and watered the ship. Rodney was not disposed to linger there, as the Spaniards were well aware that the Canaries were a convenient calling place for the English ships and it would be easy for a fleet of their great galleons to take them unawares.

So they hurried onwards, seeing on the way nothing more formidable than a whale and a school of porpoises, but they were all of them continually alert for a sight of the enemy.

Lizbeth had gradually adjusted herself to life aboard ship. At first it was a continuous chain of surprises. She had imagined, listening to tales of the adventures of

Hawkins and Drake, that she had learnt a little of what life at sea could be like.

But here, aboard the *Sea Hawk*, reality had nothing in common with her romantic dreams. The life was hard, and as soon as the fresh food was finished she found it difficult to endure the eternal diet of salt beef, salt pork, weevily biscuits and a glass of lemon juice twice a week to keep off scurvy.

It was hard to accustom herself to the rough food, but it was harder still not to reveal how surprising she found those to whom it was ordinary fare. For the first time in her life she saw men at close quarters behave as men and not as gallants. She had never before realised or even anticipated what masculine company would be like without the social veneer which had been so very apparent in all her previous encounters with them.

It was not that the men were over-coarse or in any way repellent because she saw them off their guard. The officers, with whom she associated daily, were all of them decent, cleaning-living men and not in the least lewd or repulsive in their conversation.

It was to be expected that their sense of humour was sometimes a good deal broader than it would have been had they realised her sex, and it amused her on these occasions to know that Rodney was far more embarrassed than she was herself. No, she was not shocked by anything that happened aboard; she was only surprised and even astounded by the strictness of the discipline, the exhausting, unending work there was to be done, and the stern, rigid segregation of the Captain from the rest of his crew.

He sat, it seemed, upon almost Olympian heights, and the officers as well as the men looked upon him with awe and respect. Lizbeth told herself not once but many times a day that this was no superhuman figure, but Rodney Hawkhurst who was here by the grace of her father's money and who believed himself betrothed to her half-sister, Phillida. Even so, as she echoed the 'Aye, aye, Sir' of the others aboard and waited, as the others did, for orders which must be obeyed promptly, she found herself moved by a deferential respect which she had never before accorded to a man.

At first Rodney's anger allowed him to speak to her only when other people were present and then in the most formal manner possible; but as the voyage advanced, he eventually found it impossible not to become more friendly. She alone ate at the Captain's table, as was the custom with an honoured guest. She breakfasted in her cabin off a tray that was carried to her by Hapley, but dinner and supper were taken alone with Rodney, unless he invited one of the other officers to join them.

At first they sat in silence and then gradually, because there was no one else to whom he could talk, Rodney talked to her. She realised all too clearly that it was no particular compliment that she should receive his confidences—he was more often than not thinking out loud and the subject chosen was seldom anything but plans for the future, all related to the daily running of the ship, and yet she was thankful for this small mercy.

She was aware that he was in a continual state of fear lest her identity should be discovered and therefore she made no effort to mix with the officers or even to be seen more than was absolutely necessary. She walked on the quarter-deck and even sat there in the sunshine when she felt she would not be in the way. Her obvious desire to be alone made the other officers avoid her, although when she did unavoidably come into contact with them they were friendly and, as far as she could ascertain, completely unsuspicious.

At first she allowed herself to appear cowed and suitably repentant beneath the silence of Rodney's anger; but when later he began to talk and she was allowed to answer him, she found it hard to keep in check her sense of fun or to control the mischievous twinkle in her eye. It was a pity, she thought more than once, that he was so incensed with her, because they might have enjoyed being together. They could have talked quite happily, as they had talked that first morning at Camfield when she watched him stride towards her across the park, pre-occupied with his own thoughts.

Once she forgot herself so far as to flirt with him in the soft light of the cabin's lantern, after they had dined.

'Would you rather tame a ship to your will, or a woman?' she asked daringly.

He smiled at the question and his eyes rested on her with the expression in them that had half-frightened and half-delighted her at Camfield. It was the same as that which had been there that morning by the lake when she had known he had contemplated kissing her.

'Both are exciting,' Rodney answered, 'but of course, the joy one experiences depends both on the ship—and on the woman!'

'Yet you are confident of your ability to conquer both?' She was teasing him.

'Yes, very confident—do you doubt me?'

'And if I do?'

'Perhaps I could prove myself to you—one day.'

For a moment their eyes met and were held by some-thing they both saw within the other. Then with an effort and a muttered curse, Rodney broke free and rang the bell violently for more wine.

As the voyage progressed, she began to realise the strain under which he was living and she knew it was good for him for a short while to forget his responsibilities, for always it seemed as if he must act a part, the part of an omnipotent commander, dauntless and assured, sailing his ship ever onwards to success.

It was part of his act, Lizbeth realised, for him to come on the quarter-deck now, slowly and without any sign of excitement while everyone else was staring straight ahead for the first sight of land and the rigging swarmed with Petty Officers and ratings.

'There it is, there, Sir!' Gadstone cried in a voice that rose shrill as a boy's in his excitement.

This was his first voyage and every moment of it seemed to be one of sheer delight.

'What you see is Dominica, Master Gadstone,' Rodney said coldly; 'but even so, I imagine there is quite a lot to be done before we reach there. I will trouble you to make arrangements for the filling of the water casks. Get her into the wind, Master Baxter, if you have finished straining your eyes at the sight of that quite ordinary island.'

Rodney's sarcasm was enough to make everyone bustle into activity. But Lizbeth looked at him out of the corner of her eye. A little pulse was throbbing in his neck and there was a glint in his eyes which was at variance with the deliberate calmness of his voice. He, too, was excited, she knew that. Ahead was the gateway to adventure—which must make or break him.

She had a sudden impulse to slide her hand through his arm, to tell him she understood and let him know she sympathised with the effort he made to appear calm and natural. Instead she moved away a little so that he should not see her and remember how much her presence irked him. Besides, at this moment he was incensed with her over yet another matter.

This morning she had come on deck earlier than usual. It had been a very hot night and she had found it impossible to sleep, so instead of waiting until Hapley brought her breakfast she had come from her cabin before eight bells sounded and arrived on the quarter-deck just a few minutes in advance of Rodney himself.

She was not to know the ship's routine and Master Barlow's question of 'Hands to punishment, Sir?' took her by surprise. The pipes of the boatswain's mates began to twitter.

'All hands to witness punishment!' roared a Petty Officer on the main deck and the men began to pour up from below while Rodney stood rigid by the quarter-deck rail.

The expression on his face was severe and there was something in his attitude and in the men's expectancy which made Lizbeth wish she had kept to her cabin. But she could not push past Rodney and leave the quarter-deck. She must stand and watch the boatswain's mates trice a man naked to the waist up to the main rigging. Then the drums began to roll.

In her short sheltered life Lizbeth had not imagined in her wildest dreams anything so bestial as the cat-o'-nine-tails whipping through the air, tearing at the naked flesh until the blood flowed in a crimson stream from the man's back on to the clean-scrubbed deck.

As was usual with an experienced seaman the man made no sound, but at the end of two dozen strokes he hung motionless and silent. A bucket of water was flung over him. He was cut down and hustled below.

'Hands to breakfast, Master Barlow,' Rodney commanded.

The men on deck seemed to vanish as quickly as they had come and it was only then that Rodney turned to see Lizbeth with a white face and hands that were clenched together to prevent herself from fainting.

'You are early this morning,' he remarked, but she imagined he was glad to see her weakness.

All the horror of what she had just seen boiled up into a sudden hatred of him.

'Are you a devil,' she asked passionately, 'that you should treat a human being in such a way?'

'The man had disobeyed an order,' Rodney answered coldly. 'If men were allowed to do such things without punishment, then it would be impossible to control or direct the ship.'

'It is cruel and wicked,' Lizbeth stormed.

'They all know the penalty of disobedience,' Rodney said. ' 'Tis a pity your brother Francis was not here to see it.'

He turned on his heel as he spoke and went below to his breakfast, while Lizbeth stood gripping the rail and despising herself because the tears blurred her eyes. The shock of what she had just witnessed made her whole body quiver, and she felt that the sight of that man's torn and bleeding back would haunt her all her life.

She was not to know that Rodney, sitting alone at his breakfast table, had always disliked the floggings that were the tradition of every ship that sailed the seven seas. He would rather have died than admit such a thing to Lizbeth, for he was bitterly ashamed of such weakness, but though he had seen hundreds of them, they still left him feeling sick in the pit of his stomach and any breakfast, even a more appetising one than that he was eating now, had the taste of sawdust after what he had just seen on deck.

The thought of Lizbeth's white face and trembling fingers made him push aside his plate after he had eaten only a mouthful or so.

'Curse the wench,' he said out loud. 'She has asked for it in coming. How can I help what she sees and hears?'

And yet he knew he would never be hardened to pain and suffering wherever he might find it. Just a flogging disturbed him physically every time he saw it, so Lizbeth's distress had equally the power to hurt him.

Her little face, white and strained by the shock of what she had seen, was like a dagger in his heart. Her eyes were wide and defiant of the tears that were not far away; and her lips trembled—the lips he had kissed and had never been able to forget.

He swore at himself for being a fool, and yet he could do nothing about it. He could never, it seemed to him, forget her presence aboard his ship and he told himself that his whole joy in the voyage was destroyed because of her.

Having little knowledge of women and believing them to be frail flowers who would crumple up at the first hardship, he had expected her to be ill for a few days after they got to sea, but Lizbeth had remained surprisingly well and if she had complaints, she had at least ventured no word of them to him. They had run into rough weather in the Bay of Biscay, but although she had looked drawn and white and had eaten very little at meals, she had not taken to her bed.

'Methinks Master Gillingham can be proud of his belly, Sir,' Barlow had said one evening. 'Most lads of his age would have been incapacitated by the seas we've just been through.

Rodney felt as if Barlow were reproaching him for the uncomplimentary things he had said when he heard that Francis was coming on board. He snapped back an answer and realised that Barlow thought him unjust and not ready to give credit where credit was due.

It had not made him feel any more kindly towards Lizbeth and he wished that he could encounter some ship returning to England, in which case he had every intention of putting her aboard and sending her home. Lizbeth happily did not know of this intention, and as they sighted the Island of Dominica she was looking forward to their first encounter with the Spaniards as much as any of the men on board.

She had been present when Rodney explained to his officers what his plans were. He would water his ship at the island and then catch the trade wind into the Caribbean Sea. Once there, he would make for Nombre de Dios, a small but important town, which was the terminus of the Panama gold route. The treasure was brought by Spanish ships from the harbours of Peru to Panama. There it was loaded on mules and carried across the isthmus to Nombre de Dios on the Caribbean Sea.

Drake had known of this sixteen years earlier in 1572 when he attacked the mule caravans, taking his crew over land to surprise them before they reached Nombre de Dios. He had made friends of the natives, who had helped him in every possible way, and he had left behind him a legend of kindness and justice which had never been forgotten.

But the Spaniards, having lost cargoes of great value to Drake, had taken care to preserve their gold and now not only was Nombre de Dios an armed fortress, but the treasure ships were guarded all the way back to Spain.

Privateers had given Nombre de Dios and the Caribbean Sea a rest in the past few years. It had been considered too dangerous to challenge the Spanish forces there; but Rodney thought it was worth trying to see if there was any chance of slipping into port and snatching some of the treasure before it was loaded.

If he failed in this, he could cruise down the Darien coast where there was always plunder to be found. He had hopes that natives might help him with information, but like everything else in the chancy work of privateering, one could not make too many plans ahead. One had to wait and see what circumstances were and seize an opportunity when it came.

The *Sea Hawk* reached Dominica late that afternoon and anchored in a small bay, sheltered by a high cliff. There was water in plenty, for the land was white with mountain streams. The crew were all itching to explore the tree-covered hills, but Rodney insisted on the ship being watered first before anyone was allowed to stretch their legs or look for tropical fruit. He was well aware that it was dangerous to linger near these islands. The Spaniards might be on the look-out and he gave orders that the ship was to be kept ready to sail at any moment.

Another reason for getting under sail as quickly as possible was that the inhabintants of the island, the Caribs, were cannibals. A cruel, ferocious, warlike people, they had made a stout resistance to the Spaniards and seamen of all nations calling at Dominica found it wisest to avoid any encounter with them.

The place was lonely, with only the sea birds swirling and calling overhead. They stayed the night, raised anchor the next morning and sailed into the Caribbean Sea. For the next twelve days they were without a sight of land or the sail of another ship. It was very hot, and Lizbeth felt sorry for the men who must hurry about the decks, pulling on the ropes, lowering or raising the sails with the sweat trickling down their half-naked bodies.

Yet the heat made her feel strangely sensuous. She longed for wild, impossible things which had never entered her head before. She dreamed strange dreams—dreams of Rodney, so that sometimes she blushed when she looked at him the following morning.

Once, under a star-strewn sky in the airless heat of the tropical night, they had stood close together on the deck and Lizbeth had a mad desire to touch him, to make sure he was there and not a figment of her imagination.

'What are you thinking about?' Rodney asked, and his voice was unusually deep.

'You!' Lizbeth could not help speaking the truth.

'And I am thinking of you!' he spoke the words angrily.

'Why?' she hardly breathed the question.

'Because I cannot help it; because I cannot be free of you,' he hurled the accusations at her.

She stood very still, and the phosphorescence from the sea seemed to halo her hair.

'Curse you!' Rodney cried, but there was no anger in his voice. She trembled at his words, yet it was a sweet ecstatic emotion which seemed to course through her veins.

'Lizbeth!' It was the cry of a man hard-pressed; and then the ship's bells brought them back to their senses.

Without another word Rodney turned on his heel and went below, leaving Elizabeth alone, her hands to her breasts trying to quell the tumult within her.

It was getting towards dusk on the twelfth day after leaving Dominica when the look-out shouted:

'Sail ho!'

Rodney forgot to be composed on this occasion and came running up from his cabin on to the quarter-deck.

'Where away?' he asked.

'On the port bow, Sir. A carrack, I think, Sir.'

'Yes, a carrack, Sir,' shouted another from the foretop of the gallant masthead. 'She's right to windward under all sail, Sir.'

For a few seconds no one on deck could see anything; then Rodney saw a gleaming square of white rise for a second over the horizon and then vanish again. Minutes passed and now the sails were more frequently to be seen, until at last the ship was in plain view running goose-winged before the wind.

'She is flying the Spanish colours at the main, Sir,' shouted the look-out.

Rodney nodded. He had seen that some seconds earlier, but was afraid that, if he said so, his voice would betray his excitement.

'She is at least seven hundred tons, Sir,' Barlow's voice said at his elbow.

Rodney did not answer for a moment, he was watching the ship approach. He was well aware that her guns would outmatch his. She was big, and the 'Spanish castles of the sea', as they called them, could afford to carry very heavy guns and those of a long range.

'Clear for action!'

The bulkheads came down, the ship's boys gave a cheer as they came running up with powder for the guns between which the black iron spheres were set ready for instant use. On the starboard side the guns were run out on their wooden trucks and loaded within a few seconds; on the port side the crews were ramming in the charges of shot and heaving the guns into position.

'Cleared for action, Sir,' said Barlow.

Rodney opened his lips to speak, but the words were checked by a sudden shriek from the masthead:

'Sail ho!'

Rodney jerked his head upwards as the look-out continued: 'On the starboard bow, Sir. She's right in the way of the sun—she's a lugger!'

All heads turned towards the starboard. They had been so busily engaged in watching the carrack on the port bow that the lugger had come straight over the horizon before they had seen her. She was two-masted, a pearling lugger from the Gulf of Panama, perhaps, but she would be armed and there was no question as to whose flag she was flying.

Rodney began to calculate how long it would be before the ships closed on them. From the *Sea Hawk's* masthead in the clear light of the Caribbean a ship could be seen from a distance of as much as twenty miles. But the gap between the ships and himself was shortening.

89

He had not long to make up his mind and he knew that, if he dithered and did nothing, he would be crushed between the two of them. He saw the men looking at him as Barlow waited for the orders. He knew in that split second that there was only one order he could give.

'Set the topsail, Master Barlow,' he said.

He fancied there was the slightest hesitation before Barlow repeated the order.

'Clap on more sail—ease the halliards,' Rodney added. Again Barlow relayed the order.

'Keep her steady as she goes, Master Barlow,' he said a moment later.

There was a fresh breeze blowing which caught the sails. The men were scurrying about the decks, being cursed by Petty Officers as they sprang up the rigging. The crew was ready with the sheets and braces. Gun crews were waiting as a runner might wait to start on a race.

Rodney stared across the water to the carrack. She was coming more quickly than the lugger, which was beating against the wind.

'Wind shifting, Sir,' Master Barlow said.

'Keep her steady as she goes,' Rodney replied.

'As she goes, Sir?' Barlow repeated, the faintest question in his voice.

'That was what I said, Master Barlow.'

Barlow understood for the first time what was taking place. Rodney saw his face drop, the sudden quenching of the excitement in his eyes, and then as the *Sea Hawk* responded to extra sail and gathered speed, the seamen, too, realised that they were running away.

A kind of groan went up which seemed to Rodney in that moment one of contempt rather than disappointment, but he appeared to hear nothing. He was watching the galleon approaching on one side and the lugger on the other. Sandwiched between the two there was not a chance for the *Sea Hawk*; and yet he knew only too well what his men were feeling.

'We could have tackled one,' he said to himself, 'but

not two.' Even so the carrack alone could out-class them, out-gun them; and even if they grappled with her and effected some damage, there was every chance they would find themselves at the bottom of the sea before she had finished with them.

He had made his decision, unpopular though it was, and the *Sea Hawk* with every sail strained to the uttermost was running as fast as she could across the Caribbean Sea. He was concentrating so fiercely on watching the carrack that he did not at first hear a very quiet, soft voice at his side.

'Rodney,' it said, 'Rodney!'

Even in his pre-occupation Rodney realised that Lizbeth was addressing him by his Christian name, contrary to her custom since she came aboard, of being strictly formal even in private.

'What do you want?'

The question was abrupt, almost rude.

'I heard Master Hales say we are running away! It can't be true. Surely you are going to stay and fight?'

'With two Spanish ships? It would be madness.'

He did not know why he troubled to answer her except that it was a relief to be able to express thoughts that were seething within his mind.

'Are you afraid?'

Lizbeth's question was an impertinence which he could not allow.

'Not for myself,' Rodney snarled, 'but for my ship, for the men who sail with me—for you, if it comes to that.'

'I would not have you play the coward on my behalf,' Lizbeth replied.

'Play the coward!' Rodney repeated the words beneath his breath.

Then suddenly he lost his temper. He turned and glared at Lizbeth with such fury in his expression that almost instinctively she took a step away from him.

'Will you oblige me, Master Gillingham,' he said in a voice that was perfectly audible to those standing by, 'by

91

going to your cabin and staying there? Those are my orders, Sir!'

As he finished, he turned again to his contemplation of the carrack but he knew that Lizbeth had obeyed him. And yet somehow it gave him very little satisfaction. The wind was rising, but if that was an advantage to the *Sea Hawk*, it also gave the same advantage to the Spanish ship.

She was chasing them now. There was no doubt about the fact that she had altered course and her bow was pointing straight at them. She was gaining, too, and Roger calculated that in another hour she was likely to overhaul them.

It was then he looked at the sky! Dusk was falling with the swiftness which in the Tropics turns a sunlit, cloudless day suddenly into night. It was their one hope, as he well knew. The darkness would cover their retreat and they might lose the Spaniards before the dawn.

The lugger was being left behind on the starboard bow. She, too, had given chase, maybe in response to signals from the carrack, or perhaps she was not a pearling ship as he had at first suspected but one of the *guarda costas* which the Spaniards had creeping along the coast for just such an occasion as this.

The breeze suddenly wavered and then renewed itself. Rodney watched the carrack to see if she too received the check. In the tropical waters one ship can have a fair wind while another only a few miles away can lie becalmed. Rodney began to be afraid that the wind would die away on him completely, but the *Sea Hawk* kept steadily on course while the carrack, with her greater breadth of sail, drew nearer and nearer.

And then, as he watched he suddenly saw a disc of white appear on the side of the carrack. The disc spread and became a small cloud and six seconds after its appearance the dull thud of a shot reached his ears.

'They'll be carrying two devils from hell aft on the quarter-deck,' Barlow muttered.

There was another burst of smoke from the Spanish

ship and this time a spout of water rose from the crest of a wave a little to the starboard of the *Sea Hawk*. Rodney called Baxter to him.

'See what we can do with our culverins.'

Baxter bawled the order, but the Master Gunner shook his head doubtfully as he eyed the distance between the two ships. A cannon aft was sighted. He measured out the powder charge on the fullest scale, he trained the gun again and then stood, a length of smouldering match in hand, watching the heave of the ship. Suddenly he set the match to the touch-hole, jerked the lanyard and the cannon roared out.

'Three cables short of her,' yelled a voice from the fore-top.

The Spanish ship was firing fast now. There was a sudden, splintering crash and a hole appeared in the quarter-deck bulwark amid a shower of splinters. Another shot skimmed along the planking of the fo'c'sle. A man fell with a crash and there was a sudden wave of crimson staining the deck. Rodney saw who it was as the man fell—it was Dobson, the ship's surgeon.

There was the sudden roar of the *Sea Hawk's* cannon and a flash of flame, vivid and glowing, which told Rodney that darkness had nearly fallen. In a few moments it would be completely dark. Another shot splintered below.

'Cease fire!' he shouted.

He imagined, rather than saw the surprise on Barlow's face.

'Cease fire, Sir?'

'At once, Master Barlow.'

It was too late to prevent another shot, and a second later they saw an answering flash of fire from the Spanish galleon. Rodney knew that the *Sea Hawk* could no longer be seen, for he could only locate the Spanish ship by the fire from her guns.

The wind was freshening and as he felt it blow upon his cheeks, Rodney made the second momentous decision of the evening. If they kept straight ahead, he argued with himself, the Spaniard would be able to follow them, over-haul them and keep firing where she expected them to be.

What was more, she would be near at hand, when dawn broke, to finish the destruction she had already begun. Nights were short in the Caribbean—they would not have many hours in which to get away from her. To do this and to escape he had to try methods other than the obvious. He decided to alter course and to turn nor'west, which would give them a less favourable wind but which would be the last thing the Spaniard would expect them to do.

He gave the order and knew that Barlow and the helms-man thought he was demented. He was blessing the darkness, blessing the chance of saving his ship—that was all that mattered for the moment, that the ship should be saved; and even if they had run away, they would all live to fight another day.

They had been but a few moments on their new course when there came a flash in the darkness and a shot splashed into the sea two cables to their starboard bow.

'Steady as she goes, Master Barlow,' Rodney said.

'Aye, aye, Sir.' Barlow's voice was less doubtful now. He understood what Rodney was trying to do.

The breeze was growing stronger and then, even as Rodney gave a sigh of relief, there was a crash which made the ship shudder from stem to stern.

For a moment Rodney felt himself reel on the quarter-deck.

'Are you hurt, Sir?' Barlow asked.

'No, keep her going.'

It was a wide shot that should have missed them com-pletely. Rodney's instinct told him that what he had done was right in principle, but the *Sea Hawk* had caught it broadside on and he knew a great deal of damage must have been done.

The next shot was half a mile away from them, and the next, and the next. It was lucky that the masts had survived and the *Sea Hawk* could still scud away from her oppressor. But the shot which had hit them was by

94

no means an insignificant one. Rodney wanted to go below and assess the damage, but he knew that for the moment he must stay on deck and correct their course—a course which must take them out of reach of the Spanish guns before the dawn broke.

6

Dawn came with a magical suddenness in the Caribbean Sea. One moment all was dark save for the stars twinkling overhead, and the next instant great pink hands swept the sable from the sky and it was day.

Haggard and hollow-eyed from lack of sleep, Rodney's expression, as his eyes swept the sea, was echoed by every officer and man on deck and the sigh of relief which welled up in every breast was as audible as the splash of the waves against the ship's side and the creak of the rigging as the sails bellied out above them.

There was nothing in sight. Rodney heard Barlow ejaculate, 'Praise the Lord!' and while he felt inclined to say the same, he managed to keep a dignified silence, for all that he longed to shout aloud his joy and relief.

It had been a night of unending anxiety. Almost as soon as it was dark, the wind began to blow heavily from the south-east. Rodney altered course again so that the *Sea Hawk* was carried in the direction of the American coast; but at the same time there were innumerable dangers in proceeding at such a speed in the darkness in those practically uncharted seas.

There was every likelihood of their running into an island, rocks or sandbanks that were not marked on the charts; apart from that, at the rate at which they were going they might easily reach the main shore itself. But the risk had to be taken. The Spanish ship would be on the look-out for them as soon as the dawn broke; and what was more, there was always a chance of their encountering other ships as they got nearer to the coast.

In the hours of darkness Roger had felt a depression settle upon him more intense than anything he had ever known in his life before. He had faced death hundreds of times in the past ten years, he had known sickness and had felt despairingly that he would never reach home alive; but this agony of anxiety seemed to be a foretaste of hell.

Over and over in his mind he asked himself the question whether he had done the right thing in running away. He could see again—all too vividly—the surprise and contempt in Lizbeth's eyes, the expression of astonishment on Barlow's face and what he fancied was scorn on those of his other officers.

The *Sea Hawk* had played the part of a coward; and yet Rodney could see no other course which he could possibly have taken without being foolhardy to the point of suicide. It might sound very heroic to die fighting against overwhelming odds; but Rodney wanted to live, he wanted to take the *Sea Hawk* back to Plymouth, not to leave her, a broken hull, at the bottom of the Caribbean Sea.

There was nothing else he could have done, he told himself as he set his jaw in defiance. And yet he was human enough to mind the unspoken criticism of those he commanded, to want to recapture their faith and confidence in him.

Just before dawn broke was for Rodney a most searing experience in which he knew a vast and empty loneliness and realised, as he had never realised before, that the responsibility of command was not always pleasant. His men were tired, the ship was damaged, and yet when the light came they might have to fight a bitter and bloody battle which they must win to live, for to lose meant extermination.

Then, by the blessing of God, the sea was empty! The waves, choppy from last night's wind, reflected the deep, vivid blue of the sky. For some moments Rodney waited, tense, for the voice of the look-out telling him there was a sail in sight. When no voice came from the masthead, he looked round the deck and realised there was a great deal to be done.

The quarter-deck was furrowed and grooved with jagged splinters pared off the wood. There were piles of torn rigging and wreckage on the half-deck and around the fo'c'sle. The surgeon, Master Dobson, lay where he had died, but someone had had the decency to throw some sailcloth over him.

Rodney heard Barlow give an order to two seamen who proceeded towards the shrouded corpse. There would have to be a burial service later, Rodney knew, and he wondered how many more bodies would join that of the surgeon.

But before he had time to trouble himself with the dead he must attend to the living. The *Sea Hawk* was moving heavily and was much lower in the water than she had been the day before. He looked round for Barlow and saw that he had gone below.

For a moment it appeared that the damage was not great; and yet Rodney remembered only too clearly the sound of the last shot entering the Sea Hawk's hull. He had wondered frequently through the night how much damage had been done, but he dared not leave the deck, believing that, when it came to a matter of picking up the sound of a wave beating over a rock, or sensing danger before it was quite upon them, his ears and senses were better than those he commanded. But now he began to be troubled, and Barlow's face, when he came on deck a few minutes later, told him the worst.

'How deep?' Rodney asked before Barlow could speak.

'Seven feet and more, Sir.'

'Where is the hole?'

'A foot above the water-line, Sir. She would be all right in a dead calm sea, but the waves were beating in all last night.'

'Can we fother a sail and get it over the hole?' Rodney asked.

'I'm afraid it is too bad for that, Sir. The water we

98

have already shipped will make it impossible for the men
to work below. We can try, of course, and the men are
at the pumps, but the hole is about three feet across.'

There was nothing they could do save get the ship
ashore and mend her properly. The trouble was, how?
They must find a place where they could lie undisturbed
long enough to make the necessary repairs. It was at
that moment that the look-out shouted 'Land ho, Sir!'

Rodney looked at Barlow.

'We will have to find the best place we can,' he said
briefly. 'What is the casualty list?'

'Two men killed besides Mister Dobson, Sir, and twelve
wounded.'

'Then do the best you can for them,' Rodney said, 'and
get the dead ready for burial. We must make for the
shore, the wind shows no sign of abating.'

Rodney spoke impersonally, but his eyes met Barlow's
and there was a look of perfect understanding between
them. Both knew that the ship was getting heavier and
sinking lower every minute that passed. The white crests
of the waves splashing happily against the sides of the ship
were as deadly a menace as a Spanish gun.

The pumps, small and never very effective, would be
quite useless against such a weight of water as the *Sea
Hawk* had shipped during the night and was still taking
aboard. It was something that land was in sight. That
meant they had anything from fifteen to twenty miles to
sail before they reached the nearest point, and God alone
knew if that would prove a safe harbour.

Neither Rodney nor Barlow expressed further the fears
that were locked within their breasts. The men were set
to work cleaning the decks, and the bodies of the dead
were sewn tightly into shrouds and laid in a row waiting
for Rodney to conduct the burial service.

Having instructed Master Baxter to call him if there
was the slightest difficulty in steering, if there was a sail in
sight or anything untoward happened, Rodney went below.
He would have liked to have a wash and snatch some
breakfast, for he had had nothing either to eat or drink

since the evening before when they sighted the Spanish carrack, but he knew it would be expected of him first to see the wounded.

With Barlow following him he went below decks. It was dark and the oil lamps flickering from the beams cast long dark shadows. It was desperately hot and even to Rodney, who was used to the stench and fug of a ship, the atmosphere was stifling. The wounded men lay in a row, some of them cursing blasphemously as the roll of the ship hurt their shattered limbs or made it difficult for them to retain the posture in which they lay.

It was only as he reached the men that Rodney remembered that, having seen Dobson killed, he should have appointed someone to act as surgeon in his place. It was the usual procedure when the ship's surgeon was killed, but he wondered now who on board would have the slightest conception of what that post entailed.

Rodney had not liked Dobson and could not pretend to be sorry that as a man he was dead, but from any other point of view his death was vastly inconvenient. On a voyage of this sort a ship's surgeon was a vital necessity, and although they usually killed as many men as they saved, they at least had some knowledge of their profession, however inadequate.

As he moved forward now in the darkness, disliking the heat, the smell of bilge and unwashed bodies, Rodney tried to remember all that he had learnt when he was with Drake. That amazing man had a vast knowledge of medicine. He had studied the uses of healing herbs, and the men with whom he sailed would rather have trusted him to doctor them than any surgeon, however skilled by reputation.

But as he tried to recall what he had seen and heard, Rodney felt helpless. He could not be certain that his memory was to be relied on and in reality, he thought, he was as inexperienced in the matter as the merest cabin boy.

It was then, as he reached the men, that the wavering light of the lantern showed him a kneeling figure by one

100

of them. Someone had the doctor's polished case with all its paraphernalia of bottles open on the floor. Rodney stared as the swaying lantern flickered on a red-gold head and he saw who knelt there.

Lizbeth was bandaging a man's arm while he swore one resounding oath after another at the pain his wounds were giving him.

'Quiet there! Rodney's voice was crisp and authoritative and the man was instantly silent; and then he stared down at Lizbeth, not knowing what to say.

It was a shock seeing her tending a half-naked man in such a manner. No decent or superior woman was interested or concerned with the dirty work of nursing. Gin-drinking old women might hire themselves out as mid-wives, women of the lower orders without any training or special skill took up nursing as an inferior means of livelihood; but in the main it was men's work to look after the sick, and at sea, as on the shore, the weakest and most inefficient men were ordered to such a menial and unimportant task.

And yet it was difficult in the circumstances for Rodney to know what to say. He would have liked, if he could have expressed himself naturally, to order Lizbeth to leave the man alone and go on deck immediately. And yet, even as the words framed themselves on his lips, he knew he could not say them. Someone had to take up Dobson's job and he intended to appoint a Petty Officer—the one most easily spared. But this was not the moment to do so with his supposedly-honoured guest concerning himself with the men's well-being.

'Have you any *aqua vitae* on board?' Lizbeth asked, looking up at Rodney as he stood speechless beside her.

'*Aqua vitae*?' he echoed stupidly.

'Yes, I require it for the next man.'

She nodded as she spoke to a man lying on the other side of the one she was treating. He had been hit in the shoulder—a great open wound, torn, bleeding and blackened with powder.

'Give him spirits if you have no laudanum,' Rodney

said, well aware there were only two sorts of medicine for wounded men when the pain became really unbearable.

'He has had some laudanum,' Lizbeth replied, 'and I do not wish him to drink the *aqua vitae*, I want to pour it into the wound.'

'God's light! Whatever for?' Rodney ejaculated.

There were a few bottles aboard of the precious brandy-wine, which he himself enjoyed, but he thought for a moment that Lizbeth was demented when she asked that he should sacrifice his special liquor for such a cause.

She saw his confusion and explained patiently.

'You see how dirty the wound is. When the Spanish cannonball hit him he was carrying the powder and shot between our own cannons. 'Twas spilled all over him. A wound that is as dirty as that is bound to get gangrene unless we can get it clean. If I had herbs such as I have at home, I could deal with it. A clover of garlic is excellent, but I have none here and I believe that *aqua vitae* will clean it up equally as well.'

'Who told you such things?' Rodney asked.

'I have heard men talk since I was a child of the hurts they have suffered. It was a favourite topic of conversation at my father's table. I know, too, a little of the healing properties of herbs and the cleaning value of raw spirit. Can I have the *aqua vitae*?'

Quickly, because he could not find the words to refuse her, Rodney sent a ship's boy to his cabin for a bottle.

The man cursed and swore as Lizbeth poured it on his wound, but when she had bound it up he thanked her.

There were three men left to bandage and Rodney waited until Lizbeth had finished with them. There were splinters which had to be extricated from a seaman's burly chest with very inadequate instruments in Dobson's medicine-case. Another man had lost a foot, but Lizbeth knew she could do nothing about the jagged, mutilated limb, which needed amputating. It was a job for the butcher as Dobson was dead, and was best left, Rodney decided, until they could be steady in harbour.

The last man was dead. There was a great pool of

blood on the floor beside him. There was another stream which had flowed in a sticky trickle from his mouth. His eyes were wide open, startling in their fixed stare, and Rodney's voice was harsh as he gave orders for the man to be carried on deck to join the other three bodies awaiting burial.

He knew the man well. He was a big, burly man of Devon called Clerihew and had sailed in the *Golden Hind* on Drake's brilliant exploit when they captured the *Cacafuego* and sailed home rich with plunder. Now Clerihew was dead, and Rodney felt as if he had lost an old friend. It almost surprised him how much he resented the fact that such a man should die for no good reason. They had achieved nothing, they had run away, and that in itself was more bitter than anything else.

Lizbeth's task was done. She stood up, looked at the row of men bandaged and drugged, and told a man who was not wounded to make them as comfortable as possible.

' 'Tis hot here,' she said hesitatingly, conscious of the sweat on her own forehead. 'Perhaps they could have some air?'

'They can be taken on deck later,' Rodney promised.

He would have promised anything at that moment to get Lizbeth away. He was feeling more embarrassed every moment by her proximity to the wounded men.

'Thank you, that will help them, I am sure,' Lizbeth said.

She turned to a seaman who was in attendance and asked him to carry the medicine-chest back to her cabin, and then she turned and walked along the lower deck to the companion-way.

' 'Tis best that the medicine should not be left with the men. They might be tempted to help themselves,' she remarked. 'There are many drugs there which I am sure are deadly poison.'

Rodney said nothing until they reached the upper deck, and then, as he drew a deep breath of fresh air, he said:

'I must thank you for doing your best with the men, but there is no need for you to attend to them any more.

I will appoint an Acting-Surgeon.'

He was speaking to Lizbeth, but his eyes were looking around as he spoke. There was no sign of a ship, but the coast was in sight. They had reached it none too soon, Rodney thought. He had no intention of alarming anyone, but while he had been below watching Lizbeth bandaging the wounded men, he had heard sounds which were all too ominous to a man used to ships.

There was a sound of water beneath the lower deck, he could hear the lap and swirl of it, a burbling sound which was very unlike the usual wash of the bilge. He could hear, too, the monotonous clang of the pumps, but he knew how little they would achieve. It took a lot to sink a ship such as the *Sea Hawk* and yet it was by no means an impossibility, and there were still eight or ten miles ahead of them before they could reach the coast.

Lizbeth was speaking, but for a moment he could not concentrate on what she was saying.

'Is there anybody on board who has any knowledge of medicine—real knowledge?' she asked.

'I have no idea,' Rodney replied. 'I shall have to make enquiries.'

'If there is no one, as I suspect,' Lizbeth said, 'then I shall continue to do what I can for the men. I am not afraid of blood, as some women are, and at least I shall be gentler with them than the man I found trying to move them about when I went below.'

'I forbid it,' Rodney retorted quickly.

'In this I refuse to obey you,' Lizbeth replied. 'You may be in command of the ship, but men should not be allowed to die because there is no one to care for them.'

'I have told you, it is no work for you or for any woman for that matter,' Rodney said.

'I shall look after them, and nothing you can say can stop me,' Lizbeth answered.

Tired though he was, preoccupied with other things, Rodney glared back at her. He felt so irritated by her defiance that he had half a mind to take her by the shoulders and shake her. He almost forgot in that moment

104

that she was a woman. She was instead something quite impersonal that was defying him, and Rodney was not used to being defied.

'You will do as I say or I will put you in irons.'

She laughed at him then, her head thrown back a little, the sun glinting on her red hair.

'You would not dare,' she replied.

He remembered then what she had said to him the evening before. He remembered how during the night he had thought often of how she despised him for having run away from the Spanish ships.

'Go to your cabin,' he said furiously, 'or I swear I will have you carried there!'

She did not move, but her green eyes gleamed beneath her dark lashes. They were both tense, both burning with indignation, both tingling alive with fiery anger which made everything forgotten save themselves.

An interruption came like a thunder-clap.

'Excuse me, Sir,' Barlow said at Rodney's elbow. 'There is a small fishing-boat just ahead of us with three men in it. Shall we take them on board?'

Rodney looked out to sea—nothing else was in sight.

'Take them on board, Mr. Barlow,' he said, 'but delay our passage as little as possible.'

Barlow understood and, forgetful of Lizbeth, Rodney strode up to the quarter-deck and watched the drama taking place below.

The fishing-boat was forced to heave to as the ship's boat which had been lowered drew alongside her and in a short time the three men were hauled aboard. One was an Indian—there was no doubt about that—the other two were darker-skinned with high cheek-bones, combined with thick lips and thick, fuzzy heads of hair. At first glance Rodney was sure these were Cimaroons. Bitter enemies of the Spainiareds, Cimaroons were Negro slaves who had run away from the cruelty of their masters and mated with Indians of the woods.

So many had escaped during the Spanish rule that they

had now grown into a people who lived in the forests around the Isthmus of Panama. They had their own king and were split into several tribes. But all were united by one controlling spirit—a common hatred of those who had oppressed them.

The three men were dragged across the deck. Their faces were sullen, their eyes smouldering with suppressed fires. Rodney spoke to them in Spanish. He asked them who they were and when the oldest man answered him surlily that he and his brother were Cimaroons he smiled.

'Release the prisoners,' he ordered. 'Let them stand free.'

The seamen obeyed him wonderingly. As he went on to speak in Spanish to the men he had captured, they stared in even more astonishment. For as Rodney talked, a vast change came over the three fishermen. First they looked surprised, then their mouths were wreathed in smiles and finally they were down on their knees, touching their foreheads to the deck in servitude.

For the first time in her life Lizbeth was glad that her education had been so extensive. Her father had had her taught in much the same way as Queen Elizabeth had been instructed. At the age of ten she had been learning Italian, French, Latin and Greek, and when she was twelve a tutor in Spanish had been found for her. She alone aboard the *Sea Hawk* besides Rodney knew why the fishermen had changed their attitude so quickly when Rodney spoke to them. They thought that they had been captured by the Spanish!

When they found that the ship was English and that her Captain had sailed with their friend Sir Francis Drake, they were only too willing not only to reveal any information that might be of use to the English Captain, but to offer their help.

Quickly Rodney explained their need for a harbour. The three natives looked at each other; then the oldest, the Cimaroon who had spoken first, began a long reply. Immediately ahead of them, he said, was the coast of

Nicaragua. Rodney started at that, because he had been expecting to reach land south of Panama. The night wind had blown them further than he had anticipated.

He and his brother, the Cimaroon went on, were visiting an Indian settlement; but a week ago one of the gold ships from Panama, *en route* for Havana, had been forced to seek shelter in their harbour while a split rudder was repaired. The Spaniards had forced into slavery those of the Indians whom they had not killed, they had seduced the young women, and, rather than eat the provisions with which the ship was stocked for the journey back to Spain, they had ravaged the whole countryside in search of food.

The chief of the tribe was afraid that, although the ship was nearly ready for sea, the Spaniards were in no hurry to leave because some of them thought they had missed the treasure fleet which was sailing from Havana with a powerful escort of warships, and fever had also broken out among the galley slaves.

Fearful for their lives, the Cimaroons had escaped from the settlement and taken with them for safety the Chief's son.

'If the Spaniards are there, we cannot land,' Rodney said in despair.

The Indian declared to the contrary. He knew of a smaller inlet not far from his own settlement where the *Sea Hawk* would be quite safe. The Englishmen could repair their ship in secret and the Spaniards need know nothing of their arrival. The real danger, however, the Indian warned them, was from the *guarda costas*, but many of these had gone to Havana to escort the other ships filled with gold which had been loaded at Nombre de Dios.

The Spanish ship in their harbour was the last of the gold ships to leave Nombre de Dios, and in response to a quick question from Rodney, the Indian added that no *guarda costa* had returned to look for her and the Spanish officers had commented bitterly upon this, as they thought they should have been missed by now.

107

A ship that had sailed from Nombre de Dios to Havana would be filled with silver and gold and much valuable treasure. Rodney felt a sense of excitement growing within him. Yet what could he do about it? His own ship was crippled and even with the help of the friendly natives, he estimated that it would take several days to repair her, however hard they worked. It was too soon to think of anything except reaching safety by letting the Indian guide them to a point on the coast where they could creep along under the shelter of the cliffs to the promised harbour.

Being to the north of the Panama isthmus meant that there might be ships passing, but it was a risk to which he had no alternative. At the same time he had a feeling that his luck was going to change. Nothing could have been more fortunate than that they should have captured three friendly natives at this particular moment.

Rodney remembered there had been a revolt of the Indians in Nicaragua against the intolerable oppression of the Spaniards about thirty years earlier. It had been hopeless from the start, for the Indians were unarmed and the Spanish rulers, who had explored and taken over the country after it was discovered by Christopher Columbus, had treated the insurgents with incredible cruelty. Rodney could be sure that the Indians of Nicaragua would help him strike a blow against the might and power and brutality of Spain.

It was only when the natives had finished speaking and he turned to take them aft so they could help pilot the ship that he realised that no one had understood a word that was being said. He saw Barlow's face and felt he owed him an explanation; and then as he hesitated, realizing that time was short, Lizbeth came forward.

'Shall I tell Master Barlow what has been decided?' she enquired.

'You speak Spanish?' Rodney asked in astonishment.

'Of course,' she replied, 'and several other languages if they should be of any use to you.'

It was a rebuke, but her lips were smiling and suddenly Rodney felt that he wanted to bury the hatchet. His anger and irritation with her vanished.

'Thank you, Master Gillingham. Please tell Master Barlow what has been said, and these other gentlemen as well.' Rodney included the gaping Lieutenants in his gesture.

Lizbeth translated the conversation that had taken place between Rodney and the natives.

'A Spanish ship!' Master Gadstone exclaimed, his eyes alight with excitement. 'We will capture her if it is the last thing we do.'

'Which it may easily be,' Barlow said crushingly. 'My thanks, Master Gillingham,' he added politely to Lizbeth, then hurried after Rodney.

'I want to come to grips with these damned Spaniards,' Master Gadstone said to Lizbeth. 'I have hated them ever since I was a boy when I heard of their treachery to John Hawkins at the battle of St. Juan de Ulua. I was very young at the time, but I resolved there and then that when I grew up I would make the Spaniards suffer for the cruelties they inflicted on their prisoners, for the agonies of those who died on the rack or who lay forgotten in the black prisons of Seville.'

There was almost a fanatical light in the young man's eyes as he spoke. Lizbeth put her hand on his arm.

'I understand what you feel,' she said, 'and yet hatred, like cruelty is a frightening thing.'

Master Gadstone smiled at that.

'I will teach the Spaniards about both if I get near to them with a sword in my hand,' he threatened, 'and pray heaven, our Captain will give us the chance.'

'I hope so, too,' Lizbeth agreed.

The young lieutenant was silent for a moment, and then he added:

'I was angry with him for running away yesterday, and yet he was right—it was the only possible thing to do.'

'Do you really think that?' Lizbeth asked, surprised.

'But of course. You can see what the Spaniard's guns could do to us. If we had tried to fight her, she would have pounded us into pulp before we could have got a shot home. And those luggers can do a lot of damage. Yes, the Captain was right, though I hated him for his decision at the moment it happened.'

'I felt the same thing,' Lizbeth said.

They smiled at each other like conspirators.

'He is a fine man,' Master Gadstone said. 'One day I hope to be like him and I, too, will have a ship of my own.'

There was a warmth of hero-worship in the young man's voice.

Lizbeth watched him hurry away to his duties. He was handsome enough, young, virile and doubtless extremely attractive to women, but she felt no secret stirrings within her heart as she talked with him.

With Rodney it was different; never could she be indifferent to him. He made her furiously angry, he made her tingle with apprehension. he made her tremble, but never could she ignore his presence.

She wondered why he was so different from other men, and remembered the fury in his face when she defied him— he had looked as if he would strike her. Something within Lizbeth quivered at the thought—but it was not fear she felt.

Lizbeth's expression was serious and a few minutes later she slipped up on to the after-deck. Rodney was there with the three natives. The ship, now heavy and difficult to handle, was coming slowly to the lee of the shore. The water was calm, but it was only a question of time, Rodney knew. before the ship would be completely waterlogged.

Slowly and with really brilliant seamanship he brought her. through a narrow channel of rocks into a small natural harbour. There was a sandy beach, high overhanging cliffs, and partial protection from the open sea by a coral reef.

They dropped anchor about noon and though everyone was tired from lack of sleep and Rodney felt as if his eyes were burning in his head, within an hour of their arrival they had the forge out on the beach and the smiths and the carpenters were getting ready to make the necessary repairs to the *Sea Hawk's* side.

It was not going to be an easy job, that was obvious from the first moment the damage was assessed, but skilled men could manage it. What was more worrying was that a great many of the ship's stores had been ruined by salt water. Not all their provisions were down below for space had been reserved for the cargo of gold which they hoped to bring home with them; but some had been there and Rodney was wondering how he could possibly replace them. Actually he knew the answer to all his problems, but for the moment he dared not voice it even to himself.

It was only as the afternoon passed and evening came that he took the Cimaroons and the Indian aside to talk to them where no one could overhear. No one in the ship's company could speak Spanish, but Rodney felt that caution was very necessary, especially now. Although the Spaniards were five miles away according to the Cimaroons, the men had been told to keep their voices low and make as little noise as possible, and not, under threat of dire punishment, to go beyond the bay itself.

They were prepared to obey for the moment, but Rodney knew full well that, when they were less tired and their work had advanced a little, the more adventurous of them would be up to mischief.

Here was yet another reason why there was no time to be lost. About an hour before dusk he gave Master Barlow special instructions and with a dark cloak over his shoulders and a dagger in his belt he came into the after cabin. Lizbeth, who was in there, gave him one glance and knew where he was going.

'May I come with you?' She knew it was a forlorn hope, but she had to ask the question.

'I am going alone with the Indian boy,' Rodney answered. 'He suggests it is not wise even to take his friends with him. I am just going to spy out the land, that is all.'

111

'I would still like to come,' Lizbeth said, 'but I understand.' She hesitated for a moment and raised her eyes to say shyly: 'I think I ought to apologise for what I said yesterday. You were right not to risk the lives of those you command. At the time I wanted to do battle with our enemies whatever the cost to ourselves.'

Her voice was low and, with an unexpected flash of intuition, Rodney realised what it must have cost her to apologise to him. Sometimes she might seem an irresponsible child and at others a woman. It was the woman who must humiliate herself, must bend her pride and say she was sorry to a man who had not treated her with much courtesy and certainly with little consideration.

Impulsively Rodney took a step towards her.

'I am glad you understand, Lizbeth,' he said. 'I hated you to think hardly of me, but I knew it was the right thing to do. And now perhaps I, too, should apologise for some things, and thank you for others. I am grateful to you for caring for my sick, for it is not a woman's work and I hate to see you stoop to such a filthy task.'

'Nothing is more important than the health of the crew,' Lizbeth answered. 'I am going down to the wounded now. You will not forget the man whose foot is shot off.'

Rodney felt guilty. He had forgotten him.

'I will give instructions to Barlow before I leave,' he said. 'There is no need for you to go below again. Speacock, the man you were instructing, will do all that can be done.'

'I think I am in a better position that Speacock, to judge what is best,' Lizbeth smiled; 'and besides, those who are in pain will need laudanum and I do not think I would trust Speacock to measure it properly. Tomorrow, if you will allow me, I will ask the Indian to find me some of the herbs which have healing properties.'

Her eyes were soft and gentle as she spoke and Rodney, watching her, realised that she was very pale and knew that she, too, was as much in need of sleep as he was. He wondered how Francis would have stood up to the voyage so far and realised with a sudden hint of amusement that he would far rather have Lizbeth with him than Francis.

Impulsively he bent forward and taking her small hand in his raised it to his lips.

'I thank you,' he said softly and was gone from the cabin before she could speak again.

7

No one slept much on board the *Sea Hawk* that night. Lizbeth, moving restlessly in her cabin, could hear the men pacing up and down the deck and whispering to each other when they spoke, for Rodney had commanded silence before he left.

Ashore the blacksmiths were still at their forge under an improvised tent to hide the glow of the fire. It made them so intolerably hot that every so often they must step outside to draw breaths of fresh air and wipe the sweat from their eyes.

They had been working without a stop the whole day, but no man had asked to be relieved, for each knew without being told that the life of every man aboard the *Sea Hawk* depended upon the speed of the repairs. At any moment a Spanish ship sailing near the shore might spot them or the Spaniards in the harbour further along the coast might spring upon them from the cliffs above.

The *Sea Hawk* had been brought as near in-shore as it was possible to anchor her and the crew had worked all day at the pumps to empty the water out of her hold. Even Lizbeth, ignorant as she was of seamanship, could feel that the ship was riding more lightly now and there was once again a feeling of buoyancy about her.

It was very hot in the night without a breath of air and, even apart from her anxiety over Rodney, Lizbeth thought it would have been impossible to sleep or rest in such a stifling atmosphere. She was sorry for the men still working, but she knew that any work, however tiring, however intolerable, was preferable to a Spanish prison or to being chained to a galley until one died of exhaustion.

'Rodney! Rodney!' She wanted to call his name out loud.

In a panic, she thought that she might never see him again. The Spaniards might have captured and killed him. The idea stabbed her with a physical pain and she shut her eyes against the agony of it—Rodney!

She saw the strong, clean line of his chin, the square forehead, his heavy eyebrows, straight nose and the sensitive fullness of his lips. . . . And she saw, too, his eyes looking down into hers with an expression which brought a burning flush searing its way up her body to her cheeks. Words he had spoken had suddenly a new significance.

'Dying does not matter, but it takes courage to look death in the face.'

She bit her fingers to prevent herself crying—Rodney must not die, he must not! He must live, he must come back to the ship . . . to her!

Rodney! Rodney! If only she could pray, but the very prayers she had used all her life were strangled by the tightness of her throat.

'Dear God, bring him back.' It was torture to enunciate the words but they brought her a little solace.

Rodney! Rodney! Even the darkness of the night seemed to stifle her, so that she must die herself from this agony of anxiety.

The hours passed slowly. When dawn came, there was still no sign of Rodney. He had placed sentries on the cliff before he left so that they could watch for the approach of the enemy from whichever side they might come. The men were lying half-hidden under the coconut palms amongst the luxurious vegetation with which the land appeared to be covered.

Lizbeth, from below, could see them quite clearly and she knew their heads were turned continually in one direction—the one from which they expected Rodney to return.

With daylight those on board the *Sea Hawk* under Barlow's command sprang into an accelerated activity which appeared to keep them all breathless, not only from the heat, but from the speed with which their orders must be carried out.

And then, just when Lizbeth felt she could bear it no longer, when her eyes ached from watching for the man who did not come, Rodney returned! He came so swiftly that he was down the cliff side and crossing the sandy beach almost before she was aware of his presence.

But even had she not seen him, she felt that she would have known by the attitude of everyone aboard that he was there. It was not that they stopped work; it was not that anything was said or done, but in every man there was the same reaction—a sudden relief from tension which swept through the ship as obviously as a cry.

There was a boat waiting for Rodney where the waves lapped languidly against the sands and it took but a few seconds for the seamen manning it to row him to the ship. The bo'sun's pipes shrilled as he came aboard and then, regardless of discipline, of custom and correct procedure, Lizbeth reached him first.

'Thank God you are safe! she cried.

His face was pale she noticed, but his eyes were shining with some inner excitement. His doublet was dusty and he looked as though he had lain all night in the earth or in some sandy place and had not had a moment since to brush himself clean.

Rodney looked at Lizbeth when she spoke to him, but his first words were for Barlow, who stood a little to one side as if waiting for instructions.

'Everything in order, Master Barlow?'

'The repairs should be finished by noon, Sir. We can put to sea tonight.'

Rodney smiled. This was what he wanted to hear.

'Thank you, Master Barlow. I wish to speak to the entire ship's company.'

'Now, Sir?'

Barlow glanced for the first time at Rodney's clothes.

Lizbeth knew that he was thinking of the breakfast that Hapley had waiting in the cabin. Rodney also needed a shave, but with his usual impatience with such trifles he said sharply:

'At once, Master Barlow!'

'Aye, aye, Sir.'

The command was given for 'all hands on deck' and the men came tumbling up from below with a haste which bespoke their eagerness. Only the blacksmiths, the men working with them, and the sentries on the cliffs were missing.

Rodney looked down on the crowd of faces upturned to his. They were a fine lot, he thought suddenly, English every man-Jack of them, and not one that he would not be glad to have by his side in a tight corner. He stood looking at them, waiting for that sudden pregnant silence that comes just before an orator says his first words. Then with the hot sun beating down he began to speak.

'You know where I went last night,' he said, and every man seemed to bend forward a little so that he should not miss one word. 'The Indian whom we brought aboard guided me to his village which lies about five miles to the north of us. It is built on the edge of a bay—a natural harbour, very much like the one here, only larger.

'As he and his friends had already told me, there is a Spanish ship anchored there, put in for repairs to her steering. The ship is the *Santa Perpetua*—a large galleon of over five hundred tons and loaded with treasure from Panama. She was on her way to Havana; and when she does not arrive, there is every chance that other ships will be sent in search of her.

'I am telling you now so that you will realise all that we have to guard against. Our friend, whose father is Chief of the village, thinks that she has approximately two hundred white men aboard, perhaps more. They are most of them experienced fighting men and well armed. They have posted sentries around the village and there is always an armed guard aboard the ship itself, although the officers, and the majority of the men too, have been

117

making the most of their enforced holiday, and enjoying themselves ashore. The Indian girls are not unattractive; the native wine is potent.'

Rodney paused a minute, then looking straight at his audience, he said:

'Tonight we are going to take the *Santa Perpetua.*'

A wild cheer rose to every man's lips. It was hastily checked by Master Barlow's 'Quiet there,' repeated and re-repeated by the Petty Officers.

'We must make no noise,' Rodney warned. 'Voices carry in this atmosphere. Last night, lying above the native village, I could hear conversations being carried on, orders being given, the sick groaning with fever. We have still many hours of daylight ahead of us and we must keep quiet and still for fear of discovery.

'You will all of you have your orders, you will all of you, I know, carry them out to the best of your ability. A mistake on the part of one may mean the death of all. There is no need for me to point out to you that we are greatly out-numbered in fighting strength. We despise the Spaniards but we should be foolish indeed if we under-estimate them. They have been well trained in the art of fighting hand to hand.'

Rodney paused and then, as the men seemed still to be waiting, as he felt the excitement radiating from them and saw by the expression on every face the elation they were feeling, he did not dismiss them as he intended, but continued:

'There is one other thing I would say to you. Before I left England, before I went to Plymouth to buy the *Sea Hawk* I stayed a few nights in Whitehall. I was not privileged to meet our Queen, but I saw Her Majesty, in fact I stood within a few feet of her.

'I was passing through the Stone Gallery when the Queen, surrounded by her couriers and Ladies-in-Waiting, came into the Gallery from the gardens. I had not been expecting to see Her Majesty and like the other people there I stood to one side, awed and surprised at her sudden appearance.

118

'It was a dull day, but it seemed to me as if the sun had suddenly come out. She is not tall, our Queen, and yet when one sees her, one feels that she is the greatest woman on whom one has ever set eyes. She has a dignity and grace which give her a beauty beyond words. I would like to describe her to you and yet it is impossible.

'When one is away from her, one thinks of Queen Elizabeth the woman; but when she is there, you know you are in the presence of England—this country which has bred us and which we all love because it is ours.

'I watched the Queen pass and I knew then that she was the personification of all that we struggle for, all we try to attain and all for which we will, if necessary, give our lives. She is our Queen; she is Gloriana; she is England!'

Every man listening seemed to draw a deep breath and then, without another word, Rodney turned and walked across the deck to the after cabin. There was silence for several seconds, a tribute to an orator who had moved them, to words which were echoed by every man in his heart; and then, excitedly, the chatter broke out, uncrushed by the orders for silence being given by the officers continuously long after every man was back at his duties.

Only Lizbeth did not move. She remained where she had stood listening to Rodney and only after a long time did she realise that her hands were clenched tightly together so that her fingers were bloodless, and her cheeks were burning with the same excitement that was making her heart beat almost painfully beneath her breast.

It was a new Rodney she had heard speaking, a man inspired, a man whose voice had been a thrill when he spoke of what he had seen and what he had felt. It was the first time that Lizbeth had encountered the veneration and adoration that the Queen commanded amongst the men who served her and amongst all those, indeed, with whom she came in contact.

The mere mention of her name conjured up many strange and varied memories of her past—the girl whose

119

childhood had been so helpless, her mother humiliated and executed; the shadow of the scaffold lying dark and menacing over her own obscure yet closely watched existence. Alternately caressed and neglected, she was the heir to the Throne of England at one moment and a bastard outcast the next.

London was crowded with gibbets, Smithfield's pyres were burning, but Elizabeth had survived these perils by a miracle of discretion, brilliance and courage.

Lizbeth had all her life heard talk of how those at Court were inspired by Gloriana as they had named the Queen; how Hawkins, Drake, Raleigh and a hundred others had wanted only to lay the spoils of their voyages at the feet of her whom they served. She had listened to a thousand stories of the devotion of the Queen's statesmen; and she had known, for all England speculated on it, of the affection that existed between the Queen and the Earl of Leicester. There had been chatter about stately Hatton and handsome Heneage de Vere, the dashing king of the tiltyard, and young Blount who blushed when the eye of Her Majesty was fixed upon him. There was the Earl of Essex now, tall, handsome and irresponsible, to give the gossips something to whisper about.

And yet no one, however spiteful, however malicious, could deny that Elizabeth was great. As Rodney had said, men were ready to live and, if necessary, to die for her and to count their lives either way of little consequence. And yet she was just a woman.

Lizbeth remembered the throb in Rodney's voice and felt a strange sensation she had never known before. Although the idea was almost laughable, it was almost a jealousy that any woman, even if she were a Queen, should draw men to her in such a way that she held not only their lives, but their hearts in her hands and took such devotion as her just due.

And then it seemed to Lizbeth in that moment she learned an important lesson, one which should be taught to all her sex. She learnt that in a greater or lesser degree every woman should be to a man an inspiration, a spur, an ideal and last of all, a goal to which he must strive endlessly.

For a moment Lizbeth felt frightened by the magnitude of this; and then, standing on that sun-baked deck with hands scurrying around her, the sound of the black-smith's hammer in her ears and the lap of the waves beneath her feet, she smiled with an inner satisfaction and a sense of power that she had never known before. She, too, was a woman, although for the moment no one was aware of it!

Dinner at twelve was a hastily snatched meal, but at least Lizbeth had Rodney to herself for a few minutes. They neither of them took much note of what they were eating and Rodney seemed for once to have forgotten his anger and resentment at her presence, and talked away as easily and without reserve as if they had been at Camfield. He told Lizbeth further details of his investigation the night before.

'The Indian boy went into the village to find out the latest news and then came back to where I was hidden,' he said. 'He learnt that the steering of the *Santa Perpetua* has been repaired and that the ship is to leave at dawn. But there is to be a party ashore tonight. The natives have been commanded to find half a dozen bullocks and a dozen fat pigs. They were in revolt at the idea, but I gave them money and both the bullocks and the pigs will be there and a great number of casks of native wine.'

'What is that like?' Lizbeth asked.

'Very fiery and very potent. It is made from the fermented sap of a palm tree which has leaves nearly twenty feet long, and big, golden flowers three feet high. The wine is called *Vino de Coyol*. The Spaniards got hold of some of it, but the natives have kept most of their store hidden from them. Our Indian boy brought his father, the Chief, to see me. I gave him all the money I had with me to be spent on this feast and I think the Spaniards will besurprised to see how lavish it can be.'

121

'And while they feast . . . ?' Lizbeth queried excitedly.

Rodney nodded.

'That is the point. While they are feasting we must strike!' He drummed on the table with his fingers, a habit he had when he was concentrating. 'I want to avoid as much fighting as possible; I cannot afford to lose a single man, especially if we have two ships to put to sea.'

'Do not be afraid,' Lizbeth said softly. 'The galleon will be yours, I am sure of it.'

He smiled at her then.

'You told me once before I should be successful,' he said, 'and yet yesterday you taunted me with being a coward.'

'I am ashamed of my words,' Lizbeth answered. 'I did not understand. I wanted to fight the Spaniards, to fight and win.' She hesitated for a moment and then added in a low voice: 'I had not seen then the wounds that guns can inflict on human flesh. The man with the shattered foot had it amputated last night. I did not know that men could suffer so much and live.'

Impulsively Rodney put out his hand and laid it over hers.

'I have commanded you before, leave the wounded to those who are used to such matters.'

'And I have told you that I will not obey you in this,' Lizbeth replied. 'Who else on board has any knowledge of medicine or the treatment of wounds?'

Rodney did not answer the question and Lizbeth continued triumphantly.

'You see, you cannot tell me, so I must do my best. Do you know that the man into whose wound I poured the *aqua vitae* is without fever?'

'I see that by the end of the voyage I shall be drinking water,' Rodney said.

But Lizbeth did not smile in response to his jest and her brows were knit as she said:

'If only I knew more! I have heard that the Indians know of plants with great medicinal properties. May I ask our Indian friend to find some for me?'

'You shall certainly ask him later,' Rodney replied.

Lizbeth looked at him then and the same thought was in both their minds. However confident they both might be, would there be a 'later' for either of them? Rodney got to his feet quickly.

'I must not linger here,' he said abruptly. 'There is much to be done.'

'But, please,' Lizbeth pleaded hastily, 'will you not tell me exactly what your plans are?'

'You will know in good time,' he answered.

She had a wild impulse to put out her arms to him and beg him not to go. What did a galleon matter, or the Spaniards, or the Queen herself for that matter, if Rodney were safe? Lizbeth wanted to keep him at her side. She wanted . . . but what did she want?

How impossible it was to put it into words. She only knew that her whole being was beset with conflicting emotions—pride, admiration mingled with fear, and some other feeling to which she could not put a name.

She thought of all she had endured during the night when she was afraid that he would never return, and knew that what she must suffer now would be infinitely worse. Her prayers had been answered once, but could she be sure they would be heard a second time?

'Stay here!' If only she dared suggest such a thing; and then courage returned to her. Rodney would succeed —she was sure of it—and she must inspire him, not try to make of him a coward or a weakling.

'He will be successful,' she said the words aloud to herself and then wiped the tears roughly from her eyes.

It was, however, an hour before dark before Lizbeth really understood exactly what was occurring. A little before that Rodney had asked Barlow to discover who among the men could swim. Barlow had looked surprised.

'Swim, Sir?'

The majority of seamen thought it was unlucky to learn to swim. If their ship was sunk, the sooner one went to the bottom the better. Swimming about only prolonged the agony. Rodney knew this and understood Barlow's surprise at the question.

'I want a boat's crew who can swim and swim well,' he said, 'and don't pick me anyone who will flounder about and expect to be rescued—do you understand?'

'Yes, Sir.'

Barlow came back with the information that there were twelve men aboard who could swim. A boat had only eight oars and he had, therefore, chosen the eight men he thought best suited to the work ahead.

'Eight will do, Master Barlow,' Rodney said. 'I shall go with the boat. You will be in charge of the *Sea Hawk*.'

'Can I not come with you, Sir?' Barlow asked eagerly.

Rodney shook his head.

'No. You will be in charge here and if we fail, your orders are to proceed to sea immediately. Do you understand?'

'Yes, Sir.'

'Fetch Master Gadstone to me.'

Gadstone was fetched. As he came into the cabin, he was almost dancing with excitement. He had been waiting for something like this ever since he left England.

'Now listen to me, Master Gadstone,' Rodney said. 'What I am going to give you to do is an extremely difficult task because it demands waiting, patience, initiative, and being able to run away.'

'Run away, Sir?'

'Yes, run away,' Rodney said grimly. 'Now listen to me attentively.'

He spoke sharply, and purposely with a cold authority. He wanted to calm down Gadstone's excitement and exuberance to something more sensible. It was by no means an easy task. However, he looked calmer, Rodney thought, as he saw a little band of men set off up the cliffs—Gadstone and six others, all young and long-legged and, as he said to Barlow, 'capable of running like the Devil'.

'Wait for them until the last moment, Master Barlow,' Rodney instructed, 'but you are not to jeopardise the safety of this ship for them or for anyone else.'

'Very good, Sir.'

Barlow spoke in a tone of resignation. He knew Rodney's plan was sound, even brilliant in conception, and yet he hated the part he had to play in it. He had calmly to wait aboard the *Sea Hawk* and perhaps put out to sea with the knowledge that both his Captain and Lieutenant were dead or taken prisoner.

'I shall leave in five minutes,' Rodney said.

He went into the after cabin to make a last entry in his log-book and found Lizbeth standing by the port-hole. She turned as he entered and because he was not expecting to see her, she saw his face for a moment off guard. He was smiling excitedly as a schoolboy. He might manage to speak coldly and authoritatively to those he commanded, but just for this moment he was himself—a man in search of adventure and high adventure at that, a gambler who was staking everything on a throw of the dice.

'If only I could come with you!' Lizbeth breathed the words rather than spoke them and yet Rodney heard.

It was then it seemed that he remembered who she was and what would be her position if he were killed and the ship captured. Suddenly grave, he walked across the cabin to where she stood.

'It is not my fault that you are here,' he said, 'and yet I am responsible for you. If anything happens to me, Barlow is in charge of the *Sea Hawk* and has my instructions to take her back to England. If he should fail, then I beg of you . . . do not let yourself be taken prisoner by the Spaniards.'

'What do you mean?' Lizbeth asked.

'There are cleaner ways of dying than rotting in a dungeon in Seville,' Rodney said; 'and if they should discover you to be a woman, it . . . it will not help you.'

There was no need for him to say more. They both knew the fate that would await her.

'There are several poisons, I think, in the doctor's cabinet,' Lizbeth said in a low voice.

'Let us pray they will not be used,' Rodney answered.

Lizbeth threw back her head.

'I am not afraid to die. That is why I would like to come with you.'

'I did not know that women had such courage,' Rodney said.

She smiled at that.

'I believe you know very little about women, after all.'

'Or perhaps merely very little about you,' Rodney replied.

She looked up at him at that and for a moment their eyes held each other. Then he started as if he had forgotten the time. Instinctively she put out her hands towards him.

'Take care of yourself, Rodney,' she pleaded.

He hesitated for a moment as if he would say something in reply and then he put his hand on her shoulder, an easy, affectionate gesture of good fellowship that he might have made towards Francis.

'I shall be safe enough,' he smiled.

He was gone then. A moment later Lizbeth heard him give a series of commands. Slowly she went to the door and out on to the deck. The men were already in the boat and Rodney was going over the side to join them. They had all of them stripped their shirts from their bodies, Rodney included. Their feet were bare, each wore a sword belt and cutlass and a sharp knife which he would carry in his teeth when he swam.

There was an hour yet before darkness and they had to get round the more dangerous part of the coast before they could lie in wait. Rodney had not anticipated that it would be as nerve-racking as it was, moving out to sea and then along beneath the cliff, keeping a look-out all the time for watchers from above or for a ship at sea.

The way itself was tricky, for in several places there was a deep undercurrent. There were also half-submerged coral reefs which might easily tear a hole in the boat.

But at length they came to the place which the Indian had indicated as being the best place of concealment until darkness fell.

It would not be long now, Rodney thought, and welcomed a star as it appeared above them, shimmering through the velvet sky. Still they must wait, while Rodney's thoughts were with Gadstone who, by this time, should be nearing his place of concealment above the village. An Indian would meet them there.

Gadstone and his men were to hide, watching everything that was taking place, and to do nothing if all went well until they heard three blasts on a whistle from the *Santa Perpetua*. That was the signal and when Rodney gave it they were to leave at once, running as quickly as their legs could carry them back to the *Sea Hawk* to get on board before she sailed to join the captured ship.

But if things went wrong, then Gadstone's little band was to cause a diversion. They had several fire bombs with them and each man carried a javelin tipped with tar; and although they could do little against a large number of Spaniards, they might at least cause some confusion and divert attention, if it was necessary, from the ship lying in the harbour.

That was Rodney's plan for Gadstone, and Barlow had his orders. Now there was only his own part to be executed. In a whisper he gave the order for the boat to proceed. Dipping the oars with the utmost caution, they crept round the coast and suddenly the harbour opened up before them and they saw that the party ashore was, as the Indian Chief promised, in full progress.

Four great bonfires were burning, as well as the other fires on which the bullocks and pigs were being cooked. The light was enough to reveal the merry-makers sprawling around on the soft sand, their arms encircling the flower-bedecked Indian maidens, while they ate and drank the food and wine that was being plied upon them by the older members of the village. Behind the native huts was a compound guarded by sentries in which the galley slaves were imprisoned.

In the bay lay the *Santa Perpetua*, her high masts visible against the sky. It was difficult to see anything very clearly and yet Rodney was sure she lay in deep water and he reckoned that it would take at least three or four minutes for a boat to reach her from the shore.

A burble of voices and laughter came from the party on the beach. It was quite a considerable noise, but even so Rodney hardly breathed the order which told his men to beach the boat. A few minutes later they were swimming, each man with a knife in his teeth, his cutlass bumping uncomfortably against his legs as he struck out into the darkness towards the ship. The sea was as warm as milk and Rodney, who was a good swimmer, easily passed the other men and reached the ship first. He caught hold of a rope hanging over the side and waited until the others joined him and then, slowly and as silently as they could, they began to climb.

Very slowly they raised their heads over the thick bulwarks, mercifully it was not netted, and, as Rodney had expected, the sentries left on board the ship were all standing by the taff'rail looking longingly at the festivities ashore. There was a moment of deadly peril when the Englishmen, dripping wet, must move across the whole length of the deck to strike down the men before they turned and saw them.

But even as they started creeping forward the natives ashore started to sing and dance, the noise they made deafening all other sounds.

It was all over in a matter of seconds. The six sentries each received a knife in the back and before they could shout a heavy hand was clamped over their mouths to receive their dying breath.

'Look below,' Rodney whispered.

The men came back a few minutes later shaking their heads.

'No one else aboard, Sir.'

'Very good.'

Each man had been allotted his job before they left the *Sea Hawk*. They hurried now to the halliards and braces

128

of the foresail. There had been no wind all day, but now an evening breeze was blowing off the land and the ship was rocking in her moorings as if she herself were ready to start. Rodney held his breath. Someone ashore might notice what was going on. But the Indians were dancing round one of the bonfires, their naked bodies, gyrating and pulsating, making it hard to see anything.

'Ready to weigh anchor, Sir, and she has one of them new capstans.'

It was a Petty Officer who spoke breathlessly, and Rodney, glancing round him, knew that this was the supreme moment of danger when they must weigh anchor. Every seaman knew what a noise the anchor made being wound aboard.

The merry-making was still loud and rampageous ashore—indeed it was increasing in volume as Rodney had planned with the Indian Chief, and yet—who knew? —one of the officers might have sharp eyes, one of them might not be as drunk as the majority sounded.

Slowly they began their task, their bare feet seeking a hold on the smooth deck as they bent all their weight to the capstan bars. The cable came steadily in, but the measured clank, clank of the capstan seemed to shout the news of what they were doing abroad.

Clank, clank!

Surely someone must hear it! Rodney thought in despair, sweating as he expended every ounce of his strength and muscle.

The cable was heavy as might be expected in such a big ship, but it was coming up smoothly. Clank, clank! And now at last the anchor was rising!

It was only then that Rodney dared to glance towards the shore. The natives were whirling round with the abandonment of Dervishes. Those who were not dancing were stamping their feet and clapping, the drums were beating and they all seemed to be straining their vocal powers in some fiendish ditty. The Indians were co-operating well!

'Man the mainsail yards,' Rodney commanded. He

went to the tiller himself and brought the *Santa Perpetua's* head round into the wind.

A sudden puff seemed to come at just the right moment, the sails flapped, bellied and flapped again. Rodney was conscious of the rapid beating of his heart as he watched the huge expanse of canvas. The sails were filling, the ship was moving. He could hardly believe it was true.

She heeled to the wind with a creaking and a groaning of her cordage; then Rodney heard the chuckle of the waves against her bows. The wind was increasing, veering round to nor'-east, as he and Barlow had anticipated earlier in the evening; and the *Santa Perpetua* began to gather way.

It was then that Rodney drew his whistle from his pocket and gave three loud blasts upon it. He waited another moment and blew another three, in case Gadstone could not hear him above the frenzied row on the beach. And yet he was sure the little band must have seen the *Santa Perpetua* moving.

On shore there came a sudden shout, a different sound from all the rest. Someone was pointing towards the ship; another and yet another finger came out in their direction, and men were running down to the water's edge, shouting and gesticulating. At that moment there was a flash and an explosion behind them. Rodney grinned to himself. Despite all his instructions to the contrary, he had guessed that young Gadstone would not be able to forbear letting off his fire bombs.

It was quite unnecessary and strictly against his orders, but he knew that those long hours of waiting in the darkness must have been very trying to Master Gadstone's exuberance; but he and his men would be legging it back to the *Sea Hawk*. They would be in time to catch her before she sailed.

The fire bombs, as Rodney had expected, had added to the confusion on the shore. Looking back over his shoulder, he saw that the Indians were still playing their allotted part. The natives were running about screaming;

the Spaniards, bemused, drunk and completely taken by surprise, had not the slightest idea what they should do.

The *Santa Perpetua* was out of the bay by this time and breasting the open sea. Topsails and spritsails were quickly set. But there was no hurry. Although some of the Spaniards were hurrying into the boats lying on the shore, Rodney knew they had no chance of catching up with the ship and they would soon give up the chase once they found themselves afloat in the darkness.

He set his course south. It would not be long, he reckoned, before the *Sea Hawk* came to join him and then they would sail towards the Darien coast.

The *Santa Perpetua* was big and heavy and yet Rodney found her easy to handle. It was many years since he had been at the tiller and it gave him almost a sensuous thrill to caress the smooth length of wood with his hands, to feel the ship respond to his slightest touch. There was the sweet music of the breeze in the rigging and the lapping of the waves against the side as they moved forward into the star-strewn darkness.

Rodney threw back his head and let the air out of his lungs. They had done it! He could hardly believe it was true, but they had done it! The *Santa Perpetua* was theirs. He had captured her just as he planned without the loss of one man; he had captured her for England and for—Gloriana!

8

Dawn broke at three o'clock in the morning and Rodney had not left the wheel all night. He was not conscious of feeling tired, but rather as if his body no longer belonged to him and was acting independently, so that sometimes he stared stupidly at his hands, watching them at the wheel and wondering how they knew the right thing to do.

Sometimes he talked with people who were not there, his voice low against the darkness, and somehow one with the murmur of the sea.

'Talk to me, Phillida,' he said once. 'Why do you hide from me? I will find you, wherever you go, wherever you conceal yourself. You are mine! There is no escape. I will make you love me. . . .'

But it was not Phillida he saw against the night, but Lizbeth—her green eyes mocking him, haunting his dreams, until he imagined her a devil, for surely he must be possessed by her.

Lizbeth's long lashes, downcast against her cheeks until they were raised to reveal no demure, maidenly coyness, but a flashing anger, a fury equal to his own.

Lizbeth across the dinner-table; Lizbeth in the sunshine on deck; Lizbeth so close to him that he could hear the very intake of her breath . . . or was it just the breeze?

How terribly tired he was . . . and yet he must take the ship to . . . Lizbeth!

As the light climbed up the sky and revealed the smooth pattern of the waves stretching away endlessly into a misty horizon, Rodney saw that he had brought the *Santa Perpetua* safely away from the coast and out into the open sea.

He hoped, too, that he had been successful in navigating the course that he and Barlow had planned together, their aim, of course, being to avoid the trade route from Nombre de Dios to Havana. Then, as his tired brain tried to feel some relief at the thought that for the moment there was nothing dangerous in sight, there came a hail from the main mast.

'Sail ho!'

Rodney felt himself grow alert, the mists of fatigue cleared in a moment from his mind. He did not reply, he only lifted his face and waited. He knew what he wanted to hear and yet the reassurance seemed to take an unconscionable time in coming.

'It's the *Sea Hawk*, Sir! On the starboard bow, Sir, and making straight for us, I'm sure on it,' came the cry, and Rodney gave a sigh of relief.

'A cup of wine, Sir?' a voice said at his side.

He looked down to see one of the men with a tray in his hand. On it was a jug and goblet of such exquisite workmanship that Rodney could only stare at them in amazement. Gold-chased and ornamented with precious stones which glittered in the morning sun, they seemed like something that must have come out of a palace rather than a ship's cabin. He glanced round to see the man who had brought them grinning from ear to ear.

'The after cabin's full o' such gewgaws, Sir,' he volunteered. 'Looks as 'ow we've struck it lucky.'

Rodney picked up the goblet and drank the wine. It was rich and good and he felt it gave him new life and energy.

'Let us hope this is a sample of what the rest of the cargo is like,' he said briefly, putting the goblet back on the tray. 'Get the galley fire going, we all need breakfast.'

'Aye, aye, Sir.'

The man went off at the double and for a moment

Rodney envied him—he looked so fresh and full of energy, while he felt utterly exhausted, it was no use denying it, and he despised himself for his frailty. Then he remembered that this was the third night he had been without sleep, and he felt that there was some excuse for his fatigue.

He looked towards the *Sea Hawk*. She was coming steadily towards them, but her progress would be slower than that of the *Santa Perpetua* who had the wind behind her.

Rodney was longing to go below to explore the ship, to see more of her than could be seen from where he stood behind the wheel; but he knew there was no one he could trust to take his place. Besides, every man was needed to work the sails. It had been difficult doing things in the dark, feeling their way around an unknown ship built on lines unfamiliar to British seamen.

And now Rodney noticed that they were making fast the sheets, making a decent, seaman-like job of those which had been cast off in a hurry, or left uncoiled. He knew that the men, as they hurried about, scurrying up the rigging or shouting instructions one to the other, were determined to impress their mates on board the *Sea Hawk* when she came alongside. They all desired to show off, a very human weakness in the circumstances.

Rodney grinned to himself as he realised that though the ship might look smart, he and his men were like ragamuffins—half naked, the few clothes which they had on torn or dirty with their scrambling aboard; barefoot, yet armed with cutlass and knife, they looked what they were, buccaneers and pirates.

Rodney was hungry, too; but more than food he wanted a shave, a chance to wash, and the feel of a fine linen shirt against his skin.

Already the sun was hot and he knew that in an hour or so it would be hotter still, with every prospect of the wind dying away on them. Before that they would have met the *Sea Hawk*. She was growing nearer every minute and he could imagine now the excitement and speculation on deck.

He looked up at the main mast and saw that one of the men, without instruction, had taken down the red and yellow-castled banner of Spain; and he remembered that he should have given orders for this and had forgotten it. Master Barlow would have been scanning the main mast anxiously in case the ship to which he was proceeding so confidently was not the *Santa Perpetua* but another ship manned by her rightful owners.

Now Rodney could see, or thought he could, figures standing in the fo'c'sle, and wondered if Lizbeth would be amongst them. He was sure she would be there. She would not call him a coward now: for though she had apologised for her words, they still had the power to rankle and hurt him.

In capturing the *Santa Perpetua* he had justified, if it had needed any justification, the action he took in running away from superior odds and refusing to risk his ship and the lives of his men in a fight which could only have destroyed them. He had been right—of course he had been right; and although it was childish to have a feeling of elation at having justified himself, Rodney felt childish at the moment.

The *Sea Hawk* was coming nearer every moment and now he could see those aboard her waving excitedly. Barlow was managing her well, Rodney noticed, keeping her on a steady course and making the most of every breath of wind. For the thousandth time since he left Plymouth he told himself that he was lucky in having Barlow with him. He was a man one could trust, and though he would always lack initiative and that unaccountable touch of inspiration which was necessary in every good commander, as a second-in-command he was peerless and beyond criticism.

The *Sea Hawk* was within earshot now and the men were cheering. The sound of it brought a sudden lump to Rodney's throat. It was so English, so much a touch of home, the men cheering the capture of the *Santa*

135

Perpetua as they might have cheered a game or the sight of port itself after a long voyage. They had not reproached him when he ran away from the Spanish carrack and the pearling lugger, but he knew that he had disappointed them. Now they were giving him their full-hearted approval, and he felt suddenly almost absurdly gratified and pleased that he had done what they expected of him.

It was not difficult to heave to in the open sea. The breeze had practically died away. A boat was lowered from the *Sea Hawk* and Rodney was amused to see that the first person to climb up the side of the *Santa Perpetua* was Lizbeth. She could be quiet and unobtrusive if necessary; but when it came to getting something she wanted, she took full advantage of her position as an honoured guest.

'Oh, Rodney! You've done it!'

Her hands clung to his and she was forgetful of everything, including caution, in her excitement.

'My congratulations, Sir!'

Barlow's welcome was formal, but there was no mistaking the excitement in his face, too. His eyes were roving round, taking in every detail of the galleon; her broad beam, low projecting bulkhead and square stern; her poop towering into the air like a castle; her taff'rail three and four feet thick behind which gleamed half a dozen wide-mouthed guns—polished brass culverins and demi-cannon.

Barlow gaped at the woodwork glittering with gilt insignia, elaborate carvings and armorial escutcheons, while the sculptured figureheads, the queer, tall octagonal complicity rigging were to him all figures of fun.

'By the soul of King Harry!'

It was Barlow's most expressive oath and only used when he was deeply moved.

'She's the most wonderful ship I have ever seen,' Lizbeth said, drawing in a deep breath. 'Please tell us everything. How did you capture her? Was there any fighting?'

136

'It all went according to plan,' Rodney said, looking at Barlow and not at her. 'Are Master Gadstone and his band on board?'

'Yes, Sir.'

Rodney smiled. It was the one thing about which he had been worried.

'Then let us view our new possession, after which we had best make for some quiet harbour where we can inspect her cargo undisturbed. Did the Indian return with Master Gadstone?'

Barlow nodded.

'Yes, Sir. Excited as a child he was, and Master Gadstone the same way.'

Rodney laughed.

'There was something to be excited about this time.'

He turned as he spoke to lead the way to the after cabin; and then, as they reached it, through the open door on to the deck came a man. For a moment they were all too surprised to do anything but stare at him in astonishment.

He was young, extremely good-looking, with an olive skin and dark eyes which proclaimed his Spanish origin. He wore a claret-coloured doublet and breeches of the same hue; his stockings were a lighter shade and his small ruff was piped with gold. The roses on his shoes matched his doublet and were also spangled with gold; and round his shoulders was a great chain of precious stones.

For a moment no one said anything. The strange young man stared at Barlow, Lizbeth and Rodney. The latter was suddenly conscious of his naked raggedness. Nevertheless it was for him to take the initiative. Straightening his shoulders, and with a swagger he was far from feeling, he stepped forward.

'Your name, Señor?'

He spoke in Spanish and the young man answered him in the same language.

'I am Don Miguel, son of the Marquis de Suavez, owner of this ship.'

Rodney inclined his head.

137

'I am Rodney Hawkhurst, servant of Her Majesty Queen Elizabeth of England, Commander of the *Sea Hawk,* and also, due to capture, of the *Santa Perpetua.'*

'I understand, Sir.'

The Spaniard's tone was quiet and level. He put his hand to the sword which hung at his side. He unstrapped the belt and lifting it, handed it to Rodney in the time-honoured gesture of those who have been conquered.

Rodney took it from him and handed it to Barlow.

'Thank you, Señor de Suavez,' he said. 'You will of course, consider yourself my prisoner, but we will make you as comfortable as possible until we return to England.'

The Spaniard gave a little wry smile, as if he knew only too well the hardships of prison life that awaited him there.

'You are most gracious, Sir,' he said. 'I regret I did not hear you come aboard. Unfortunately I have been ill of the fever and the ship's doctor prescribed a sedative of such potency that I must have slept while the battle was taking place.' He hesitated for a moment and then continued. 'You will forgive my curiosity, but were many of the officers and men of the *Santa Perpetua* killed?'

'I am glad to set your mind at rest. No one was killed,' Rodney replied, 'except the six sentries left on board while the rest of the crew were feasting on the beach.'

For the first time an emotion showed on the young man's face.

'I told them feasting was unnecessary and quite ridiculous,' he said irritably. 'We had nothing to celebrate but a broken rudder.'

'I will, of course, be only too glad to tell you all that occurred when we have more time,' Rodney said, 'but at the moment there is much for me and my officers to do. I would be grateful, Señor, if you would return to your cabin and stay there.'

The Spaniard bowed and, passing through the after

138

cabin, crossed to a small door on the other side. It was the fact that his sleeping cabin was through the after cabin which had prevented the men who searched the ship from finding him the night before. The other cabins were empty and Rodney's eyes lit up with pleasure when he saw the log-books, maps and charts which lay about in the Captain's quarters.

He had never seen or anticipated anything so luxurious as the officers' accommodation aboard the *Santa Perpetua*. He noticed with astonishment that the bunks were furnished with the finest linen sheets and there were feather mattresses too—things he had never before seen at sea. Certainly the Spaniards knew how to make themselves comfortable.

The furnishings of the after cabin brought forth exclamations of awe from both Lizbeth and Barlow. Huge tables, carved and painted, were laden with a profusion of gold and silver ornaments, while it was obvious that the Captain of the ship and his guests habitually ate off gold plate. There were soft rugs on the floor and hangings of rich velvet over the portholes, while tapestries and pictures relieved the darkness of the panelled walls.

But such wealth cried aloud danger, for the Spaniards were not likely to let such a valuable ship as the *Santa Perpetua* disappear from sight without a search for her.

Without wasting time Rodney told Barlow to man the *Santa Perpetua* with the best hands that could be spared from the *Sea Hawk*. He had already decided, contrary to the usual procedure, to take over the *Santa Perpetua* himself rather than to put in a subordinate to take charge and run it with a prize crew. There was no one else, he thought, capable of navigating such a large ship; besides, he could anticipate how useful her great armament and heavy guns might be to them.

Already new, ambitious plans were forming in his mind, but for the moment the only thing which mattered was to get away with the least delay possible. The Indian boy and the Cimaroons who were to pilot them to the Darien coast came aboard. Rodney thanked the Indian for what he had achieved last night in making the capture of the *Santa Perpetua* possible and promised him as a reward for himself and his village a sum of pesos which made him gasp with excitement and gratitude.

Rodney had not so much money in his possession, but he was certain that there would be plenty of money both in gold and silver aboard the *Santa Perpetua*; and he was not mistaken. When they reached a small, concealed harbour south of the Isthmus of Panama and had time to inspect the Spanish ship, they discovered four hundred thousand pieces of gold, fifteen chests of coined silver, thirty tons of silver in bars, two hundred pounds of raw gold, apart from a cargo of amber and ambergris, ivory, musk, wines, Chinese silks, perfumes, laces, rare preserved fruits, fine porcelain and many other valuable and beautiful things.

A proportion of this they transferred to the *Sea Hawk* to divide the risk, and the men were wild with excitement at the thought of the share of the prize they would receive when they returned home and the ship's cargo was sold and divided.

With two ships to handle they were, of course, shorthanded. Rodney sent the Cimaroons ashore to search for volunteers. He was bitterly opposed to Barlow's suggestion that they should, as was usual, kidnap a number of the natives and make them their slaves. It was the custom amongst ships of all nations, but Rodney had an ingrained dislike of slaves, and though his officers thought he was crazy, he stuck firmly to his idea that he wished the men to volunteer and he would employ them and pay for their services.

Apart from this course of action being quixotic and extraordinary, Master Barlow as well as the other officers thought it unlikely that the Cimaroon would obtain a single volunteer amongst his kind. Rodney knew, although they dared to say little to him, fearing his anger, that the officers as well as the men laid bets with each other against his enticing any native by such methods, even if they were sickly or deformed and therefore of little use to their tribe.

And yet on the third day they were in harbour Rodney's optimism was justified. The Cimaroon returned at dusk with twenty men and the news that there would be, perhaps, double the number waiting further down the coast where there was a bigger native village.

'They are young,' he explained to Rodney, 'but they are strong and keen, and I promised that they could trust your word that they would be paid. No one has ever paid them before,' he added a little wistfully, 'and some of them would like to go to sea and learn how to handle a ship.'

'I am grateful to you for helping me in this matter,' Rodney said. 'My officers were certain that few of your tribe would wish to leave their own shores.'

The Cimaroon shook his head.

'It is not much of a life for a young man,' he said. 'There are Spaniards everywhere. They increase from year to year. If a man works hard and is prosperous enough to have a few cows and pigs, the Spaniards come and take them from him. They have raiding parties to find slaves not only for their ships, but for the mines on the other side of the isthmus. Our young men grow afraid; but they trust you. You are the friend of our friend, Sir Francis Drake.'

It was not surprising that Rodney was pleased with himself, Lizbeth thought that night at supper, as he sat at the head of the great polished table. The candlelight glittered on the gold and jewelled ornaments. Don Miguel dined with them, for Rodney had learned in the *Golden Hind* with what courtesy and generosity he should treat important prisoners.

They soon found that the young Spaniard could speak English, and more fluently than they could speak Spanish. He was aged twenty-three years and this was his first voyage to inspect his father's property on the Spanish Main. He told them a little of the wealth and treasure that had been carried from Nombre de Dios to Havana in the six ships which had preceded him, with which he would have been sailing now had it not been for the broken rudder.

'No wonder Spain is arrogant with such riches at her command!' Rodney muttered.

'We have tried to be the friend of England,' Don Miguel said.

'You tried to rule us,' Rodney retorted.

The Spaniard shrugged his shoulders.

'Friendships between nations is like marriage,' he said. 'One always has to be the master.'

Rodney laughed.

'Your King might master Mary,' he said, 'but Elizabeth is a different proposition. No man will ever get the better of her, as no nation will ever get the better of England.'

'We shall see,' the Spaniard remarked, and both Lizbeth and Rodney knew that he was thinking of the Armada.

For a moment there was a touch of fear in both their hearts. What might not have happened while they had been away from England? Lizbeth was silent as she remembered the stories she had heard of the great galleons twice the size of the *Santa Perpetua*, waiting their chance to come sailing up the Channel with all the power, majesty and wealth of Spain behind them.

But Rodney was recalling how Drake had 'singed the beard of the King of Spain' in his assault on Cadiz harbour last year. The Spanish galleons, ponderous and unwieldy, encumbered by the very heaviness of their armament, had been useless against the speed, quickness and manœuvrability of Drake's smaller ships. Over a hundred ships had been destroyed that day. The Spanish Armada might appear formidable, but the English would outwit the Spaniards wherever they might meet them, he decided; but out of courtesy he did not voice such sentiments aloud.

It was impossible, even though he might be an enemy, to dislike Don Miguel. He had a charm which nothing could deny, not even the blind hatred of those who averred that every Spaniard was a devil and a brute.

Lizbeth had grown so used to hearing the most horrible and bestial things about the Spaniards that at first she shrank from Don Miguel, allowing her preconceived ideas to smother her instinct; but later as she met him day after day at meals, as they walked together on the deck of the *Santa Perpetua,* because, neither of them having anything to do, they were perforce thrown together more than was usual in such circumstances, she began to treat him as she might have treated any young man of his age whom she met at Camfield.

It was impossible to talk all the time of ponderous and dull things such as war and national enmities; and instead, because they were both young, they talked of life and of living, and of all the things that interested them both.

Don Miguel was a fine horseman and Lizbeth had ridden since she could walk and loved horses almost more than anything else in life. From being stiff and resentful in Don Miguel's company Lizbeth began to look forward to the times when they could be together.

When they were in harbour, except for meals, he was confined to his cabin and had a guard at the door; but when they were at sea he had the freedom of the ship, for Rodney knew it was impossible for him to escape. And so they talked, Lizbeth and the young Spaniard, sometimes in English and sometimes in Spanish, and occasionally they would try their French and Latin together, laughing over each other's mistakes.

The harbour where Rodney examined the cargo was too near to the Panama Isthmus for it to be safe to linger there for more than a few days, so with the native seamen aboard they set off down the coast, finding it more than beautiful, mile by mile.

There were great forests stretching away as far as the eye could see, with rich tropical vegetation from which, when they went ashore, Lizbeth obtained many of the herbs she required for the wounded men. There were turtles' eggs, coconuts, plantains, bananas and pineapples to be found; and they cooked and salted a turtle which was surprisingly pleasant to eat. There were other things, too, which were brought aboard which made the food on the first part of their voyage from England seem only a bad dream.

Pheasants flourished in great profusion on the Darien coast. They passed the port where Drake had landed and which he had called Port Pheasant because there were so many of those beautiful birds to be seen there. Here it was definitely not safe to linger, for the Spaniards had never forgotten Drake's raids from Port Pheasant, so they slipped by it, hoping that they passed unobserved.

There were wild birds, venison, hens and pigs to be obtained from the natives. Rodney insisted on paying for everything he took; and in consequence, when the new volunteer seamen went ashore, they often returned with a friend or two who also wished to join the English crew.

They were happy ships, both of them, and though sometimes there were floggings when a man got too obstreperous and had to be punished as an example to the others, Lizbeth knew that Don Miguel often looked in surprise at the smiling faces of the men hurrying about the decks and up the rigging, singing and whistling as they worked with a carefree lightheartedness which bespoke their contentment.

'They are happy,' he said one afternoon as he and Lizbeth sat in the after cabin just before sunset.

It was a burst of song which brought forth his remark, a sea shanty which every man aboard had known since babyhood and in which all joined at the very tops of their voices.

'Yes, they are happy,' Lizbeth answered. 'They are well fed and successful, and there will be good prize money for every man when we return to Plymouth.' She spoke without thinking, and feeling she might have hurt him by referring to the loss of his ship, she said, 'I am sorry—sorry for you, I mean.'

144

He smiled at her then and his eyes watched her as she sat half-curled in an armchair, her chin resting on her hand, her hair, which had grown longer since they had been at sea, curling almost to her shoulders. It was vivid against the dark velvet of the chair in which she sat and now, wondering at his silence, she raised her eyes to his and saw something there which made her feel suddenly tense.

'You are very pretty,' he said softly in English.

She felt the blood rising in her cheeks.

'What do you mean?' she stammered.

'Did you really think you were deceiving me?' he asked. 'I knew, I think, from the first moment I saw you. Are Englishmen really so blind, or are they just pretending?'

Lizbeth did not attempt to misunderstand him.

'Rodney knows,' she said, 'but not the others.'

Don Miguel made a little gesture with his hands.

'I always knew the English were stupid, but *Sacremento!* to imagine such loveliness could belong to a boy—that is madness!'

Lizbeth laughed. She could not help herself.

'Promise me you will say nothing,' she begged. 'I will explain to you why I came here.'

She told him her story, although to spare his feelings she glossed over her father's anger with Francis' friendship with Dr. Keen. She told him how she had taken Francis' place and of Rodney's fury when he discovered how he had been tricked; and of how, expecting her to be a boy, the men had accepted her and as far as she knew, had never had the slightest doubt as to her sex.

Don Miguel listened carefully and then he bent forward in his chair.

'Are you content to be a boy?' he asked.

'Perfectly.' Lizbeth answered a little defiantly. ''Twas strange at first, but now I am used to it.'

'And yet, if you were a woman, how different the atmosphere on this ship would be! They would all be trying to please you; the officers would vie for your favours—there would be a gallantry about every man

145

and about everything they did. Men work best when they have a woman to please.'

'What you are saying would shock Rodney,' Lizbeth said. 'He does not approve of women aboard ship—and who shall blame him? Only the worst captains and the worst women sail together in English ships.'

'The English are always unpredictable,' Don Miguel replied. 'But I cannot understand how you could deceive them for one moment when you are so lovely. I would like to see you dressed in some of the rich silks which lie below us now. There is silk from China so fine that it can pass through a ring, so soft that the mere touch of it seems to caress the skin. There is silk there the colour of an emerald and there are emeralds, too, which would look entrancing round your white neck.'

He got to his feet suddenly and glanced towards the door on to the outer deck. It was closed, the men were still singing; overhead they would hear the slow steps of the officer of the watch.

'I will show you something,' Don Miguel said.

He crossed the room and, taking a picture from the wall, laid it on the floor. The panelling behind the picture was the same as the rest of the room. He pressed a secret spring and a portion of it flew open. It was a place of hiding skilfully contrived so that no one could guess of it.

Lizbeth gave a little gasp of excitement. From the hole in the panel Don Miguel took a carved and ornamented box. It was padlocked and he drew from around his neck a ribbon on which hung a gold key. The small padlock, which was also made of gold, opened, and now the lid of the box was turned back and Lizbeth gave a cry of sheer astonishment, for the box was filled with jewels of every sort and description.

There were pearls of all sizes and shapes, some strung, some just as they had been taken from the oyster. There were great sapphires set in carved silver and a necklace of emeralds set in gold, which Don Miguel held for her to see. It was the loveliest thing she had ever seen.

Instinctively her hands went out towards it.

'I would like to see it against your neck,' he said.

'They are lovely,' Lizbeth exclaimed, not really listening to him. 'I have never seen such big emeralds before.'

'There is a bracelet and ring as well,' Don Miguel told her.

'They seem to have a strange fire,' Lizbeth said.

'But that is true. Do you not know that the fire in an emerald is the reflection of the fire in a man's heart when he sees the woman he really loves?' Don Miguel asked. 'Rubies are for passion, but in Spain emeralds stand for a love that is greater than passion.'

As he spoke, he drew the ring from the box—a great, square-cut emerald with a shaft of gold carved in a strange, tortuous design. Don Miguel reached out and took Lizbeth's hand in his; and before she realised what he was doing, he had slipped the ring on her finger.

For a moment she looked at it, and then Don Miguel raised her fingers and she felt the touch of his lips on them.

'It is yours,' he said. 'Keep it somewhere secret because I have given it to you.'

With a violence that took him by surprise, Lizbeth snatched her hand from his.

'How can you think I would do such a thing?' she asked angrily, and pulling the ring from her finger, she threw it back into the box. 'Do you not understand that everything in this ship belongs not to one person but to all? Part goes in prize money to those who man her, the rest to the shareholders who have financed the voyage. If I took the ring that you offer me, I should be stealing. What is more, now you have shown me where it is, you must tell Rodney about the secret hiding place.'

Don Miguel seemed to hesitate.

'If you do not do so, I must,' Lizbeth said.

He smiled at her then and somehow she found her anger evaporating.

'Pray do not be angry with me,' he pleaded. 'I did not think you had such strict ideas of justice. What is a

147

ring, one way or another, in this great cargo, which is worth thousands of English pounds? I wanted to give you something that is mine. I forgot I have nothing.'

Lizbeth was touched then by the humility in his voice.

'I should not have spoken as I did,' she said quickly. 'It was kind of you to wish to give me a present and I thank you for the thought even while I can take nothing.'

'But you have already taken something,' the Spaniard replied.

He shut the emeralds back in the box as he spoke and his voice was low and serious.

'What have I taken?' Lizbeth asked, puzzled.

'My heart,' he answered.

For a moment she could hardly credit what he was saying, and then, as her eyes stared at him in surprise, she saw the expression in his, saw the sudden fire behind the seriousness of his gaze—a fire such as she had seen in the depths of the emeralds.

'Oh, no! no!' she exclaimed impulsively.

'It is true,' Don Miguel affirmed. 'Surely you cannot be so modest as to think that I could be with you day after day, that I could see you, listen to you, talk to you and not fall in love with you? Do you not know how attractive you are?'

'No, of course not.'

In spite of her distress at what he was saying, Lizbeth could not prevent the dimples appearing in her cheeks.

'You are lovely—you are entrancing—you enchant me every moment I am with you,' the Spaniard said. 'You are English and, before, I believed that all English women were cold and staid and very, very dull; but you are like quicksilver, your hair draws me as the warmth of a real fire draws a man who is cold. I need your warmth, little Lizbeth. I am lonely and cold and far from home. I need you.'

Lizbeth put her hands to her ears.

'This is wrong. You must not talk to me like this. I must not listen to you.'

'Why not when we are both lonely people?' Don

148

Miguel asked. He came a little nearer to her as she spoke, and now to answer him she must look up at him.

He was very much taller than she, yet as she saw his face, soft and tender with his longing and his love, she felt a sudden desire to put her arms around him and hold him close. He was only a boy after all—a boy like Francis, far from home, being brave and keeping a stiff upper lip under the most difficult circumstances in which a man could find himself—a prisoner in his own ship with no one of his own nationality to speak to or to keep him company.

For a moment Lizbeth forget that he was an enemy, forgot his secrecy about the jewels and even her surprise at hearing that he loved her. She remembered only that he was young and lonely and that she had thought not once but many times that he was making the best of an almost insupportable position.

'Poor Miguel,' she said, using his name for the first time before she could stop herself. 'I wish I could help you.'

She spoke from the depth of her heart and only as she saw the expression on his face did she realise the construction he might put on her kindness.

Before she could say anything more, before she could prevent his doing so, he had swept her into his arms. She felt his strength for the first time and was surprised at it because she had not thought of him as a man; and then his lips were on hers, and he was kissing her tenderly, yet with a demanding passion which took her breath away.

9

On the quarter-deck Rodney was humming softly to himself as he walked to and fro. It was swelteringly hot and the ship was moving very slowly, for the breeze was almost indiscernible and most of the time the sails hung limp and empty, while the sea itself was so still that the water seemed to cling against the wooden sides of the *Santa Perpetua*.

The *Sea Hawk* about half a mile away was in the same plight. Rodney could see Barlow gazing agitatedly at his top-sails. Barlow always worried unduly when there was a dead calm; it seemed unnatural to him somehow, while a tempest left him unmoved and quite unperturbed as to what might be the result of it.

Rodney, on the other hand, rather enjoyed periods of calm seas and sunlit skies. There was nothing to do except wait until the wind blew again and at the moment it was a relief to be able to relax after the excitement and agitation of the last few days.

With two ships to worry about he found himself unable to sleep at night, rising half a dozen times to look for the lights of the *Sea Hawk* shining across the intervening water. He would not have admitted this weakness to anyone, but he felt that he could not bear to lose either of his ships after his triumphant success in capturing the *Santa Perpetua*.

Their position until they were well away from Nombre de Dios and the Panama Isthmus was extremely precarious. The Spaniards had a fleet of ships at Havana and nothing could be more likely than that two of them or maybe more might be sent in search of the *Santa Perpetua*.

Don Miguel, too, was a person of importance. Rodney had learned that his father was one of the greatest landowners on the Spanish Main and master of many of the ships which sailed for home laden with the treasures brought down to Panama from Peru and the gold mines. It was not to be expected that the only son of the Marquis de Suavez could be lost without causing great commotion not only in Havana, but in Spain itself.

Don Miguel had, with extraordinary self-control, taken his capture with a dignity which had forced everyone aboard, even the fire-eating Master Gadstone, into an unwilling but sincere admiration of him.

But his compatriots might feel very differently, Rodney thought, and it was not until they were many miles from the danger zone that he began to breathe more freely and feel that he could move about without continually looking back over his shoulder to watch for a sail looming over the horizon.

It grew hotter and the vegetation on the mainland become more tropical and more exotic. Yet the birds of brilliant plumage could not equal the wondrous variety and colour of the fish which swam around them in the clear water—fish of every size and shape, of every pattern and hue.

Rodney felt he would never grow tired of looking at them, and it amused him to see the efforts of the big, rough sailors to capture some of these delicate, fairy-like creatures and keep them aboard. But in earthenware or pewter vessels they soon lost their beauty and their lives, and the men had to content themselves with making a pet of a giant tortoise and with buying the vivid-feathered parrots, macaws and toucans which, when they went ashore, the natives were only too ready to sell for the smallest possible piece of silver, whatever nation had minted it.

There were flowers in great profusion ; and Rodney, noting now a strange white blossom not unlike a lily

151

tucked behind the ear of one of the native volunteers as he ran lightly up the rigging, thought suddenly of Phillida. He had compared her with a lily when he first saw her.

With that clear white skin and hair that was gold as the wheat when it first ripens in the sun, her loveliness had left him breathless; and yet he remembered guiltily that it was a long time since he had last thought of her or even remembered her existence. It was difficult in the warmth of the Caribbean to recapture the thrill her beauty had given him.

Somehow he could only find himself remembering the expression in her eyes. They had nothing in common with the warm, glowing blue of the sea over which he sailed. They were the blue of the English sky in spring—a cold, rather chilly blue which made no effort to arouse and warm the blood in a man's veins.

Mentally Rodney shook himself as he walked across the quarter-deck. Phillida was the most beautiful thing he had ever seen, and he had seen a great many women one way and another as he wandered round the world with Drake. But there had been no one even in Whitehall to rival her —he was sure of it. Though he had spent but a short time in London, he had managed to see most of the acclaimed beauties—Lady Mary Howard, Elizabeth Throgmorton and the Countess of Warwick. Phillida was lovelier than any of them, and when he returned, rich and successful from this voyage, she would belong to him.

He tried to imagine what it would be like to hold her in his arms, to seek her lips, to feel the soft silkiness of her skin beneath his hands. Yet somehow, try as he would, his imagination would not serve him rightly and he could only remember Phillida pleading with him on the terrace at Camfield that their marriage should not take place too soon.

There had been fear in her expression then, and something else that he had not understood, something which made him feel vaguely uneasy.

He strode across the deck and back again, thinking how much more comfortable it was to have the greater space

152

of the *Santa Perpetua* in which to stretch his legs rather than the more confined space of the *Sea Hawk*. His brain raced away on this new subject as if glad to be released from concentrating on Phillida.

It ranged over the great guns of the *Santa Perpetua* which had never ceased to thrill the Master Gunner and at which the men practised every morning; and remembered the precious cargo lying in the hold. Now Rodney turned his head and looked back to where the *Santa Perpetua* trailed their last capture—a small pinnace. They had taken her yesterday from her Spanish owner with his crew of six natives.

She was laden with hens, hogs and honey, a cargo which had been rapidly transferred to the *Santa Perpetua*. Rodney was towing her now, meaning to use her if she could be of service while they cruised down the coast, and then intending to do as Drake had always done, break her up before he left for England. These small pinnace were useless in the open sea but useful enough to the Spaniards in their coast work and she could not, therefore, be left intact.

The Cimaroons coveted the ironwork and Rodney had already promised this to their friend the pilot. He had been hoping today that they would encounter a pearling lugger and get a chance of taking the pearls before they were deposited at Nombre de Dios ready for shipment to Spain. He would collect a necklace for Phillida's white neck, he thought, and knew, even as he decided it, that this was but a sop to his guilty conscience; and then he smiled at his own self-accusations.

Men, when they were engaged on difficult and dangerous tasks, had little time for women. When he returned home, things would be different. He would teach Phillida then what love meant. He would waken her to a passion as warm and as ardent as his own. At the moment there were more important things to do.

He took another turn about the deck. The *Santa Perpetua* was almost still now, but Rodney knew that the wind would rise in the night. It was too dangerous to

153

proceed far in the darkness, but they could always set sail immediately dawn broke and keep forging ahead until the heat of the day drove the breeze away and once again they rocked becalmed on a glassy sea.

He took a quick look at the *Sea Hawk* and at the empty sea—there was nothing they could do but wait for the wind. They were near the shore but the water was deep. The only real danger was from hidden coral reefs. The man with the lead was chanting the depth. Rodney could hear his voice.

'No bottom,' he called.

Rodney looked over the side. He could see the clearness of the water and the fish swimming beside the ship. There was no danger anywhere, only sunshine and the still heaviness of the atmosphere unrelieved by a breeze. On the *Sea Hawk* Barlow was staring up at his topsails. Barlow would be itching to get under way, and suddenly Rodney was not certain that he himself did not feel the same way. He felt restless suddenly, though why he could not say.

He wondered what Lizbeth was doing. At this hour of the evening she usually came on deck. Rodney had grown used to seeing her there and he knew now that her presence no longer irritated him as it had done at first. He even looked forward to the meals at which they could talk together, and since he had captured the *Santa Perpetua* he had found frequent cause to be grateful for her presence.

It would not have been easy to sit alone with Don Miguel, eating his food at his table off his gold plate. Lizbeth's presence had relieved the tension which he felt would have existed between him and his reluctant guest. Her suspicion and resentment of the Spaniard had been short-lived and soon they were all three talking together as if they were old friends.

Don Miguel told them of his life in Spain and Rodney had replied by describing his voyages round the world with Drake without dwelling too obviously on their battles with the Spaniards. Lizbeth had spoken of her horses and of her home and, with what Rodney thought was great cleverness, had avoided pitfalls which might have revealed her as having been brought up in a very strange way for a young man.

There was no doubt about it, Rodney thought now as he left the quarter-deck, meals aboard the *Santa Perpetua* had been uncommonly pleasant, and he was wondering as he opened the door of the after cabin what there would be for supper that night.

It was then that he stood transfixed, unable to do anything but stand and stare. Lizbeth was in the Spaniard's arms and he was kissing her. Rodney stood with his hand on the door for what seemed to him a long time but was in reality only the flashing of a second. And then, as if his presence made itself felt to the other occupants of the cabin without words and without sound, for they had not heard him enter, Don Miguel raised his head.

His movement released Lizbeth from his arms, though whether she would have moved away without his interruption Rodney could not make up his mind. And then they were facing each other. Rodney still standing in the doorway, Don Miguel and Lizbeth on the other side of the cabin waiting, so it seemed, for Rodney to speak first.

He closed the door behind him and then slowly advanced across the cabin. He appeared calm and rigidly self-controlled, as he did when he went into battle; but actually his anger was mounting hot and furious within him and he could almost feel the red fire of it burning behind his eyes.

With an effort he kept himself in check. He had a sudden wild desire to draw his sword, to run the Spaniard through with it as he stood with what seemed to Rodney to be an insolent smile upon his face. His hand edged towards the hilt and then he remembered that this man was his prisoner—it was against every code of decency that he should attack him or even challenge him to honourable combat.

'You will oblige me, Señor de Suavez,' he said, 'by

going to your cabin and remaining there until I send for you.'

Don Miguel made what was to Rodney a mocking bow of obedience.

'I will of course obey you, Sir,' he said, 'but before I go, I would like to say that my love for your future sister-in-law is a very honourable one.'

It seemed to Rodney as if there was deliberate defiance in the Spaniard's words. How dare he refer to Lizbeth as his 'future sister-in-law'—putting him, it seemed, in the dull and unimaginative role of a guardian brother, someone spiritless and of little importance in her life!

'You will obey me without argument,' Rodney said sharply.

Again Don Miguel bowed, and then, turning to Lizbeth standing silent by his side, he raised her hand to his lips.

'My life is at your feet,' he said softly; then turning, he walked across the cabin with his lips smiling, his head held high.

For a moment the eyes of the two men met as he passed Rodney. There was a clash of wills—a battle deeper and more violent than anything that appeared on the surface of their expressionless faces; and then as Don Miguel turned towards the door, he waved his hand with a theatrical gesture towards the box of jewels standing on the table.

'Another offering for the Conqueror,' he said.

The cabin door closed behind him. There was a long silence—a silence in which it seemed to Lizbeth as if Rodney must hear her heart beating. She had never before seen him look so stern, and she thought for the first time that she was really afraid of him. And then hastily she told herself that such an attitude was ridiculous.

With an effort she forced herself to point towards the box on the table which Don Miguel had indicated as he left.

'There are jewels there, Rodney,' she said, trying to speak naturally, but her voice quavered. 'Jewels that you had not yet seen.'

'I am not interested in jewels,' Rodney answered. 'I am waiting for an explanation.'

He was like a stern tutor, Lizbeth thought suddenly, and despite the beating of her heart she managed to answer him.

'I am sorry that he should have discovered that I am not a boy,' she said. 'I promise you that I did not tell him. He just knew it. I think perhaps that foreigners are more perceptive than Englishmen.'

'How did he discover it?' Rodney asked.

'I have no idea,' Lizbeth replied. 'He told me that he had known it almost from the first moment that he saw me.' She looked at Rodney's face, and seeing the anger in his eyes and the tightness of his lips, added again, 'I . . . I am sorry, Rodney.'

'God's words! Sorry!' He almost shouted the words at her. 'So it appears when I come in here to find you in a Spaniard's arms.'

Lizbeth had expected him to refer to this and yet, now he had done so, the colour came flooding up into her little face. It made her eyes seem vividly green, as with a tremendous effort she forced herself to face him and say in a low voice:

'I am sorry for that, too. It . . . it was quite unexpected . . . and uninvited.'

'I am glad to think that it has not been happening for some time behind my back,' Rodney remarked sarcastically.

'No—never before,' Lizbeth answered. 'I . . . I had no idea that . . . Don Miguel was in love with me.'

'In love with you!' As if to relieve his feelings, Rodney unbuckled his sword and flung it down on the table with a crash. 'This is what comes of having a woman aboard a ship. In love with you! A Spaniard, a man who is our bitterest enemy, a man belonging to a nation which has tortured our people, a man you should loathe, despise and hate with a consuming bitterness! And yet, instead, what do I find? I find you in his arms!'

'I know I should feel all that,' Lizbeth answered, 'but, Rodney, somehow it is impossible. I thought all Spaniards were brutes, devils in human form; but you know as well as I do that one cannot feel that about Don Miguel. He is only a boy—a boy away from home for the first time in his life, lonely without his mother, missing his father and his sister, and falling in love with me, I dare say, because there is no other woman here for him to talk with.'

Lizbeth had come near to Rodney as she spoke, and now she stood looking up at him, her hands clapsed together, her green eyes raised to his, her soft red lips parted. Rodney stared down at her. He had not realised before how lovely she was—her hair released during her embrace with Don Miguel was soft about her face, it seemed to glow almost like a fire against the dark oak of the cabin.

'You are lovely,' he said beneath his breath, speaking to himself; and yet Lizbeth heard him.

Yes, she was lovely, he thought, and then suddenly the anger which had consumed him, the burning fury within his chest, which had raged there since he first came into the cabin, could be controlled no longer. He stretched forth his hands and gripped her shoulders, dragging her closer to him so that he could look down into her face.

'You are very eloquent when it comes to pleading for some swine of a Spaniard,' he said. 'But what about you? If it is kisses you are hungering for, cannot English ones satisfy you?'

His voice was hoarse and brutal; and then, before Lizbeth could guess what he was about, one arm was round her and with his free hand he tipped her head back against his shoulder and his lips were on hers.

This kiss was very different from the one she had from him before. His mouth bruised hers, his arms were like bands of steel so that she must gasp for breath. He held her as if he would never let her go; he held her as if he was a man starved and hungry. His kiss was frightening; and when at length he raised his lips from hers, he did not relax his hold upon her. For a moment she could not speak; then, as he looked down at her, she saw the cruelty in his eyes and the hard savagery of his mouth; and then he kissed her again, kissed her until at last she must cry for mercy.

158

'Rodney, please . . . let me go! I beg of you'—but he was past hearing her.

This was not the Rodney she had known and liked, the Rodney she trusted—but another man, a stranger, a devil, it seemed, who had taken possession of the man she had thought of as a friend.

'Rodney, I pray you! God's mercy, but . . .'

She began to cry, tears of sheer fright and terror spilling themselves from her eyes and running down her cheeks so that his lips were salt with them. Then at last it seemed as though he awakened to a sudden realisation of what he was doing. With a cry, which startled her by the very violence of his voice echoing round the cabin, he flung her from him.

She fell on the floor, bruised and breathless, too blinded by her own tears to see what he was doing. Then she heard the slam of the cabin door and realised that she was alone. For a moment she lay there, sobbing almost broken-heartedly, and it was the sound of her own tears which restored her self-control, which brought her to her feet.

At any moment, she remembered, Hapley might come to lay the supper table. She could not be found in such a state. She felt for her handkerchief, mopped her eyes and forced herself to quell the sobs which kept rising in her throat; and then, unsteadily, as if the sea were rough, she made her way to her own cabin. There she locked the door and flung herself face downwards on the bunk.

How thrilled and proud she had been of her new quarters on the *Santa Perpetua*! But now she hated them, hated the softness of her bed, the luxury of the linen sheets, the feather pillow and warmly-woven blankets. She wished she were back in the *Sea Hawk* with its swinging hammock in an airless cabin which smelt perpetually of bilge.

There she had been happy. Even though Rodney had been angry with her at first, they had gradually become friends. She thought of how he had talked to her confidingly and easily as they sat alone at dinner and supper.

They had both of them thought excitedly of the adventures that lay ahead.

This was what adventures ended in, Lizbeth thought. This sense of unhappiness and misery, this sense of being degraded and humiliated by someone one loved. Lizbeth sat up suddenly. What was it she had said to herself? And then she knew, knew clearly and unmistakably—she was in love with Rodney! She must have been in love with him for a long time, she thought, perhaps even before she had left England; yet she had not known it.

How blind she had been, how idiotic, not to have guessed the true state of her own feelings! She thought now, as she raised her fingers to her bruised mouth, that she had loved him since that first moment when he had caught her among the rhododendron bushes and kissed her because she had spoiled his hat.

There was blood on her lips now, his kiss had been the brutal exhibition of a man who had completely lost control of his finer feelings; and yet, Lizbeth felt she could understand. Like Don Miguel, he was missing the women he had known and loved and who had loved him; and unlike Don Miguel, he was incensed by her presence to the point of exasperation, so that he longed to hurt her and make her suffer because in some very different and obscure manner she was making him suffer by her presence.

If she had been a man and he could have punished her for annoying him, the whole episode would have been forgotten; but because she was a woman, he must revenge himself upon her in a very different manner. Lizbeth began to cry again.

Her tears were not the fearful ones she had cried in Rodney's arms, they were the gentle, wistful tears of a woman in love, a woman who knows that her love is unrequited and suffers the awful pain of loving, incurably, the man who does not want her.

Was there ever such a tangle, Lizbeth asked herself. Rodney in love with Phillida—for she had no illusions about that; and Phillida disliking Rodney and all men, wishing only to be a Nun; while she—she loved Rodney

160

as she had never deemed it possible to love anyone in the whole of her life.

She thought now that she had been waiting for this ever since she had begun to dream of love and of men and to imagine the type of man who would be her hero and to whom eventually she would surrender herself for all time. They had been the imaginative dreams of girlhood, dreams which ended with the sound of wedding bells, dreams in which no darkness clouded the face of happiness.

But reality was different. Lizbeth wept because she was lonely, because her arms ached for the man who had thrown her roughly from him and who, she knew, hated her rather than returned her love. And in that moment it seemed to Lizbeth that she grew up. She was no longer a child, no longer the same wholehearted, happy girl who had ridden in the early dew at Camfield, who had played pranks on her stepmother and got into trouble because she would not do her tasks in the stillroom.

It was Lizbeth the woman who sat here in the cabin of a captured ship, far away in the Caribbean Sea, and saw that love was not in the least bit what she had imagined it to be, In a very short space of time this evening she had aroused love in a man she did not want, and lust in a man she loved.

She saw then in that moment the difference between right and wrong, between good love and bad, and knew where her choice lay, however much heartbreak it must bring her.

Her tears stopped after a while and then she washed her face and started to change her clothes for the evening meal. For a moment she wondered whether she could face either Rodney or Don Miguel again, and then she knew that to stay in her cabin tonight would only make matters worse. Tomorrow must come. There was no escape from people aboard ship. They must meet and they must behave as if nothing had happened, because, however much their hearts might ache and break, they were two months' voyage from home.

For the first time since she had come to sea Lizbeth

felt that things would be easier could she appear as herself. This terrible state of affairs of pretending to be Mister Gillingham in front of the officers and the men was beginning to be distasteful and irksome, and she wished that tonight of all nights she could be Lizbeth both to Rodney who hated her and to Don Miguel who loved her.

It was vanity that made her choose Francis' best doublet of blue satin, the sleeves slashed and puffed; the ruff which went with it was edged with silver, and when she looked at herself in the burnished mirror, Lizbeth was not ashamed of her appearance.

All the same, she saw herself for a moment in her mind's eye in the green Chinese silk that Don Miguel had described to her and she imagined the emeralds clasped around her neck, the bracelet on her wrist and the ring on her finger; and she wondered if she came into the cabin in such attire Rodney's eyes would light at the sight of her and he would say again the words he had spoken but a few hours ago in astonished surprise.

'You are lovely!'

She could hear his voice, and yet she knew the words were not spoken as she would have him say them! With a jerk she called a halt to her imagination. Rodney belonged to Phillida her half-sister. They were betrothed and Phillida was pledged to him whether she wished it or not.

With a little sigh Lizbeth put up her hands to her face and then defiantly she threw back her head and opened the door. She might do many things that were wrong, but she was not a coward. She would face Rodney tonight, and Don Miguel, however much she might shrink from doing so, however great the hurt to her heart.

She went into the after cabin. Supper was being brought to the table, and as she expected, Rodney and Don Miguel were waiting for her. Both were pale and grim and both men seemed uncomfortable at her presence. As Hapley came into the room carrying the heavy gold dishes for the first course, Rodney took his place at the head of the table, with Lizbeth on his right and Don Miguel on his left.

162

Supper was eaten in silence. Lizbeth afterwards had no idea what she ate or what was set before her. It was only when the servants had withdrawn and they were left alone in the soft candle-light that Rodney emptied his goblet of wine and set it down with a sudden thud on the table.

He had been waiting for this moment, Lizbeth thought, waiting until he could speak freely. She knew that what he was going to say would be unpleasant.

'I have spoken to Señor de Suavez,' he said to Lizbeth, 'and I have told him that, since he cannot conduct himself as a gentleman, he will no longer have the liberty of the ship. He will have his meals here with us, but otherwise he will be confined to his cabin. The door will be locked and a sentry will be on guard both night and day. In these circumstances it is not necessary for me to tell you that you are to have no intercourse whatever with him. If you wish to address this man, you will do so in front of me.'

'Rodney, you cannot do this!' Lizbeth protested heartily. 'It is unjust. Don Miguel has done nothing to offend me, and if he has spoken of love that is my business and his. It has nothing to do with you.'

'It has a great deal to do with me,' Rodney retorted.

Lizbeth knew by the pulse beating in his throat that his calm, unhurried manner of speaking was only a pose. He was still angry, as angry as he had been a little while earlier when he flung her to the floor.

'You are here as a guest on my ship,' Rodney continued, 'and de Suavez is my prisoner. I should be within my rights if I clapped him in irons and left him down in the depths of the ship. Out of decency I have given him a place at my table, I have allowed him the freedom to talk with you and with the other officers aboard. He has abused my generosity by attempting to seduce an Englishwoman, an honoured guest, the daughter of the man who has a part share in the ship in which we sailed from England.'

'I still say that what you are doing is unfair,' Lizbeth said quietly. 'It is unfortunate for Don Miguel that an Englishwoman should be aboard. That is my fault, not

163

his; and if you wish to punish anyone, you should punish me.'

Her words did nothing to mitigate Rodney's anger.

'You are talking nonsense,' he answered harshly. 'Besides, I am not inclined to argue with you. I have told de Suavez what to expect, a guard has already been put outside his cabin; there it will stay till I can hand him over to the authorities in England.'

It seemed to Lizbeth that Don Miguel paled a little. He made no protest, but Lizbeth was not prepared to be over-ridden by Rodney's authority. She loved him, she thought, watching his face in the light of the candle, and yet she was able to see his faults. He was being hard and ungenerous over this. He was being unjust and using his authority in the wrong way just because his anger was aroused.

Perhaps there was something of pride in it, she thought, and perhaps pique, too, because Don Miguel had discovered the secret of her sex. Whatever his reasons, she was not prepared to accept them; and pushing back her chair a little now, she said:

'To make different arrangements now as to the custody of Don Miguel will cause comment in the ship. The men will begin to speculate as to what has happened; and if people are anxious to solve a mystery, there is usually a mystery to be solved.

'We all make mistakes, and perhaps Don Miguel made one this evening when he told me of his feelings. Shall we say that he should have controlled them; but other people also lose control of themselves but are not punished so harshly.'

She was being particularly daring in what she was saying, she knew that. Nevertheless she knew that her arguments were having their effect on Rodney. He was frowning, his brows knit together. She could see him considering her words, and wondering if in reality he was being unwise to alter the arrangements about his prisoner.

'Very well,' he said at length, 'I will agree to this on one condition only, that you both give me your word of honour that you will never be alone together in this cabin or in any other place where you are not within hearing of someone else.'

There was a little pause and then quickly, because Lizbeth knew that the concession had been a great effort to Rodney's pride, she said:

'I agree. Don Miguel and I will not be alone. When we talk together, there shall always be someone within hearing.'

'And it will please me if you talk as little as possible. Do you promise, de Suavez?'

'I give you my word of honour.' Don Miguel answered.

His dark eyes met Lizbeth's across the table as he spoke, and she could have cried out at the misery within them. There was nothing more she could do for the moment. She had interceded with Rodney and been successful; but she knew that he was still angry and was afraid of provoking him further.

Don Miguel rose to his feet.

'If you will permit me, I will retire to my own cabin.'

'You have my permission,' Rodney answered coldly. 'The guard will be removed.'

'Thank you.'

Don Miguel's bow was frigid; then he bowed to Lizbeth and left the cabin.

'Thank you,' Lizbeth said softly to Rodney.

He struck his clenched fist down on the table fiercely.

'Faith! but don't thank me,' he cried. 'If I had my way, I would hang the Spaniard from the yard-arm; but I will have no one else on board guessing who you are and why you came here. There is trouble from it as it is.'

Lizbeth did not answer, but rose to her feet and walking across the cabin, stood for a moment looking at the picture behind which lay Don Miguel's secret hiding place. She saw that the box of jewels had been removed from the table when it was laid for supper and put on a chest beneath the picture itself. She wondered if Rodney had looked at them or whether in his anger he had ignored

them as he had done when she first tried to tell him about
them.

And then she started as she heard his voice behind her,
not having realised that he had risen from the table.

'Lizbeth, I am sorry.'

His voice was quite humble now and there was no anger
in it. She looked up at him and saw that his face had
changed—the arrogance had gone, instead he looked like
himself again.

'I am sorry,' he repeated. 'I should not have behaved
to you as I did, but you drove me beyond endurance.'

'We will forget it,' Lizbeth said in a low voice. knowing
as she spoke that she would never forget the hardness of
Rodney's lips on hers, the strength of his arms around her.

'That is all right, then,' Rodney answered in tones of
relief.

Like every man he was anxious to get away from the
embarrassing subject and he put out his hand to take up
the box of jewels.

'You were going to tell me about these,' he suggested.

'They were hidden behind that picture,' Lizbeth
answered, striving to speak naturally. 'Don Miguel
showed them to me.'

Rodney opened the box, which had not been locked
again, and now he drew in his breath as he saw the jewels
and realised a little of their value.

'These are worth a fortune,' he exclaimed, then added,
'You say de Suavez showed them to you?'

'Yes,' Lizbeth replied. 'They were hidden behind this
picture. There is a secret panel in the wall.'

'I wonder why he showed them to you . . .?' Rodney
began.

Lizbeth looked away from him a little anxiously.

'But of course I know!' he added sharply. 'He wanted
to give them to you. He is in love with you, he has
admitted as much.'

'I refused them,' Lizbeth said quickly.

'How dare he?' Rodney asked. 'He knows as well as I
do that the spoils of a ship all belong to a common pool.'

'I doubt if you would ever have found these,' Lizbeth told him quietly. 'If he had not shown me, I would never have guessed that anything was hidden there. You had no idea either.'

Rodney looked down at the emeralds in the box and then at Lizbeth.

'He must love you very much. Were you tempted to accept them?'

'Of course not!'

Lizbeth's tone was indignant.

'I wish I could believe you,' Rodney said. 'Perhaps my entrance into the cabin was more inopportune than I realised at the time!'

'I think you are being insulting,' Lizbeth said. 'I told you that I had already refused the jewels. There is no point in our discussing it further.'

She walked away as she spoke. She hoped, as she reached the door, that he would call her back. But he said nothing and she left him with the box of jewels in his hands, staring down at the great square-cut emerald.

10

The men were cheering, half ironically, as a pearling lugger was brought alongside the *Santa Perpetua*. There were six Spaniards in charge of it, and as they were brought aboard Lizbeth could see that they were the type she had imagined all Spaniards to be before she met Don Miguel.

Their faces were coarse and bestial, their deportment arrogant; and that they were brutal was obvious when one looked at the natives they had commanded in the lugger. Every man had open wounds across his back where he had been struck with the many-thonged leather whips which the Spaniards used so cruelly on their slaves.

They were very different indeed from the natives whom Rodney had asked to volunteer for service on the English ships; cowed and broken both in body and spirit, they did not seem to care what happened to them, and the fact that their ship had been captured seemed to leave them only apathetic.

Rodney called the Cimaroon to his side.

'Do you know these men?' he asked.

The Cimaroon nodded.

'They are not of my tribe,' he said. 'They come from further south.'

'They will be of little use even if they consent to sail with us,' Rodney said. 'If I put them ashore, will they manage to get back to their own people?'

The Cimaroon shrugged.

'Those who survive will doubtless find their way home,' he said.

'So be it!'

Rodney gave the order for the boats to take the captured slaves and put them ashore; but even this hardly seemed to rouse the Indians from their lethargy; and the Spaniards, watching what appeared to them the mercifulness of a madman, sneered openly. Their hard faces and bold eyes made Lizbeth shudder.

She remembered how Rodney had told her to poison herself rather than be captured by the Spaniards, and now she saw the reason for this suggestion. Death was infinitely preferable to being at the mercy of men such as these. She was even relieved as she heard Rodney give the order for them to be taken below and put in chains.

The contents of the lugger were brought aboard. There was a small amount of silver and a quantity of wine that was being taken to the Governor of a settlement farther north; but these were unimportant beside the pearls which the lugger was conveying to Nombre de Dios to be ready for the sailing of the next gold fleet.

There were canvas bags full of them hidden in a safe place in the Captain's cabin. All were valuable; but there were not. Rodney decided, any exceptionally fine specimens among them, until a further search of the lugger revealed a small tin box hidden beneath the boards of the cabin. There were only six pearls in the box, but they were enough to make Rodney exclaim in astonishment, for he knew that these indeed were treasure trove. Softly-pink as the morning sky, they shimmered iridescent in the sunlight, so delicate, so lovely in their texture that even the most inexperienced beholder must have some idea of their intrinsic value.

Rodney placed them in his own cabin for safety and giving orders that they would tow the lugger until they could find a convenient place to break her up, he signalled the *Sea Hawk* that he wished to talk with Barlow.

It was not long before Barlow came aboard with a smile of pleasure on his face at the thought that Rodney wished to see him. Lizbeth, sitting in the sunshine, watched the two men meet and saw them go into the after cabin.

She could guess fairly accurately what they would discuss, for she knew, although Rodney had not said so openly, that he was considering returning home.

The day before they had attacked a small Spanish settlement which had been built beside one of the many natural harbours that the mainland provided. There were no ships in the harbour as the *Santa Perpetua* nosed her way along the coast, but the Cimaroon had told Rodney that there would be plunder to be had at the settlement, and he made his plans accordingly.

He had sent a boat loaded with eighteen English arquebuses and archers ashore north of the harbour. They had instructions to watch the roads leaving the settlement and prevent the Spaniards from escaping with their treasure before Rodney could capture it. He was well aware that, if attacked from the sea by superior odds, the inhabitants of the settlement would run away as quickly as possible, taking with them everything of value they could lay their hands on.

Soon after his men had landed, Rodney sailed the *Santa Perpetua* boldly into the harbour, knowing that at the first sight of her the Governor and the people would expect her to be manned by Spaniards. It was only when they were anchored and his men were already rowing ashore that Rodney ran up the flag of St. George.

There was some hand-to-hand fighting; but when Rodney threatened the Spaniards with a taste of the *Santa Perpetua's* guns, they surrendered unconditionally.

It was not an important settlement, but there was a large quantity of gold and silver, both in coinage and domestic utensils, and some very fine bales of silk which the Governor had purchased to send back to Spain. There were cedar boards, too, and Spanish weapons which Rodney knew had a value in England.

While they were there, they also took the opportunity of replenishing both the *Santa Perpetua* and the *Sea Hawk* with provisions and good Chile wine. It was not wise to linger long in case they were surprised by Spanish warships; so having taken everything they could aboard,

Rodney sailed away, leaving the Spaniards furious but powerless to do anything to prevent their going.

The *Sea Hawk* was now weighted down with cargo, as was the *Santa Perpetua*, and Lizbeth guessed there would not be much point in delaying their passage home. She was sure that was why Rodney was having a conference with Barlow at this very moment; then, as she watched the boats returning from the shore where they had deposited the slaves from the pearling lugger, she heard a footstep and looking up, she saw that Don Miguel had come up on the quarter-deck.

He had been confined to his cabin during the encounter with the pearling lugger and now she supposed he had been released and she smiled up at him, conscious at the same time that Mister Gadstone was within earshot.

'Another capture I hear,' Don Miguel said.

Lizbeth nodded.

'A pearling lugger,' she replied.

'A good haul?' he enquired.

'I do not know,' Lizbeth lied, because somehow she could not bear to tell him about those six pearls.

There was no reason for her to keep it secret, but she did not want to boast to Don Miguel of Rodney's success. She was proud of what they had done, and yet the newly-awakened love within herself made her understand much that Don Miguel was feeling.

He, too, wanted to be successful. He, too, wanted to show her that he could conquer and be the conqueror. She could understand, as she would not have understood before, the pain in his voice and the sudden harshness of his tone as he said:

'Master Hawkhurst has the blessing of the gods—good fortune is always at his shoulder.'

'We are not yet home,' Lizbeth answered.

Don Miguel glanced towards Master Gadstone who, although he was watching the boats returning from the shore, obviously had an interest in their conversation.

'And when we reach what you call home,' Don Miguel said, and now he spoke in Spanish, 'I shall never see you

171

again. Do you not think that I remember that, every moment, every second of the day and night? I am a prisoner here in my own ship, but in some ways I, too, am fortunate, for I know that you are not far from me, and there are moments like this when I can keep looking at you.'

'Hush, we must be careful.'

Lizbeth hardly breathed the words above a whisper. She was alarmed. She saw the quick glance Master Gadstone gave Don Miguel when he started to speak in Spanish. Whatever language he used, there was no disguising the soft, caressing tone of his voice or the expression in his eyes when he looked at her.

'We must be careful,' Lizbeth whispered again.

She rose to her feet as she spoke and walked across the quarter-deck, climbing the companion-way to the poop, which was as far away from everyone as she could get. Don Miguel followed her, and now as they stood side by side high above the sea, he said:

'I love you!'

'If Rodney should hear, you would be confined to your cabin,' Lizbeth warned him.

Don Miguel shrugged his shoulders.

'Master Hawkhurst is jealous. That is why he behaves as he does.'

Lizbeth shook her head.

'No, he is not jealous,' she contradicted him.

She wished with all her heart that he was. Rodney's anger was hard to bear and she had been more unhappy this past week than she had ever been in her life. Her love had brought her no clear understanding of the man she loved. Rodney's was a strange, complex character she decided. She only knew that his moods wounded and distressed her and that she had no power over him, as she had over Don Miguel, to make him happy or unhappy by a smile or a frown.

Rodney was incensed with her and she knew it every time they sat down to a meal. She could not have believed that he could change so completely and be so different from the laughing, easy companion with whom she had shared the voyage until Don Miguel disrupted their friendship.

He had been angry with her when they left Plymouth and his offhand silence had been uncomfortable soon after leaving England. But Rodney had recovered and his silence had broken down under his own need of conversation.

But this was different. Now he spoke bitterly, harshly and often with a cold sarcasm that was more hurtful than blows. He seemed not only suspicious of her, Lizbeth thought, but also there was something in his manner which made her feel that he despised her. She found herself longing to plead with him, to ask his forgiveness, to swear, if he wished it, that she would never speak to Don Miguel again. Then, even as the words trembled on her lips, pride came to her aid.

She would not demean herself so far to any man, even though she loved him as she loved Rodney. He was being unjust, he was at fault in what he suspected, but she swore that she would not humble herself to seek his favours. Yet she could not prevent herself being wounded and made desperately unhappy by the situation.

She saw Rodney at meals, but Don Miguel was invariably with them. At other times he usually ignored her presence. She might, she thought miserably, have been invisible or something lower than a slave from the way he seemed obviously not to see her as he walked about the deck.

Alone in her cabin, Lizbeth cried many bitter tears. Love, she thought, had brought her no happiness, only a loneliness beyond anything she had ever imagined. It was hard, in the circumstances, not to want to seek comfort where she might find it, and despite herself she did find Don Miguel's love for her comforting.

'I love you!'

There was a magic in those very words, even though they were spoken by a man she did not love. And yet, she thought, in a way she did love Don Miguel. She

173

loved him with an affection that was almost maternal in its warmth. She wanted to comfort him, she wanted to protect him from the horror and misery that lay ahead of him in the future.

He was so young—not in age, but in outlook and character—and she knew from the stories he told her of his childhood that he had been cosseted by his mother and kept from encountering the hardships which other boys of his age took as a matter of course. He had always known luxury and comfort, the security of family life, the adoration of his womenfolk.

It was his father who had insisted that he should go abroad and had suggested a visit to the Spanish Main. The *Santa Perpetua* had sailed from Spain with several other vessels and was to return guarded by the fleet of warships—what could have been safer? How, indeed, could they have anticipated that any accident might happen to Don Miguel?

He had character, Lizbeth thought, even though it was not as yet fully developed; but he had experienced very little emotion in his life, and she knew, even without his telling her so, that his love for her was something overwhelming and completely unsettling.

'I love you.'

She had never realised before how many intonations, how much suppressed longing could be expressed in those three simple words, whether they were spoken in English or Spanish, they still meant the same thing, the throbbing of a man's heart, the yearning of his whole soul.

She wished, as she had wished several times before, that she could reciprocate his love. Perhaps then, for a very short while, they might have found happiness and joy together. She might, indeed, have given him some memories to comfort him when he was imprisoned; but try as she would, she could not pretent to love Don Miguel when her heart was already given to Rodney.

He had no use for it. If he thought of any woman, he thought of Phillida; and yet Lizbeth loved him, loved him even when he sat angry and glowering at the dinner table,

174

making the atmosphere so unpleasant that she was un-aware of what she ate and indeed felt her throat close against food as if it poisoned her.

Only Don Miguel seemed unaffected by Rodney's anger. He said little, but his eyes watched her face with an intensity which he know without being told infuriated Rodney more than anything else.

'I love you.'

Don Miguel's voice struck across Lizbeth's thoughts as she stood now on the poop. Then, as she turned from a contemplation of the sea, she saw Master Barlow come from the after cabin, across the half-deck and go down the side of the ship into his waiting boat with an air of haste and purpose about him which confirmed her idea that they were turning for home.

She was about to speak to Don Miguel when she saw Rodney come on to the quarter-deck and heard his voice giving orders to Master Gadstone. The ship suddenly sprang to activity, boats were being taken alongside, men were climbing up the rigging.

Lizbeth looked at Don Miguel. His face was very pale, his eyes dark and wounded.

'You are going home,' he said, quietly, 'and you are glad. I saw the sudden light come into your eyes when you were sure of it. You will forget me; but as long as there is a living breath in my body, I shall never forget you.'

'Nor I you,' Lizbeth said quickly. 'I shall think of you and . . . pray for you.'

She saw that her words had been no comfort to him, and she added:

'Perhaps the war will be over very quickly. Perhaps you will not be a prisoner for long—perhaps not at all. The Queen will send you home to Spain and then you will be with your family again.'

Don Miguel did not reply in words, he only gave a sharp, humourless laugh and Lizbeth realised how absurd her suggestions were. There was no Spanish Ambassador in England now to plead his case, even if he had one. For

175

years, perhaps for a lifetime, he might linger, forgotten and neglected in some dark prison, even as hundreds of Englishmen suffered in Spanish hands.

Lizbeth remembered her own feelings when she first came aboard the *Sea Hawk*, when she wanted to fight every Spaniard. Then there was not even pity in her heart for those who died, and she knew that public feeling in England was as strong as hers had been, if not stronger.

She thought of the Spaniards who had been taken off the pearling lugger and knew she would not ask mercy for them. They were cruel and bestial. It was only Don Miguel who was different, and that perhaps was merely because she knew him and because he loved her. It was when human relationships entered into politics, she thought suddenly, that things became difficult.

It was easy to hate one's enemy until he became a man in love. She felt it was all too difficult for her to understand, too difficult to argue about. She only wanted to save Don Miguel from his inevitable fate and she had no idea how to do it.

She saw Rodney glance up at them as they stood there silhouetted against the sunlit sky, and she saw that, as he looked, his eyes were hard and his lips tightened in the way that she most feared. Instinctively Lizbeth moved forward and Don Miguel followed her.

Men were hurrying about the decks and Rodney stood watching them. There was something in his attitude, in the breadth of his shoulders and the carriage of his head which made Lizbeth feel suddenly proud of him. He was a born commander. She had not been at sea with him for over two months without learning that his methods might be unorthodox, but they ensured results; that the men not only adored him, they also trusted him. They were ready, Lizbeth knew, now, to do anything that he asked of them, and the same could be said of his officers.

He had the power of leadership; and as she watched him now, Lizbeth knew that in Rodney lay the makings of a great Englishman. He was young yet, but one day, she thought with a sudden perceptive clairvoyance, he would rank with Drake, Frobisher and Hawkins and all those others who were already acknowledged heroes—Elizabeth's men, who were making the name of England feared and venerated, loved and envied over the whole known world.

'I believe in you!'

She wanted to cry the words aloud, she wanted to run to him, to look up into his eyes and tell him that she had faith in him, not only because she loved him, but also because some finer, more spiritual part of herself recognised the potential greatness of him.

And yet she could do nothing but stand there with turmoil all around her, small and insignificant in a world of hurrying and purposeful men. As if something of the intensity of her feelings communicated itself to Rodney, he turned and walked over to where she stood. Ignoring Don Miguel, he spoke only to her.

'We are for home,' he said.

The gladness in his own face found an echo in hers.

'You have achieved all you set out to do,' she answered, thinking only of him.

He looked across the sea, then at the *Sea Hawk*, and then back to the wide decks and the rich ornamentation of the *Santa Perpetua*.

'I shall not be ashamed to sail into Plymouth,' he said, and there was a smile on his lips.

'I shall be proud—exceedingly proud—to be with you,' Lizbeth told him in a voice deep with emotion.

For a moment Rodney looked at her. His eyes seemed to search her face as if wordlessly he asked her a question; and then, before he could speak, Don Miguel interrupted them.

'How many days will it take, do you think?' he asked.

It was an ordinary question and yet somehow Lizbeth felt as if it were a sword thrust between her and Rodney. She could not explain why, but she knew that something beautiful and intangible had been shattered by that careless enquiry.

177

Rodney did not answer for a moment. He looked at Don Miguel and his eyes darkened.

'Soon enough, Señor, as far as you are concerned,' he said and turned and walked across the deck.

Don Miguel shrugged his shoulders. He thought Rodney merely rude, which indeed he had been; but Lizbeth knew there was more to it than that.

She made an excuse to Don Miguel and went below to her cabin. There she sat down on her bunk and stared at the burnished metal mirror which hung on the wall opposite. Her small, straight nose was powdered with freckles and her skin had turned faintly golden where it had been exposed to the sun. She thought then that such traces of the voyage could easily be hidden by paint and powder. But nothing could change or disguise the feelings which lay within her heart and which had not been there when the voyage started.

She loved Rodney. She felt herself quiver at his approach. She felt her whole body yearn for him as he stood near to her so that it was hard to hold her feelings in check and keep him from guessing her secret. She thought now that she would die of shame if he were to learn that she loved him.

It was Phillida to whom he was betrothed and she wondered how she could bear to treat him as a brother-in-law for the rest of her life. He and Phillida could be married as soon as they wished. The cargo of the two ships would be sold and after the prize money had been awarded, the shareholders would receive the rest. Rodney's share of the prize awards and his part as a shareholder would come to a truly magnificent sum.

Yes, he and Phillida could be married, and she, Lizbeth, would be left behind at Camfield to bear the ill-humour of Catherine and the miseries of Francis. Phillida talked of going into a Nunnery, but Lizbeth knew that such wild ideas had not the least likelihood of fulfilment.

No, Phillida would marry Rodney whether she wished it or not. Perhaps, when she was married, she would forget her yearning for religion and settle down and be content with the task of being a wife and mother.

With a little sob Lizbeth put her face in her hands—she wanted to bear Rodney's child, she wanted to belong to him as a woman belongs to a man. She wanted to feel the strength of his arms around her again ; and then, as she remembered how fiercely he had held her, she felt the tears trickle through her fingers. Even brutal kisses were better than no kisses at all. She wanted him at that moment until her whole body ached.

How long she sat in her cabin she did not know, but after a long while she heard the ship's bell strike and knew it was nearly time for supper. For the first time since she had left England she longed for the voyage to be over. This suffering within herself was too much to be borne long. It was best for her to be home, to be somewhere she could, if only for a few moments, forget Rodney and what he meant to her.

She was to think the same thing not once, but a hundred times in the next thirty days. They sailed across the Caribbean Sea without incident, watered at Dominica as they had done on the way out, and then set sail for the Canary Islands.

The men were all excited at the thought of returning home and, though Rodney's moods were changeable, he was on the whole good-tempered and pleasant. Lizbeth should have enjoyed herself, but instead she was torn by conflicting feelings which were at war within herself. It was a bitter-sweet happiness to be with Rodney, to watch him and to hear his voice and yet to know that his feelings for her were no deeper than those of an ordinary friendship . . . a friendship such as he might have accorded to Francis if he had come on this voyage as Sir Harry had commanded.

It was misery to listen to Don Miguel's protestations of love, to know that he was desperately unhappy, and to realise that every mile nearer home was a mile nearer to a prison for him. If she had had something to occupy her time, Lizbeth felt that the voyage might have passed more easily. As it was, she could only think and feel and suffer, and pray that this torture would soon be at an end.

She grew pale and unable to eat and her eyes seemed too large for her small face; and although Rodney insisted on her drinking some of the rich wine that was brought to the table for every meal, it did her no good and she could not tell him what was the real cause of her frailty.

The Canaries were seen by the look-out two hours before dusk. Rodney set all possible sail on the *Santa Perpetua* so as to get her in the shelter of the cliffs before night. They watched for the sight of any Spanish ships, but the seas were deserted.

'Luck is with me,' Rodney boasted. 'We are in need of water and I should have been sorry to pass the islands without calling there.'

He was speaking to Lizbeth and Master Gadstone who were both standing beside him on the quarter-deck.

'The Spaniards must find them as convenient as we do,' Master Gadstone remarked.

'That is true enough,' Rodney answered. 'I expected to see half a dozen galleons as we came over the horizon. Maybe our Spanish guest was praying for the sight of a red and yellow pennant,' he added a little unkindly.

Lizbeth started. Rodney's words had given her an idea. Slowly, so as not to betray her haste, she walked across the deck to where Don Miguel was standing, his hand on the rigging, looking out towards the islands. She felt instinctively that Rodney frowned at her as she went, but for once she did not care.

She reached Don Miguel's side and saw by the expression in his eyes and the droop of his lips that he was depressed and sad.

'Those are the Canary Islands,' she said in a voice loud enough for Rodney and Master Gadstone to hear. Then in a voice almost beneath her breath she asked, 'Can you swim?'

There was a sudden tenseness about Don Miguel which told her that he understood the reason for her question.

'Yes, I can.'

'Well?'

'Well enough.'

'They are going to water our ships there,' Lizbeth said, aloud, still pointing. 'Be ready any time after dark,' she whispered.

It was dangerous to say more. She turned back and walked towards Rodney who was watching the wind in the sails, his face preoccupied, and she did not speak to him again.

Dusk was falling as they weighed anchor in the same place as on their outward voyage. Water casks were got ready to be filled at dawn and then the ship's crew watched for the *Sea Hawk* to come alongside them.

Supper was served as soon as Rodney was free to leave the deck. Lizbeth tried to chat brightly and easily both to him and Don Miguel. The latter she knew was on edge and she was half afraid that Rodney would guess the reason. Supper seemed an interminable meal as course succeeded course and the goblets were filled with wine again and again.

The food was not as good as it had been when they were cruising down the Darien coast, but there was fresh fish caught that very day and the salt pork which was carried aboard the *Santa Perpetua* was superior in every way to what Rodney had bought at Plymouth.

When the meal was finished, the guard was waiting outside the door to escort Don Miguel to his cabin on deck and lock him in for the night. He had not used the inside cabin since Rodney had taken command of the ship.

'Good night, Sir.'

'Good night, Señor.'

Don Miguel bowed to Rodney and then to Lizbeth. There was a meaning in his eyes which belied the words and she prayed then that she would not fail him. She stayed on in the cabin talking to Rodney for a little while and at length she rose to say good night and saw him, before she left, moving to his own quarters.

She waited for a moment outside the cabin. There was a light from several lanterns, but the shadows were deep and mysterious. When she was sure that Rodney was safely behind a closed door, she hurried as swiftly as she could towards Don Miguel's cabin.

The guard was one of the seamen whom she knew quite well by sight. He was leaning against the doorpost, his arms folded, a look of boredom on his face. There was music coming from the fo'c'sle and Lizbeth guessed that he wished he could be there, singing or playing cards with the other men.

She hurried up to him with the air of one who carries an important message.

'The Captain has dropped a chart on the quarter-deck,' she said. 'He asks you to take a lantern, search for it, and take it to him immediately in his cabin.'

'Aye, aye, Zur,' the seaman answered in the slow, soft voice of a countryman which he had never lost despite years at sea; and then he glanced towards the cabin door. 'Oi be on guard, ye know, Zur.'

'Yes, I know,' Lizbeth replied. 'I told the Captain I would take your place.'

'Thank 'ee, Zur.'

The seaman reached up, unhooked a lantern and ran up the companion-way to the quarter-deck. It was now a question of seconds, as Lizbeth knew well. She moved swiftly to the cabin door, having already noted that the key was in the lock. She turned it quickly and then the door was open and Don Miguel stood there. They could hardly see each other in the darkness, but she felt his arms go round her, felt the pressure of his lips against hers.

'Thank you, my love, my life,' he whispered before, with a swiftness she could hardly believe possible, he had sped across the deck and dived into the sea.

She heard the splash as he reached the water and then one of the sentries gave a shout. It was answered by another on the other side of the ship.

'Man overboard! Man overboard!'

The seaman with the lantern came running down the companion-way.

'What be a-happenin', Zur?'

The question died on his lips as he saw the open cabin door. He must have guessed what had happened or he may have seen Don Miguel himself as he dived overboard. After that it seemed to Lizbeth that everything became incoherent. Men were shouting and running about the decks. As she knew only too well, few of them could swim and the few who could waited for definite orders before going after the escaped prisoner.

By the time Rodney had been fetched from his cabin Don Miguel had a good start.

'What has happened? I do not want all of you to speak at once,' he said sharply as a babel of sound arose. 'Master Gadstone, perhaps you will explain?'

Gadstone had come running up only a few moments before Rodney himself and knew only one important fact.

'The prisoner has gone, Sir.'

'Who? de Suavez?' Rodney asked, and then saw the open cabin door and the men crowded round it.

It took him only a few moments to get the facts from the seaman who had been on guard. There was no need to ask Lizbeth what had happened. Her face betrayed her and after one look at her Rodney realised what she had done.

He looked out into the blackness of the night which lay all around them.

'Nothing can be done tonight,' he said. 'If we have time tomorrow, we will look for him; but I doubt if we shall find him again.'

He turned as he spoke to walk back to his cabin. He did not command Lizbeth to follow him, but she did so. In the light of the candles she could see his face grim and set and for a moment she was afraid of him physically. He stood waiting and it was with a tremendous effort that she forced her eyes to meet his.

'You let him go,' Rodney said.

It was a statement, not a question. Lizbeth nodded. She felt somehow she could not explain to Rodney what she felt about Don Miguel. For one thing, he would not understand. He was used to hardship and he would only despise a man who could find the hardships of prison intolerable.

'You loved him?'

Rodney's question took her completely by surprise. She had expected a tirade against her for being a traitor, but not this simple question. She was thankful she could answer him truthfully.

'No, I did not love Don Miguel,' she answered, 'but I was sorry for him. He was young and vulnerable. Now he will get back to Spain to his family.'

'You loved him!'

There was both accusation and contempt in the words.

'If I had, I might have gone with him,' Lizbeth replied.

She saw a startled look in Rodney's face and the astonishment in his eyes; then suddenly an anger that she had not felt before seemed to well up within her.

'Can you not be content with what you have got already without wanting more?' she asked. 'You could have been generous and put him ashore as you put those native men who had been ill-treated. But you wanted to drag him back to England for your glorification. You wanted to flaunt your conquest. Well, you have enough without him. He is only a boy, for all that he bears a great name and owns great possessions. You have taken so much from him already, that you could at least leave him his life.'

Still Rodney stood staring at her. Then before he could answer her, before he could say anything, Lizbeth stamped her foot and her hair flew around her face in the candlelight.

'I think I hate you!' she cried, and as her voice broke on a sob she ran from the cabin, slamming the door behind her.

11

The mist was thick and the sea was rough. The roll of the *Santa Perpetua* as she ploughed through the grey water was a very different movement from that of the *Sea Hawk* and Rodney found himself regretting that he was not on the smaller ship.

They were still eight days out from home and now every man's mind was racing ahead at the thought of harbour and the excitement of setting foot on English soil again. There was an urgency and an impatience about the seamen which showed itself in everything they did. Even the sound of their voices raised in chorus or whistling as they worked, seemed to be accelerated and imbued with impatience.

It was not only the thought of the share of the prize which would be theirs when they got ashore. Although all of them would be rich until the money was spent and they were forced back to sea again in hopes of other gains, there was something deeper and more fundamental in their minds than money. Perhaps a part of it was the unexpressed fear that even now their spoils might be snatched from them.

They were in dangerous waters. There was not a man on board who was so stupid as not to realise that fact, except perhaps the native volunteers, and they, poor devils, were too preoccupied with the change of weather to feel anything but physically miserable.

It was not only the cold that was affecting them. The *Sea Hawk* had ten cases of yellow fever aboard soon after they left the Canaries.

Barlow had reported the matter to Rodney, who had said little about it aboard the *Santa Perpetua*, for he knew that, if Lizbeth heard of it, she would insist on trying to nurse the men. There was little that could be done for yellow fever, as Rodney well knew. The ten men had died and there was every likelihood that the rest of the natives would succumb before they reached Plymouth.

The crew of the *Santa Perpetua* had been extraordinarily lucky to date. Only five Englishmen and seven natives had died since they had captured her. The proportion was exceedingly small compared with the usual death rate on such a voyage as they had undertaken. But luck could change overnight and Rodney had the feeling that he was hanging on by the skin of his teeth to his good fortune and that he must not relax his grip on it for a single second until they were safely into the English Channel.

There was a keen wind blowing this morning. It was welcome, for they were making a good speed, but Rodney felt himself shiver as it whipped its way through his thin doublet. No wonder the natives were cold, he thought, used as they were to the warm tropical temperature they had now left behind them.

They would not linger long in England. He would pay them well and they would doubtless run amok in Plymouth for a week or so and then find a ship sailing west, if they were not unfortunate enough to be pressed into the Navy in the meantime.

The mist was lifting a little. He could see now that the skies were dark and lowering. There would be rain later in the day. He spoke to the man at the tiller, telling him to set his course two points to larboard; and then, as he moved away, anxious to exercise his shivering limbs, he heard a sudden wild yell from the main mast.

'Sail in sight—two of them, Sir. It's . . . it's the enemy!'

There was hardly any need for the look-out, for, as the mists lifted, Rodney had himself seen the ships at the same moment not more than five miles away and sailing straight for them. They were Spanish galleons as large as, if not larger than, the *Santa Perpetua,* and Rodney guessed that they were heading for the Canary Islands.

More than likely they were merchantment on their way back to Havana, in which case, Rodney's brain calculated quickly, they would be empty and of no value from the point of view of plunder; but they were Spanish and that was enough to make him square his chin and set his lips in a hard line of determination.

'Spaniards, Sir, Spaniards!' Master Gadstone was saying at Rodney's elbow, his eyes dancing with excitement, his feet hardly able to keep still.

'Yes, I know, Master Gadstone. Clear for action!'

There was hardly any need to give the word, the men were already running out the guns, laughing and joking as they did so.

The mist was moving low over the sea in clumps so that one moment the ships would be quite clear and the next moment they would be blotted out completely. In a moment of clearness Rodney saw that the nearest galleon was flying her ensign in friendly innocence, dipping it again and again. He was thankful then that he had placed no pennant upon the *Santa Perpetua.* She was flagless. They would wait until the last moment before running up the red cross of St. George and leaving the Spaniards in no doubt to what nation they belonged.

'Keep her steady, Master Gadstone,' Rodney said sharply.

'Aye, aye, Sir!' Gadstone replied with a lilt in his voice as if Rodney had given him a bag of gold rather than an order.

Rodney had taken Master Gadstone on board the *Santa Perpetua* purposely, feeling that he was better able than Barlow to keep the young man's exuberance in check. Now he was glad of his enthusiasm. In Gadstone's opinion there was only one thing to be done with Spaniards—attack them whatever the risk, whatever the odds against success.

Rodney know without looking or asking the look-out

that the *Sea Hawk* was not yet in sight. She had hove-to for some slight repairs and although with her superior speed she would catch up with them later in the day, it was no use waiting for her now. If they were going to grapple with the Spaniards, it was now or never. He set himself to plan the manœuvres of the encounter which would be upon them all too shortly.

The wind was with the *Santa Perpetua*, the galleons were having to tack into wind. He saw one of them broadside on now and realised that he had underestimated her size. She was much larger than the *Santa Perpetua* and her guns would be correspondingly more deadly. The other was about the same tonnage. They were lying as close to each other as was possible, as was the habit of the Spaniards. He would go between them he decided and he gave his orders accordingly.

'Man the braces, Master Gadstone, and every man is to hold his fire.'

The men at the guns could hear him and they knew what he intended. They knew as well as he did that a premature broadside would ruin the whole operation. Rodney called the men with the arquebuses and the archers on deck. They came running up just as the mist swept down again and he told them to crouch down behind the heavy bulwarks and not to be seen till the last moment.

He had a good look at the galleons a few minutes later as the mist lifted. They carried four-storied deck-houses which gave them a unique and very impressive appearance. Like many of the Spanish ships they were almost as high as they were long, with netting over their half-decks to prevent boarding. This would have been a deterrent had Rodney intended to board them, but he knew there was no chance of capturing the galleons as there were two of them. There was only one thing he could do for the glory of England and that was either to sink them or make them so unseaworthy they would sink by themselves in the storm which lay ahead.

Galleons were hard to manage in rough weather, slow

of pace and almost helpless against a head wind, but that did not make Rodney underestimate the deadliness of their cannon at close quarters. They also carried an armoury of curious catapults and the Spanish men-at-arms were notoriously accurate with their arquebuses.

The ships were growing nearer to each other and the mist was blowing away at the same moment. Rodney could see the glitter of the Spaniards' armour as they crowded towards the bow. They were getting curious, Rodney guessed, as to why the *Santa Perpetua* did not reply to their signals. She was approaching the two galleons unwaveringly.

Rodney gave the order and the men sprang up the rigging. They were hauling up the cross of St. George and in a few seconds there would be no doubt to whom the *Santa Perpetua* belonged.

'Hold your fire!' he shouted warningly to Master Gadstone.

In the course of the next few seconds the *Santa Perpetua's* bow-chasers would begin to bear. They were bow to bow now, and moving as brightly as a girl at her first dance, she slid between the two galleons.

Rodney could see the Spanish officers pointing at the *Santa Perpetua's* main mast. He heard orders being yelled, a note of panic in their voices. The men on the fo'c'sle cannon were stooping to look along the sights. Then Master Gadstone gave the order. The *Santa Perpetua's* broadsides burst into thunder, flame and smoke.

'Keep her at it, men!' Rodney shouted.

And now those hours of drill under the gruelling sun in the Caribbean Sea were justified. The very second the sponges were withdrawn the powder, rammer and shot were ready for insertion down the muzzles of the guns. The crews flung themselves on the tackles and the guns roared out again.

The men with the arquebuses and the archers had picked their men. The cannon, too, were sweeping the decks and thundering low against the galleons' sides.

As the smoke cleared, Rodney could see that the galleon

189

on the larboard side had suffered the most. She had been nearer than the other. Her main mast was tipping forward like a broken wing, the deck was a swirling mass of spars and canvas, with dead men lying in heaps beneath them.

The other galleon had lost her mizzen mast and there were several ugly, gaping holes in her hull; but her crew was the quicker of the two and now the *Santa Perpetua* was jarred by the impact of the shot from her cannon. The rigging parted in several places above Rodney's head. There was a shower of splinters which were more deadly than the shot from the Spanish muskets; then they were out of reach.

'Starboard!' Rodney roared to the helmsman. 'Stand by your guns on the larboard side!'

It was a difficult manœuvre to bring the *Santa Perpetua* round and to train her guns on the galleons' great over-ornamented sterns, but they managed it. A few seconds later, raked from astern, the second galleon was as helpless as her companion. Her mizzen mast was down, the sails trailed over her sides and down into the sea; and though her stern guns were still firing, the shots were wild and quite ineffectual. Rodney guessed that the crew was demoralised, as so often happened with the Spaniards when one came to grips with them.

'Stand by to go about!' he commanded, and the crew cheered as they realised that the battle was over and the *Santa Perpetua* was homeward bound again.

But the victory had not been achieved without casualties. The deck was splintered and the ornamental woodwork which must have been the pride of those who carved it was battered and slashed in a thousand places, the sails were split and holed, and amongst the debris on deck lay the men who had fallen beneath the Spanish fire.

There were a number of them, Rodney thought, and with an exclamation of horror he saw that Gadstone was amongst them. He was sitting propped against the taffrail with his legs crumpled under him, and a great crimson stain spreading over his doublet above his heart told its own story.

Lizbeth was kneeling beside him. It was only later that Rodney learned that she had been on deck during the whole action. She had gone to the side of the first man who fell, only to find, as she touched him, that he was dead.

It was then above the roar of the guns that she realised that a seaman was speaking to her.

'Master Gadstone, Sir! He's fallen.'

She ran across the deck to Gadstone's side. As she went, a splinter struck her shoulder, but was prevented from hurting her by the slashed puffing of her sleeve. She felt it prick her skin, but she paid no heed. It was Master Gadstone of whom she was thinking.

She crouched down beside him, instinctively keeping her head below the bulwarks.

'We've beaten them, haven't we?' Gadstone asked weakly.

'Yes, of course,' Lizbeth answered.

''Tis a victory!' He tried to cheer, but his voice croacked in his throat. 'A victory against those damned Spaniards. . . .'

His voice trailed away before the end of the words. As he slumped forward against her, Lizbeth knew that he was dead; but she held his head against her breast, not knowing what else she could do. She was deafened by the noise and din and dazed by the sight of death all around her.

She found herself praying, praying out loud as she held Master Gadstone's dead body to her. It was a long time after, when she opened her eyes to find Rodney standing beside her, that she realised it was for him and not for herself that she had been praying.

The quiet now was almost painful after the roar of the guns. Her eyes were smarting from smoke; it caught in her throat and made her cough; and then despite her every resolution she knew she was crying. She felt Rodney pull her to her feet, heard him give the order for Gad-

191

stone's body to be carried away, as he half-supported, half-carried her into the after cabin.

Everything was in confusion. Pictures had fallen, gold ornaments were scattered over the floor, chairs were overturned.

'Drink this wine,' Rodney said quietly, and there was something in the calmness of his voice which pulled Lizbeth together far more effectively than the wine he forced between her lips.

'Sit here,' he commanded. 'I must go on deck. There is much for me to do.'

He was gone almost before he finished speaking, and in a few minutes Lizbeth had followed him.

'Fifteen men killed and thirty wounded, Sir,' the Master Gunner told her.

Here was her task and she set herself to do it, realising as she worked that the conditions on the *Santa Perpetua* were much better than those she had encountered on the *Sea Hawk*.

She had inspected the surgeon's cabin after they had captured the ship and had marvelled at what she found there. There was no need to ask Rodney this time for *aqua vitae*, for the Spaniards had a special vinegar which they used to clean and cool wounds and Lizbeth had already proved its efficacy on men who had cut or injured themselves while in the execution of their duties.

There were rolls of fine linen to use as bandages, pots and bottles of healing lotions and pastes, some of which were too strange for her to risk employing them; others of whose qualities she had already formed a good opinion.

It was several hours later before she had finished with the wounded or before Rodney remembered to ask where she was. He sent for her just as she had finished bandaging the last man. When she came on deck, she realised that the ship was rolling badly and that the waves were breaking over the decks, but even in that short time the remaining crew of the *Santa Perpetua* had worked miracles and the main deck was cleared of many of the traces of the fight.

The boatswain and his mates were still splicing the rigging and the carpenter was at work, but the sailmaker had already set new sails for those which were too tattered to be left aloft. It must have been hard work, against the heave and pitch of the ship, but they had managed it; and now with the swell leaping and rolling under them and the spray soaking all those who remained on deck, the only real danger lay from the fact that the crew was almost too small to bring the *Santa Perpetua* into port.

As Lizbeth was helped across the deck and had reached the safety of the after cabin, Rodney came running out, almost colliding with her in his speed.

'Silence!' he shouted at her, though she had not spoken. 'Do you hear anything?'

It was difficult to hear anything, Lizbeth thought, above the shriek of the wind, the splash of the waves and the creaking of the ship's timbers. But a seaman who had heard Rodney's question answered.

' 'Tis guns, Sir; guns t' the sou' of us!'

Lizbeth could hear them now and they seemed for a moment an echo of those which had rung in her ears a few hours ago.

'It's the *Sea Hawk*!' Rodney exclaimed. 'I would know the sound of her thirty-pounders anywhere. 'Tis the *Sea Hawk* and she is finishing off the Spanish galleons.'

It was a guess of course, but a guess that was proved right when just before dusk fell the *Sea Hawk* caught up with them. Rodney had heaved to and waited with an anxiety which he had managed to conceal from everyone but Lizbeth, who knew only too well the signs of strain around his eyes and mouth.

The men were not so controlled, and despite the bad weather most of them were on deck when the *Sea Hawk* finally appeared.

'Ship ho!' yelled the look-out, and a moment later

came the cry that Rodney was waiting for—'It's the *Sea Hawk*, Sir!'

They cheered then, and below decks a minute or so later Lizbeth heard the wounded men cheering, for the word had been carried to them.

'She is safe!' Lizbeth spoke the words in heartfelt tones of thankfulness.

Rodney turned to look down at her. The wind was whipping her hair about her cheeks and it made her look so feminine that a few months ago he would have been filled with terror lest someone guess her identity.

Now, the emotion which filled him was a different one. Her courage made him feel proud, her tired little face made him feel very protective.

'And you, too, are safe!' He spoke softly, but she heard him above the roar of the wind.

'Rodney, you have been wonderful!' She could not help telling him of the wonder and admiration within her heart. He put his arm within hers and with an expression of sheer jubilation cried:

'Together, little Lizbeth, we have done it!'

She felt as if he had placed a crown upon her head. 'Together'—the word had a thrill of glory about it, and she loved him—loved him with every beat of her heart, with every breath she drew, with every drop of blood in her veins. Rodney, the conqueror, the victor—the man of her dreams!

The men were still cheering, for it was the *Sea Hawk* right enough with nothing more dangerous to report than a split topmast and a dozen holes in her sails. The sea, which had been running high, abated enough for Master Barlow to come aboard and tell the whole story in detail.

'They fired over the top of us, Sir,' he said, which explained the lack of serious damage to the *Sea Hawk*.

It was one of the faults of the high galleons that they invariably missed the hull of a smaller ship which lay close in beside them.

'We heard your guns, Sir, and guessed what was happenning,' Barlow went on. 'When we came upon the galleons ourselves, they were shipping water and drifting helplessly. We thought it was unlikely that either of them would make port, but thought it best to make sure of it.'

'Quite right, Master Barlow—well done!' Rodney approved.

Extra hands from the *Sea Hawk* came to relieve the crew of the *Santa Perpetua* and, when dawn broke, both ships were on their way again. Carpenters were working on the damage done below decks until the day before they sighted Land's End and after that there was nothing more to do but to dress the ship and bring her into Plymouth Harbour with all flags flying.

For Lizbeth the last few days passed with an incredible swiftness. It seemed to her that she hardly had a moment to think, with thirty wounded men requiring so much attention that, when she went to bed, hardly an hour passed without someone rapping on her door. Five men died, but the rest, despite dangerous wounds, were, she believed, well on the road to recovery as they rounded Rame Head.

Those who could walk or crawl dragged themselves on deck. No one wanted to miss that moment of satisfaction when the crews of other vessels entering or leaving the harbour would stare in stupefaction at the *Santa Perpetua* and know her for a prize.

Rodney was as busy as Lizbeth was, but as they sat together on the last night in the big oak-panelled after cabin, Lizbeth felt a sudden constriction of her heart as she realised that the voyage was ended. and this was perhaps the last time she would be alone with Rodney.

Her love for him was as hard to bear, she had thought several times that week, as the wounds of the men she tended so carefully. They were now on the road to recovery, but she would never recover. Her love for Rodney went too deep, and she knew with that strange clairvoyance which had been hers since childhood that, whatever the future might hold for either of them, she would love him until she died.

She was not sure how she knew this; she was only

195

aware that every nerve and vein in her body was a part of him. It did not matter whether he was angry or pleased with her, whether he was brutal or tender, she would still belong to him; and nothing but death, she thought, whimsically, would cure her of the hurt he had inflicted on her.

They sat talking over supper the last night until the candles gutted low. They talked, not of the future, but of the past, of what had happened since they left England a hundred and sixty-six days before, of the amusing little incidents which had happened during the voyage, which made them laugh again as they had laughed at the time. There were memories of Master Gadstone, of his enthusiasm and of his hatred for the Spaniards, which brought tears springing to Lizbeth's eyes and a grave note to Rodney's voice.

They remembered the blue skies and the clear sea of the Caribbean, the parrots and macaws with their brilliant plumage, many of which had also died on the voyage home, and the fish which swam amongst the coral reefs and could never be transferred from their natural haunts and kept alive, even for a few hours, however hard they tried.

But somehow in the greyness of the English autumn it was hard to remember the dazzling beauty of the tropical seas, and Lizbeth sometimes wondered if the cargo, too, would lose its glitter and value when they unshipped it on the prosaic docks of Plymouth where it could no longer be seen against the luxuriant vegetation and the golden sands of the Caribbean shore.

Even the bejewelled ornaments on the table, she thought, seemed duller and less sparkling; and then she realised that it was her own sadness at having to say good-bye that was colouring everything. For one wild moment she contemplated telling Rodney what she felt about him so that she could sail again with him on another voyage.

It was but a passing madness and she smiled at the idea even as it came to her; and yet she dreaded the moment when she must leave him and return to her real life as a woman. In retrospect the voyage all became a wonderful dream; the heartache, the anxieties and even the miseries were forgotten or paled into insignificance beside the happiness and the laughter and the times when Rodney and she had shared a companionship such as she had never known in the whole of her life before. She would never know it again, she thought. She must go back to Camfield, to her father and stepmother, to Phillida and Francis and the safe security of her home.

It all seemed so petty and trivial and unimportant compared with the life she had lived aboard Rodney's ships and at Rodney's side. But they would be in port tomorrow. There was nothing for her to do but say good-bye with as much dignity and control as she could achieve.

Rodney was looking at her as she sat with her elbows on the table, her little chin resting on her hands. The white starched linen which had been Francis' ruff framed her hair and the green satin of her doublet echoed her eyes.

'Are you content with what we have achieved?'

He asked the question although he knew the answer.

'No one could have done more!'

There was a thrill in her voice and he felt absurdly pleased by her praise even while he expected it.

'I have been singularly fortunate.'

'As I foretold!'

He smiled.

'You will be burnt as a witch. Faith, but I am afraid of your predictions!'

'Why, when they are in your favour?' Lizbeth asked.

'You yourself are unpredictable—you come aboard my ship in disguise. You are a woman and yet you bring me good luck. If it had been otherwise, I should have suspected you of the evil eye.'

'Instead—how will you reward me?'

Lizbeth was teasing him, the candlelight revealed the sparkle in her eyes.

'What shall I give you? The emerald necklace?'

197

It was the first time he had referred to the jewels since they had fought over them and his suspicions of her.

'It belongs to the shareholders,' she said coolly.

'Of which I am one; also I am the Captain of a successful ship who can take his first pick of the spoils. If I remember rightly, Drake was given goods to the value of ten thousand pounds before the cargo of the *Golden Hind* was divided.'

'I thank you—but I have no wish to own the emeralds!' Lizbeth told him.

She could never look at them, she thought, without remembering Don Miguel—she could hear his voice all too clearly as he spoke of his love, and see the pain in his eyes.

'No, I will have nothing,' she cried suddenly.

'Only your memories,' Rodney said, and his voice was hard.

He knew, she thought, why she would not take the emeralds, why she shrank even from the thought of them.

'Yes, those are mine—for ever.'

Lizbeth's answer was defiant, her chin raised a little; but in reply Rodney held out his hand towards her with a generous, affectionate gesture she had not expected.

'Forgive me, Lizbeth—there is nothing I can offer which could reward you for all you have done . . . for your kindness to my wounded, for your courage in every danger, for the way you have never complained, never grumbled.'

Her hand was in his and his fingers warm and strong made her breath come more quickly.

'To Lizbeth!'

He was raising a goblet of wine with his other hand.

'I thank you.'

Her voice trembled on the simple words, her whole body was quivering beneath his touch and she was afraid he would notice her agitation. He put down the goblet and looked down at her fingers lying in his palm.

'So little,' he said, and added softly, 'and so brave.'

He did not mean what he said, Lizbeth thought; it was

just a moment of sentimentality because the voyage was at an end. She drew her hand away and lifted high her own goblet of wine.

'To the future,' she said, 'and may it bring you everything you ask of it.'

She thought of Phillida as she spoke and putting down her wine, rose from the table.

' 'Tis time to turn in,' she said, her tone deliberately commonplace.

If he was kind to her again, she thought in a sudden panic, she would burst into tears.

'Good night, sweet witch. God bless you!'

She found it difficult to find the door. She managed it, though the tears were running down her cheeks by the time she reached the privacy of her own cabin.

But they were happy tears—Rodney had thanked her! She had never expected so much from him; yet how, she asked herself, could she face saying good-bye to him tomorrow, knowing her weakness, collapsing as she did beneath his kindness where she had never quailed before his anger?

She lay awake all night, distracted by her own feelings; and yet when the morning came, nothing was so difficult as she had anticipated. Things had begun happening from the moment they reached the Sound and Rodney, leaning over the side, had shouted to a passing vessel whose crew were staring open-mouthed:

'Is the Queen alive?'

He asked the question deliberately, copying Drake, who had made the same enquiry on return home from his voyage around the world. The answer to his question came roaring across the waves:

'She's alive.'

'We've beaten the thrice-cursed Spaniards!'

'The Armada has been defeated and wrecked.'

It was difficult to separate the various answers, but when they had done so, Rodney and Lizbeth looked at each other and each drew a deep breath. The Armada had been defeated, that much was clear at any rate; they

199

could wait for details until they reached Plymouth.

They came into Harbour with the music lilting on deck and Rodney waving his hat wildly to the assembled crowds. There were thousands of people on the quay, cheering and waving to welcome them, and messengers were sent posting to London to Sir Francis Walsingham and to the Plymouth authorities to tell them of what lay in the holds of the *Santa Perpetua* and the *Sea Hawk*.

The news of their return and the success of their voyage was not likely to be kept secret with the *Santa Perpetua* anchored in the harbour and looking strangely out of place among the smaller and more severe British ships. And every seaman on board her and the *Sea Hawk* seemed to have not one tongue but two as they talked of the spoils of the voyage and the richness of the promised prize money.

'Here come th' carrion crows,' one man laughed as the women of Plymouth seemed to turn out as it were in one body—wife and mistress, maiden and prostitute—pushing and fighting with each other in their efforts to get near to the returned buccaneers.

In the turmoil and excitement of it all, it was easy for Lizbeth to slip away. She had told Rodney the night before that she would leave for Camfield as soon as possible. He agreed heartily with her decision, for he was anxious that no one should know that she had been on board.

It would be some time, he knew, before he could join her. There was the cargo to be registered, and when the prize money had been distributed, the rest had to be sold and divided among the shareholders. It all meant a great deal of work; but when that was done, he would come hurrying to Camfield.

And so, as the gold-laced officials streamed on board the *Santa Perpetua*, Lizbeth left her. Two ordinary seamen set her baggage in the boat and shook her hand in farewell. She would like to have spoken to Master Barlow, to Baxter, to Hales, to the Master Gunner and all the other men with whom she had sailed; but she knew they would not expect it—they were far too busy at this moment to be looking for her.

The sun was shining on the water as the ship's boat took her to the quay. It was a pale, insipid sun with no warmth in it, which seemed to make no difference to the chill on the wind or the promise of rain in the clouds blowing across the grey sky.

Rodney had meant, Lizbeth knew, to make arrangements for her return. He had planned to find horses and servants to escort her on the long journey from Plymouth to Camfield. She felt she would rather make these arrangements herself than trouble him, so she went to the inn where she and Francis had stayed the night before she went aboard the *Sea Hawk*. The landlord took her for her brother and was quite prepared to find her decent horses and trustworthy men to accompany her on her journey. She paid him well and knew that she need not worry that he would rob her more than he was entitled to do.

When everything was arranged, she went to bed and lay sleepless, finding it impossible to rest because the room was steady and there was no creaking timber or rattle of the rigging to which she had grown accustomed without realising it. She hated the stillness of the night and was glad when dawn came and she could say that she was ready to leave an hour before the time appointed.

It was drizzling with rain, a fine drizzle which made her face wet and glistened on her eyelashes. Yet, as she turned round in her saddle to look back at the town, the harbour and the grey waves of the sea, she knew it was not the drizzle that was blinding her eyes, but tears of regret and loneliness, of a longing which seemed to make her whole body ache for the man she had left behind her.

12

It was growing dark and the scuds of rain seemed to make it darker still. The horses were tired, as were the riders, for Lizbeth had pushed them hard. For the past hour she had recognised the way and had ridden ahead of her little band of servants and pack-horses, hurrying forward with an eagerness which made it hard to keep up with her; but she was shivering as she turned into the twisting, muddy road which led to Camfield.

She found herself longing for the warmth of the tropical sun, and in her tiredness she tried to imagine herself on the quarter-deck of the *Santa Perpetua* sailing down the coast over a sea as brilliantly blue as the sky above it. She could visualise Rodney walking up and down deep in thought, his hands clasped behind his back, his expression serious and preoccupied.

In contrast she saw him as she had seen him last, waving his hat to the cheering crowds, his eyes alight, his head thrown back with the excitement and exuberance that all the crew were feeling at their return home.

Gone was his pose of being calm and unperturbed by anything that occurred. He was setting no check on his feelings, and she thought how young and handsome he looked when he was off his guard. Rodney! Rodney! It seemed to Lizbeth that every picture in her mind was of Rodney! And yet how little she knew about him! He had rarely spoken of his past. Of Drake's exploits he could talk by the hour, but he seldom included himself in those adventures.

She guessed rather than knew that there had been many women in his life and she felt the sharp pangs of jealousy as she thought of them—women who must have loved and ached for Rodney even as she loved and ached for him!

Of his childhood she had learnt only that he was unhappy at home. His mother had died when he was only a child, and his father bullied both him and his elder brothers and sisters. A brilliant scholar, Rodney's father had expected those who bore his name to follow in his erudite footsteps and resented it when they had other interests.

One by one the older members of the family had left home and finally Rodney himself had run away to join the Navy, preferring physical hardship to mental cruelty.

This was all Lizbeth had learned of his early life, for the miserable years of a lonely adolescence were still too vivid for him to speak lightly of them. But remembering the aching void that the death of her own mother had left in her life, Lizbeth sensed and understood much that he left unsaid.

Rodney! Rodney! The very wind in the trees seemed to whisper his name.

Only half a mile to Camfield Place! But there was somewhere else she must go first. She gave the word to halt. The horses seemed to obey her gratefully, while the servants looked at her askance.

'Wait here for me,' she commanded. 'There is someone I must see. I shall not be long.'

They would have demurred if they had dared, at this delay in reaching shelter and food; but Lizbeth's air of authority and the promise of good pay she made them had persuaded the hired men at the very beginning of the journey that she was someone of importance. Nevertheless she could hear them muttering to themselves as she turned off the road and rode quickly down an untidy, badly-kept drive towards Dr. Keen's house.

Built of grey stone it stood in a small garden surrounded by ancient trees. It had never been an attractive house and now to Lizbeth it appeared sinister and repellent as in the dying light she could see that its windows were shuttered and that there was no welcoming gleam of light.

She rode right up to the front door, then dismounted and rapped with the handle of her riding-whip on its rough, oak-studded surface. The sound of her knocking seemed blunted by the wind and after a moment she rapped again. A strand of ivy was flapping in an untidy manner on the side of the house, a puddle of water had accumulated near the front door, and there was over all an air of neglect and depression which began to affect Lizbeth.

Could Dr. Keen have left? she asked herself. Perhaps the house was empty? And then, even as she framed the question her mind, she was certain it was not. She had a feeling, a strong, unmistakable conviction that someone was within. The windows were shuttered, the rooms must be in darkness, and yet someone must be listening.

She could not account to herself for her absolute certainty of this; but because she was so sure, she knocked again, and this time she raised her voice and called to the upper windows:

'Elita! Elita!'

The only answer was the whistling of the wind and the tap of the ivy; but again Lizbeth called.

'Elita, are you there? I want to speak with you.'

Her voice sounded strange even to her own ears. As she waited, she heard the sound of a shutter being opened very softly. It was too dark to see clearly, but she felt sure that someone was looking out at her from the windows on the first floor; and now she called again:

'Elita! Elita!'

This time she was answered. The casement over the front door moved a few inches and Elita's voice, low and hoarse, asked:

'What do you want?'

'It is I, Lizbeth. I wanted to speak with you. Let me in.'

Elita did not answer for a moment and Lizbeth had the feeling that she was contemplating a refusal. Hastily she called:

'Come down, Elita, I must speak with you. 'Tis of the utmost importance. There is no one with me.'

'No one?' Elita questioned. 'You are alone?'

'Yes, I am absolutely alone,' Lizbeth answered. 'Marry, can you not see there is no one here?'

She felt that Elita peered into the shadows to reassure herself; then the window was closed. After a few moments Lizbeth could hear footsteps on the stone floor of the hall and the chains and bolts being undone. After what seemed a long time the door was opened a few inches.

'What do you want?' Elita's voice was surly; and now through the darkness Lizbeth could vaguely see the white oval of her face, her dark eyes, suspicious and wary.

'Where is Francis?'

To Lizbeth's surprise she did not receive an answer. Instead it seemed to her a flicker of fear passed over Elita's face, but it might have been merely a trick of the darkness.

'Let me in,' Lizbeth said impatiently. 'It is impossible to stand here where we cannot see each other.'

She loosed hold of the bridle of her horse as she spoke.

'He will not wander far,' she said more to herself than to Elita. 'He is too tired.'

She stepped towards the door as if she would enter the house. It did not open for her as she expected. Instead, Elita appeared to bar the way, only a portion of her showing through the partially-opened door.

'You must go away,' she said, in a low, fierce voice. 'I would not have answered you had I not feared you would wake the whole neighbourhood with your shouting.'

'Why are you behaving like this?' Lizbeth asked. 'Let me in, Elita. We cannot talk to each other out here in the cold.'

Her persistence seemed to make Elita decide to do what she was asked. The door was opened and a second later

Lizbeth stood in the hall. The door was closed behind her. Both the girls were in the darkness for a moment while Elita fumbled about and eventually lit a candle.

It burned slowly and fitfully, but by its light Lizbeth could see Elita for the first time. She was astonished by what she saw. The girl was obviously ill, thin and emaciated, her cheek-bones etched sharply against her face, her eyes burning dark and feverishly in their sockets. She looked very different from the exotic Elita whom Lizbeth had suspected of seducing Francis for her own ends.

There was something radically wrong, Lizbeth could see that at a glance, and she noticed that Elita's hands were trembling as she turned to face her. The hall smelt dank and cold and somehow an atmosphere of horror seemed to creep over Lizbeth. It was in a voice hardly above a whisper that she managed to ask:

'Where is Francis?'

There was no doubt now that Elita was frightened. She was trembling all over as she glanced towards the door as if she expected someone to be standing there who could overhear what she had to tell. Now grotesquely her face seemed contorted and Lizbeth realised that her teeth were chattering. Lizbeth felt fear rising within her.

'Answer me!' she commanded. 'Answer me! Where is Francis?'

'He is dead!'

Lizbeth knew then that she had anticipated the words before Elita spoke them.

'When did he die? What has happened?'

She heard her own voice ringing out and echoing away through the shadows.

'Hush, someone might hear you!'

Elita looked over her shoulder and her teeth chattered audibly.

'How did he die?' Lizbeth asked in a lower tone.

'He went with my father to a friend's house in Northampton,' Elita answered. 'There was a . . . a meeting there, but it was discovered. . . . The soldiers came. . . ." Elita

206

put her hands suddenly to her eyes and her voice died away harshly in her throat.

'Yes, yes, go on!' Lizbeth said impatiently. 'By a meeting I suppose you mean that my brother was taking part in some conspiracy against the Queen?'

Elita did not trouble to deny this; instead, she continued hoarsely:

'They were tried and condemned to death . . . all who were there. . . . My father . . . gave a false name, and so . . . did Francis.'

'They were hanged?' Lizbeth asked.

Elita nodded. 'And drawn . . . and quartered . . .' she whispered.

Her eyes seemed almost mad with terror for the moment, but Lizbeth managed to speak calmly despite the horror within her heart.

'When did this happen?' she asked.

'A month ago,' Elita replied. 'I have stayed here hidden ever since . . . But I have got to get away, someone has got to help me . . . I have friends who will take me . . . to Spain. I shall be safe there . . . from those . . . who have . . . murdered my father. . . . Yes . . . murdered him!'

She was sobbing now, harsh, heartrending sobs that seemed to shake her whole body as if with an ague.

'Who knows of this?' Lizbeth asked; and then, as Elita seemed not to hear, she put her hand on the girl's shoulder as if to command her attention.

'Who knows of this?' she repeated.

Elita raised her haunted, tear-stained face.

'How do I know who knows of it? They may be playing with me; they may be trying to trap me; but if they think the house is empty, they will go away and I shall be safe . . . safe.'

She was half-crazed with terror, Lizbeth could see that, but for the moment she had no pity, only a desire to learn more of Francis.

'You say that Francis gave a false name,' she said. 'Who knows that his name was false?'

'Only those who were there that night,' Elita replied.

207

Two of them escaped. They came here and told me what had happened. My father was . . . dead by then and they had lain hidden in a friend's house in the neighbourhood until the chase was over. They told me what had occurred and then they . . . left me. I pleaded with them to take me with them, but . . . they would not do so.'

There was despair in Elita's voice now.

'I am safe as long as they can't find me . . . safe until I can reach Spain.' She put her hands to her face.

Lizbeth turned towards the door. Francis was dead. The realisation of what Elita had told her was beginning to seep through the numbness which had been hers from the moment when the blow struck home. Francis was dead—lazy, indolent, easy-going Francis, who had wanted only to lie in the sun and write poems.

He had died because he had let himself be persuaded by his so-called friends into taking a part in their nefarious schemes. Francis was no intriguer, he was not clever enough for that, and yet he had paid the supreme penalty of all traitors. She hoped he had died bravely, but she did not dare to ask the question for fear that she might hear to the contrary.

Her hand was on the latch as Elita spoke again.

'Help me . . . please help me!'

The words seemed to come croakingly from her throat; and now her hands, claw-like in their intensity, were groping towards Lizbeth.

'Help me,' she was pleading, grovelling, beset by her own fear and terror.

'I cannot help you,' Lizbeth said slowly. 'And if I could, I would not do so! You have killed my brother.'

She went from the house without a backward glance. She pulled the door to behind her; and before she had found her horse in the darkness and mounted him, she heard the bolts being shot home and the chains jangling. The light in the hall was extinguished, Elita was alone in the darkness, alone with her own fears and her conscience.

Slowly Lizbeth rode up the drive. It was raining again now, but she did not feel it against her face. She was thinking of Francis, of how close she had been to him in the past, of how she had promised their mother that she would look after him. But she had failed—failed utterly. Francis lay in a traitor's grave, drawn and quartered.

She thought of him as she had last seen him, slipping away from the Inn at Plymouth, eager to be gone, content that she should take his place aboard the *Sea Hawk,* evading, as he had evaded all his life, the responsibility of doing the things he ought to do and getting someone else to do them for him.

Weak and irresponsible, yet she loved him. Yes, she had loved Francis, Lizbeth thought suddenly, as if he were her son rather than her brother. Always she felt she must protect him, and yet in the hour of his death she had not been there. It was not her fault and yet she blamed herself. Somehow, in some cleverer way than she knew, she should have insisted on his going to sea as their father had commanded. But Francis' hysteria at the idea had made it impossible for her to insist that he should do so.

He had forced her into helping him to escape, but what he had encountered had been so very much worse than what he had avoided. He would have been afraid to die, Lizbeth knew that. She felt both despondency and despair at the thought of what he must have suffered ; and then like a gleam of light in the darkness came the thought that, though he had stood his trial and been condemned, he had not revealed who he was. He had not sent for his father and asked him to use what influence he had to save him. Lizbeth felt a sudden lightening of her misery at the thought. In the end Francis had been brave. He had been brave enough to remain anonymous to save the honour of his name even though by keeping silent he destroyed the only faint hope there might have been of his own salvation.

He had been brave at the end—the footsteps of Lizbeth's horse seemed to echo the words—he had been brave.

She reached the servants and the pack-horses standing wet and miserable at the end of the drive.

'Only a short distance now,' she said, surprised that her voice could sound quite cheerful.

They seemed to brighten at this and followed her as she rode ahead of them. They came to the gates of Camfield Place and she passed through them, thinking as she did so that in a few minutes now she would be facing her father and her step-mother. They would ask her about Francis and she would have to answer them.

Her brain seemed cloudy so that even her thoughts came incoherently, jumbled and without sense or sequence. Francis was dead. She had to repeat the words to herself to be sure that she believed them. He was dead and yet he had died bravely. She thought of him being hanged with a party of traitors. She had always suspected that Dr. Keen was seditious. Plot after plot had been discovered amongst the Spanish sympathisers in England who wished to rid themselves of a Protestant Queen. It was only surprising that Dr. Keen had not been discovered before.

Lizbeth, remembering his shifty eyes and thin, pale lips which seemed to distort the most simple truth, felt that she had always been suspicious of him. He had been clever, but not clever enough, and he had embroiled Francis in his perfidy.

Lizbeth drew a deep breath. She had reached the door of the house. She had not even been aware of the dear familiarity of the drive and gardens as she came through them. Now, with a sudden throb of her heart she realised that she was home. She looked up at the gables, at the great width of the house stretching out on either side of her. It seemed almost as if the walls embraced her, the place where she was born and where she had lived all her life.

From within there was a sound of dogs barking and footsteps hurrying towards the door. She felt then a sense of panic—she had returned home, but alone. What was she going to say? And quite suddenly, as if in answer to the frantic searchings of her own mind, she felt as vividly as if it was still happening the noise, thunder and flame of battle around her and the heaviness of Master Gadstone's head against her breast. She knew then, as she dismounted from her horse and strode forward into the house, what she must say.

The servants were curtseying and smiling at the sight of her, the dogs were jumping up, barking a joyous welcome at her return. Now her father was hurrying towards her across the floor of the Great Chamber, Catherine behind him, her face avid with curiosity.

'My child, I am indeed relieved to see you,' Sir Harry exclaimed.

His great arms encompassed his daughter and he placed heavy smacking kisses on both her cheeks.

'Lizbeth, you are a bad girl to go sneaking off like that,' Catherine scolded.

There was no venom in her voice and Lizbeth knew suddenly she was no longer afraid of her stepmother. The room seemed big and vast. She realised that it was in contrast with the cabin of the *Santa Perpetua*.

'And where is Francis?' her father boomed, his eyes on the door.

The moment had come when she must answer this question.

'Francis is dead,' Lizbeth replied quietly.

'Dead?'

She could feel their eyes resting on her face.

'Yes, dead. He died fighting the Spaniards in our last battle. He was very brave and gallant. You would have been proud of him, Father.'

'I am proud of him.'

It seemed to Lizbeth as though Sir Harry breathed the words rather than spoke them, and now, as she looked up into his face, she saw an expression there which she did not understand. It was almost as if it were relief; yet how could it be that? She wondered then for one fleeting second whether he knew or whether he suspected that there was some mystery about Francis' death; and then she forced herself to sweep such ideas from her mind.

Francis had died fighting the Spaniards. She would

swear to it if it must be her dying oath and she would force Rodney, when she saw him, to agree to the same story. He would not refuse her, she was sure of it.

'I am indeed sad to hear about poor Francis,' Catherine was saying, wiping the corner of her eyes with her lace-edged kerchief.

'What results from the voyage?' Sir Harry asked.

At this question Lizbeth started—she had almost forgotten the news she had to bring to her father. She told him of the precious cargo lying in the holds of the *Santa Perpetua* and the *Sea Hawk,* of how Rodney was dealing with such matters at Plymouth and that as soon as the registration and sale were completed he would come to Camfield.

Sir Harry cried out with delight at that, asking again and again for details of the plunder, for the description of the pearls which they had captured from the lugger, and the value of the loot they had taken from the Spanish settlement.

She found herself thrilling to the story of their adventures, and to speak of Rodney somehow made the ache in her breast a little easier.

'Rodney said . . . Rodney commanded . . . Rodney conquered . . . Rodney! Rodney! Rodney!'

It was a bitter-sweet joy to say his name, to conjure up those months when she had been able to see and hear him. How, she wondered, could she bear the desolate, empty future without him? But she must not think of that yet, only of the glorious past.

'I love him!' she wanted to tell her father. 'I love him. If he wanted me I would cross the world barefooted to be at his side. I would die for him . . . and God in his heaven knows that I cannot live without him!'

Instead, she must speak his name calmly and hope that her voice and eyes would not betray her.

Food and wine were brought to Lizbeth while she still sat talking. It was a long time later before she suggested that she should go upstairs and change her clothes which were wet and dirty from the long ride. It was then, as she rose a little stiffly to her feet, that she dared to ask a question that had been trembling on her own lips for a long time.

'Where is Phillida?' she enquired.

For a moment there was silence. Then her father roared out the answer.

'God's pity that I should be inflicted with such a daughter. There she lies, malingering in bed when she should be on her way to Whitehall. I was angry with you, my girl, I am not pretending I was not, when I heard that you had slipped off with Francis. It threw me into a fine rage, I can tell you now; but I am ready to forgive you with the good news you have brought with you, but— Phillida!'

He threw up his arms in an expressive gesture and now Lizbeth looked towards her stepmother.

'What is wrong with her?' she asked.

Catherine shrugged her shoulders expressively.

'Nothing that we know of or that any physician can find,' she answered tartly. 'She lies and cries and will not obey your father's wishes.'

'My wishes!' roared Sir Harry. 'You would have thought that any normal wench would be honoured by such a distinction, but not my daughter. Oh, no! She must lie puling and whining in a bed of sickness and bring disgrace upon us all.'

'Do tell me what this is all about,' Lizbeth begged.

Her father's eyes suddenly lit up.

'By my sword! I have the answer. Lizbeth is home. What can be better? She can take Phillida's place. The letter said "your daughter" and mentioned no name. And Lizbeth is my daughter as surely as Phillida is, and a vast deal better one.' He paused for breath and then added: 'This settles everything. Catherine, my dear, see to it. The girl must be fitly clothed.'

'And in what way am I to take Phillida's place?' Lizbeth asked, looking from one to the other.

'My child, we have been honoured by Her Majesty the Queen,' Sir Harry explained at last. 'I am invited to send my daughter as Maid of Honour to the Queen's Grace.'

'As Maid of Honour!' Lizbeth repeated, a little dazed, and not quite certain whether the information, now she had it, was good or bad.

'To Whitehall,' Sir Harry added solemnly; 'and Phillida weeps and swears she is too ill to undertake the journey.'

'I will go and talk with her,' Lizbeth said, suddenly eager to see her half-sister.

She ran from the Great Chamber and upstairs to Phillida's room. She burst in, too impatient to knock or announce her arrival. There were two candles flickering by the beside and Phillida lay behind the shrouded curtains hanging from the heavy canopy.

'Phillida, I am home. It is I, Lizbeth.'

With a cry, Phillida lifted her head from the pillows, and then her arms were outstretched towards her half-sister and tears were streaming down her white face.

'Oh, darling, what is the matter with you?' Lizbeth asked.

She saw Phillida glance over her shoulder before she spoke, to see if the door was closed. Then she began to whisper:

'Lizbeth, I am thankful you have returned. I have missed you more than I deemed it possible. But now you have come back, you must help me. Please help me, for I cannot go to Whitehall.'

'There is no need, now I am home,' Lizbeth answered.

Phillida sat up suddenly.

'Oh, Lizbeth, I understand! You will take my place. Sweet, kind Lizbeth, I am happy for the first time since you went away.'

'Tell me all about everything,' Lizbeth asked. 'I am bewildered.'

'Lizbeth, try to understand,' Phillida answered. 'How could I go to Whitehall feeling as I do?'

'When I left you had just written to Mister Andrews,' Lizbeth replied. 'He did not help you?'

Phillida shook her head sadly. She was as lovely as ever Lizbeth noticed in the candlelight, and she had

214

grown thinner and the corners of her mouth drooped wistfully.

'No, could not help me or was afraid,' Phillida replied; 'and so there was nothing I could do but stay here and wait for ... your return.'

There was a quiver in her voice which made Lizbeth know that in her mind Phillida had substituted another name. Impulsively she took the bull by the horns.

'Rodney has been very successful,' she said. 'He has brought back a very valuable cargo. He will be a rich man, Phillida.'

'When is he coming here?'

Phillida was so pale that Lizbeth thought she might faint.

'As soon as everything is settled at Plymouth,' she answered.

Phillida closed her eyes. She was beautiful, Lizbeth thought, beautiful, and Rodney loved her. They would be married, however much Phillida might shrink from the thought of it.

'I will go to London and take your place as Maid of Honour,' she said.

'I do not know which is the worse of the two evils,' Phillida whispered. 'I could not bear the thought of waiting on the Queen, but now, perhaps, it is preferable to ... to ...'

Lizbeth knew what she was going to say and interrupted her.

'Rodney is a wonderful person, Phillida,' she said. 'You must make up your mind to marry him. I have been with him these past few months and I know there is no one like him in the whole world.'

She could not help the throb which came into her voice as she spoke; but she hoped that Phillida, sunk in her misery, had not noticed it.

'And what of Francis?' Phillida asked suddenly. 'Has the voyage made a man of him?'

Just for a moment Lizbeth hesitated. Then she told Phillida, as she had told her father, that Francis had died in action against the Spaniards.

'May his soul and the souls of all the Faithful departed, through the mercy of God, rest in peace,' Phillida prayed, and added: 'I know you loved your brother, Lizbeth. His death must have been a great sorrow to you.'

Lizbeth rose to her feet. She felt as if she could bear no further talk of Francis. It was hard enough to know the ache within herself without having other people speak of it.

'I must go and bathe,' she said, 'and change my clothes.'

'I am thankful you are home, Lizbeth,' Phillida said. 'But in a way, it makes things worse—it brings nearer . . .' Her voice broke. She could not bring herself to say the word 'marriage'.

Lizbeth suddenly felt impatient with her half-sister's tears and shrinking. If only she herself could marry Rodney, instead of the reluctant Phillida, yearning for the cold loneliness of a convent cell!

'I must go,' Lizbeth said; 'Father is waiting for me.'

She was free at last, running swiftly to her room to find her Nanna awaiting her; but perhaps because she was tired and because her heart seemed to be torn in a thousand different ways, instead of greeting her with a smile, she flung her arms round the old woman and burst into tears.

'There, there, dearie,' Nanna said, ''tis the excitement of coming home. And you've had a deal to put up with, I'll be bound. Not but what you deserve—a-rushing off like that and giving us all a turn when we heard as how you'd sailed with Master Francis.'

'Was everyone very surprised?' Lizbeth asked, smiling in spite of herself through her tears.

'We were all agape,' Nanna answered. 'Sir Harry was bellowing downstairs like a bull and Her Ladyship trying to soothe him down, and as for Mistress Phillida, she went white as a sheet when she heard you wasn't coming back. It may be that which made her take to her bed, I wouldn't be surprised. But there, she always was a deep one and you never can be sure of what she's thinking.'

Lizbeth sat down in a chair and Nanna began to take off her riding-boots.

'Now, tell me all about it, dearie,' she said as she worked, 'and how did Master Francis get along with all those rough sailors?'

It was then Lizbeth realised that her ordeal was not over. Nanna had to be told about Francis, and the old nurse wept bitterly to think that her baby was dead and she would never see him again.

It was easy to tell a lie, Lizbeth thought, but hard to sustain one. So many people would want to talk of Francis, and having made him into a hero, she had got to support the picture with tales of heroism that must go on for ever.

She realised suddenly that she was tired to the point of exhaustion. It had been a long, hard ride from Plymouth and with the restlessness of her own thoughts she had not spared herself or the servants who accompanied her. Now her body was beginning to take revenge on her. She wanted more than anything else to slip between the cool linen sheets of her bed and be alone with her own thoughts.

But she knew that tonight that was impossible. Her father would be bitterly disappointed if she did not go downstairs to tell him more of the voyage and sit up, perhaps until the early hours of the morning, chatting, about the cargo, the battle against the Spaniards, and of Francis' death.

Lizbeth thought of Elita then—alone with her terror in the darkness of the empty house, yet try as she would, she could not feel sorry for her. She had seen and heard what the Queen meant to such men as Rodney. They were ready to die for England and for Gloriana, and it was not to be endured that people like Dr. Keen and his daughter should plot and scheme to destroy that which they valued so highly.

Lizbeth went slowly downstairs in a dress of green velvet

trailing over the polished boards behind her. It felt strange to be a woman again, to feel the softness of the velvet against her skin, and the nakedness of her low-cut dress seemed indecent after months of wearing a ruff. Nanna had exclaimed at the shortness of her hair, but Lizbeth had made the excuse that it was too hot in the Caribbean Sea to wear her hair longer, and now that it was braided and held with pearl-headed pins, it was hard to realise that it had ever been cut to make her look like a boy.

As she had expected, her father and stepmother were sitting waiting for her in the Great Chamber.

'Your skin is freckled,' Catherine remarked critically, as Lizbeth sat down beside them in front of the big log fire.

'I am ashamed of both my nose and my hands,' she answered laughingly.

'We will prepare a lotion of cucumbers and calamine flowers tomorrow,' Catherine promised. 'You cannot go to Whitehall looking like a kitchen wench.'

'I have spoken with Phillida, Father,' Lizbeth said, 'and I will take her place; but I cannot leave before Rodney has returned. He will be here very shortly and I wish to see him again before I go to London.'

'Have you not seen enough of him these past months?' Sir Harry asked cheerfully.

'It is not a matter of that,' Lizbeth answered coolly, well aware that Catherine was looking at her suspiciously. 'There were certain arrangements made during the voyage regarding some of the crew which he asked me to keep in mind. I had no chance to remind him of these before I left Plymouth, but I thought it of little consequence as I was certain to be seeing him here in a very short time. Now you tell me I am to go to London. I am ready to go, only after I have seen Rodney Hawkhurst.'

'Very well, very well, I have already sent a message saying that Phillida is indisposed, and a few days more will not matter one way or another,' Sir Harry conceded.

'And we shall need time to make Lizbeth some gowns,' Catherine said.

'Gowns! That's all you women think about,' Sir Harry roared. 'But have it your own way. The day after Hawkhurst arrives Lizbeth can leave for Whitehall.'

'Thank you, Father,' Lizbeth said, 'and now what else shall I tell you about the voyage?'

She had got her own way; Francis' memory was saved so long as she could speak to Rodney Hawkhurst before he saw the others; and yet to be honest with herself, she knew that her relief and joy at having gained this concession from her father was not only because she revered the memory of her brother. She wanted, too, to see Rodney.

All the way from Plymouth her heart had ached with the thought of him and she had missed his presence more than she believed possible. Child-like she had thought that the ache would pass when she got home. It was almost as if she ran to Camfield as she might have run to a mother's arms for healing and for comfort.

But now she was here, she knew that she still yearned agonisingly for the man she had left behind. She knew then, as she had known really all the time, that nothing and nobody could help her to forget her love. It was an indivisible part of her, she lived and breathed, dreamed and woke to nothing else.

Love, love for Rodney, love for her future brother-in-law! It was in some ways a painful joy to be able to talk of him, to sit in the Great Chamber holding both Sir Harry and Catherine spellbound with her tales of the Caribbean Sea and of the voyage there and back.

She could hear her own voice talking on and on as the hours passed; and now she was no longer tired, but lost in a world of her own, a world in which Rodney was the Captain and she a part of his ship's company. She spoke of Don Miguel and followed him into the darkness of the Canary Islands. It was easy to gloss over the reasons why he had escaped, more difficult to wrench her own

219

thoughts from that moment when Rodney had accused her of loving him.

She could see again the anger in his eyes, the fury of his square chin and tightened lips. She wondered sometimes as she talked whether Catherine and her father would notice discrepancies in her story, the sudden gaps when she dared tell no more, the moments when she must sheer away from the personal dramas which loomed up now as big and important in her mind as the ships they had captured and the battles they had fought.

But Sir Harry and Catherine were as entranced as children listening to a fairy story. Sir Harry's eyes were bright and he rubbed his hands at the thought of the dividends that would soon be paid him. Catherine wanted to be told again and again about the silks and perfumes aboard the *Santa Perpetua* and the pearls which Rodney had taken from the Spanish lugger.

'I must go to bed,' Lizbeth sighed at length.

It was no use denying the tiredness of her body any further. It was nearly two o'clock and she knew that she could talk no more, but must sleep even though her life depended on keeping awake.

'Be off with you, then,' Sir Harry cried. 'I am glad to have you back, my child, and I am proud of you—as proud as if you had been my son.'

Again there was that strange expression in his eyes, but Lizbeth was too tired to worry about it. She curtsied to him, kissed Catherine perfunctorily as women who really dislike each other manage to do with a superficial show of affection. Then at last she reached the sanctuary of her own room and Nanna was there to undress her.

With her eyes half-closed, she crept into bed; but perversely, when the candles were out, sleep eluded her. She could only see Elita shaking and chattering in her terror and hear her voice saying over and over again that Francis was dead. Yes, Francis whom she had promised to protect and care for, was dead. He had died the death of a traitor, having been hanged, drawn and quartered. . . .

13

It was some hours after the *Santa Perpetua* and the *Sea Hawk* had arrived at Plymouth before Rodney realised that Lizbeth had gone.

He saw to the mooring of the ship, interviewed numerous officials, told the story of his voyage a dozen times, and had his hand shaken again and again by people he had never seen before and whom he felt would have had little interest in him had his voyage not proved successful.

Finally the tumult and excitement died down a little and when Hapley told him that dinner was served he walked into the after cabin expecting to find Lizbeth waiting for him. He had refused several invitations to eat ashore, saying that first he must make arrangements for the removal of the cargo.

Feasting and celebration banquets lay ahead of him, and for the moment he wanted nothing more elaborate than a meal of the salt pork he had found so monotonous on the voyage.

He was feeling depressed as he came into the after cabin, for he realised that this was perhaps his last meal aboard the *Santa Perpetua*. Ungainly, over-ornamented and hard to handle after the *Sea Hawk*, he had yet grown fond of her; and now as a prize ship she would doubtless be taken into the Queen's service or bought by some rich company of merchants.

It was sad to think that he would never sail in her again and he wondered if Lizbeth would feel the same about her. Even as he thought of Lizbeth, he realised that she was not there, and at the same time he saw that the table was laid with only one place and that his own.

'Where is Master Gillingham?' he asked Hapley.

'Master Gillingham left several hours ago, Sir.'

'Left, where for?'

'I've no idea, Sir. He went ashore. He said good-bye to me!'

There was a reminiscent smile on Hapley's face which told Rodney that Lizbeth had tipped him well. Suddenly angry, he seated himself in the big armchair that Hapley held out for him and drummed his fingers on the table.

So Lizbeth had gone without a word, without a farewell. He felt incensed at the way she had slipped away. He thought now he wanted to talk to her, to plan what they should say to Sir Harry. It was inconsiderate, Rodney decided; and then quite unexpectedly his anger and irritation changed into a sense of loss.

It was not surprising that he should miss her, he thought to himself. He had grown used to seeing her small oval face on his right at meals, her red hair brilliant against the dark walls of the cabin, her eyes, bright and vivid in their unexpected colour as some precious jewel, raised to his.

He thought now that the many meals they had had together had been extremely pleasant ones. He could remember how Lizbeth's laugh had rung out clear and musical when something which had been said amused her.

Petulantly Rodney pushed his plate away from him. He was not hungry, eating alone had a corrective effect on his appetite. He wanted to ask Lizbeth what she thought of their reception at Plymouth. He wanted to tell her of the compliments which had been paid him by the officials who had hurried down to welcome the ships. There were so many things that he would have liked to recount to her, to see her reaction by the expression on her face.

He drank down a glass of wine and waved Hapley away when he would have brought him more to eat. He walked across the cabin and thought again how loth he was to leave the *Santa Perpetua*. It was not only the luxury and comfort of her. It was something deeper and more fundamental, as if in the short time he had commanded her she had become a part of his life.

Perhaps that would be true of every voyage and of every ship he commanded, but this was his first experience of the nostalgia which more experienced Captains would have told him was an inevitable reaction on reaching port.

Rodney walked across the cabin again. He was remembering that moment of excitement when he and his men had climbed on board the *Santa Perpetua*. He could experience once more the exertion of his strength as he struck his dagger into the back of the Spanish sentry watching the festivities ashore. He could feel the man's breath hot against his hand as he closed it hard over his mouth.

How much there was to remember! The movement of the wheel beneath his hands and the wind that carried them out to sea! That moment when morning came and they saw the sails of the *Sea Hawk* coming to meet them! Lizbeth climbing aboard! He could see her face now, her eyes shining like stars, her lips parted in excitement. How lovely she was at such a time! And then with a sudden pain like the stab of a dagger, Rodney remembered her face, white and stained with tears as she shrank from the brutality of his kisses. He could feel her struggle against him, the efforts she made weak and ineffectual against his superior strength.

Now he could hear her voice pleading with him, crying for mercy. Rodney kicked savagely at an oak stool which lay in his path. Why did he have to remember such things now? She had been afraid of him after that. He had known it in the way she started a little when he came upon her unexpectedly, by the anxiety in her eyes and the way the colour rose in her cheeks.

And yet she had not been afraid to release Don Miguel from a locked cabin, to trick the guard, to remain behind and face his anger. Again Rodney kicked at the oak stool, and this time it turned over, its short, carved legs pointing in the air. He hated the Spaniard, Rodney decided, hated him. He had been too suave and good-looking, too elegant and civilised to be tolerated by a man of action such as he was himself.

And yet in justice he must recall the times when he had found Don Miguel a genial companion, when it had been almost impossible to remember his nationality. They had laughed together, yet now he hated him. He could feel again that sudden constriction within himself that he had felt when he came into the after cabin and found Lizbeth in Don Miguel's arms.

There had been something in the Spaniard's attitude, the strained intensity of his bent head and encircling arms, which had robbed Rodney for the moment of the power to speak or even to move. It had not been only Don Miguel's need for a woman or the spur of passion which had driven him to kiss Lizbeth—he loved her. Rodney was sure of that—not then, but later. Yes, Don Miguel loved Lizbeth.

It had been obvious in the way he looked at her and the caressing tone of his voice when he addressed her. Rodney had hated Don Miguel then. He had longed not once but a hundred times to challenge him to a duel, to clap him into irons, to send him below decks where Lizbeth could never see him, or to throw him overboard at some dangerous, shark-infested part of the ocean.

Yes, he had hated Don Miguel then and still did with a bitterness and a fury which he felt now could be relieved only by the news that the Spaniard was dead. Striding up and down, Rodney recaptured his fury as he had seen Don Miguel and Lizbeth together talking, laughing and whispering.

Then as he felt his anger and his hatred rise within him in a crimson flood, he suddenly knew the truth, knew why he felt like this, knew why at the thought of Don Miguel his whole body was a-tremble with the desire for revenge—it was because he himself loved Lizbeth.

He had not known it till this moment. He had not realised it until she was gone and the loss of her brought home to him what she had meant to him these past few months. He had grown so used to having her there that he had taken her presence for granted. Now he could curse himself for having been so blind, so obtuse.

It was easy to look back and see that so much of the pleasure he had experienced in capturing the *Santa Perpetua*, in plundering the Spanish settlement, in boarding the pearling lugger, was because Lizbeth could see his success and praise his victories. He knew now that she had been at the back of his thoughts almost the whole time. On the surface he had told himself that he was annoyed with her for having tricked him in coming on the voyage, that he had no use for women on a ship and never for a moment would he waver in his determination to treat her as a boy.

But the femininity of her crept under his guard and into his consciousness. Without meaning to do so and without admitting it to himself he thought of her as Lizbeth and a woman, and it was only with the arrival of Don Miguel aboard that his hypocrisy had been shattered. He saw now that the emotion which had been aroused within him at the sight of Lizbeth in Don Miguel's arms had been one of the oldest in the world.

It had been jealousy—sheer, unbridled jealousy—and it had driven him into being brutal to Lizbeth and imagining that he hated her as bitterly as he hated Don Miguel. How wrong and blind and idiotic he had been! He saw it all now, as, quite humbly, he acknowledged to himself the truth, that he loved her.

He wanted at that moment to go down on his knees before her and lay his face in her cool hands and ask her forgiveness. He thought of her with a tenderness and a sweetness that had never come before into their relationship with one another.

And then, as he remembered the softness of her lips, the smooth white column of her throat, the soft curves of her body and the seduction of her flaming hair, he felt the blood rise within his veins. He wanted her, he wanted her passionately and possessively as a man wants a woman. He wanted to conquer her as he had conquered so many other things, he wanted to take her into his arms and tell her fiercely that she belonged to him and to no one else.

He wished at that moment that he could cry aloud his love, his joy, his happiness. Lizbeth was his, and he would claim her before the whole world. And then as suddenly as it had arisen his elation passed. He remembered that Lizbeth was not his and never could be, for he was betrothed to Phillida.

With something suspiciously like a groan Rodney flung himself down on the chair, his brows drawn to a frown. He wondered how he could ever have contemplated marriage with a woman whom he did not love and who he was certain did not love him.

It had seemed sensible and expedient when first his godfather suggested it. It had seemed the obvious thing to do when he suggested it to her father and Sir Harry had agreed that he and Phillida should be married. Now every nerve in his body cried out against it.

Phillida would be waiting for him at Camfield and Lizbeth was her half-sister. Drumming with his fingers on the arm of the chair, Rodney sat staring into space until the twitter of the bo'sun's pipes told him that distinguished visitors were coming aboard.

Then he had to bring his thoughts back to the present and to all that had to be done regarding the ships and their cargoes. This was no time for him to sit brooding in the cabin. Lizbeth had gone and for the moment he must put her out of his mind.

It seemed to Rodney as he rose to his feet that the glory of his return was already tarnished. It was as if the sun had gone from the sky and he felt instead the chill wind of loneliness sweep round him.

It was hard to make haste when the whole of officialdom was against it. Rodney, fretting and fuming at Plymouth, could not hurry matters more quickly than clerks could make an inventory in their spidery writing with their squeaking quill pens.

Lizbeth, waiting for him at Camfield, felt as if the delay of his arrival grew more and more intolerable as the days passed. She found it hard to concentrate on the clothes that were being made for her on her step-mother's instructions. There were gowns of satin, bro-cades and velvet and embroidery finer than anything she had ever owned in the whole of her life, but somehow they seemed as shadowy as everything else that existed either in the present or in the future.

It was the past that was real, the past that she was remembering every moment of the day and night, hugging it close in her heart as if it were some secret no one could share with her. Even Phillida's pale, frightened face and her whispered terror of being married seemed somehow insubstantial beside her own memories of Rod-ney.

That he who was so virile, so endowed with vigour and enthusiasm, should have anything in common with the limp, miserable Phillida was not to be credited. Her half-sister had never seemed a very strong personality to Lizbeth, and now she took on a ghost-like air as she lay weeping in the shadows of her curtained bed or knelt beseechingly at her *prie-dieu*—praying, Lizbeth knew, for deliverance from Rodney.

Even though Lizbeth was aware that her love was hopeless, she could not mope and moan as Phillida did. Love, even frustrated love, seemed to vitalise her so that she wanted to shout and laugh and clap her hands and tell the world that she loved Rodney. She knew now that one of the things they had in common was that they were both so thrillingly alive. They were both young in an age when there was adventure, excitement, fine deeds to be done and great victories to be won.

She felt that if only she could see Rodney she could tell him this, but she knew that, when he did come, she must stand aside and watch him take Phillida in his arms.

She persuaded her half-sister to rise from her bed, to

227

come downstairs and sit by the log fire in the Great Chamber. Weak with weeping and apprehension, frail with fear, Phillida was still beautiful, Lizbeth thought with a pang. Her eyes, vividly blue against the transparency of her white skin, seemed to shine with the intensity of her feelings and the yearning of her soul for things that were of the spirit. Her hair, pale gold as the sunshine after rain, framed her face, which was pale and thin but had not lost its exquisite contours.

Yes, Phillida was beautiful, Lizbeth thought, more beautiful than when Rodney had last seen her.

Sir Harry was pressing Lizbeth to leave for London, but she dared not go from Camfield until Rodney arrived. He must know of her lies about Francis before he shattered them by a careless or unconsidered word.

From the night she had arrived she had not gone near the Keens' house nor made any enquiries about Elita. Sometimes she wondered if the girl was starving to death behind the shutters or whether her friends had come to rescue her and had smuggled her away to Spain. Cruel though it might be, she did not care what happened. She was concerned now with preserving the honour of the family and her father's illusions about Francis' death.

Rodney would help her in this, she was certain of that ; and yet the days were passing and he did not come, while Sir Harry was afraid lest the post of Maid of Honour at Whitehall should be filled.

Lizbeth had little time to think of what awaited her when she arrived in London. She could think only of Rodney and the moment when she must see him again.

It was evening when he came—a blustering, cold night with a hint of snow in the wind. Lizbeth had been hoping that he would arrive in the daytime. She had arranged that the servants on the estate should be continually on the look-out for him, promising that they should be rewarded should they inform her before anyone else that the visitor was approaching the house, but it was impossible to arrange for them to watch at night.

They were at supper when Sir Harry was informed of

Rodney's arrival. They all hurried then from the Banqueting Hall into the Great Chamber to find Rodney already in the house, standing with his back to the fire waiting to greet them.

Lizbeth felt her heart turn over at the sight of him. She felt that she had forgotten how handsome he was, how broad of shoulder, how graceful in his movements. She watched him shake hands with her father, saw him bend over Catherine's hand; and then, as he turned towards Phillida, she shut her eyes. She could not bear to see the expression in Rodney's face as he beheld Phillida's pale beauty again.

She heard him say something she did not catch, and then she heard his voice, alive, gay and compelling, cry her own name:

'Lizbeth! Little Lizbeth, have you forgotten me already?'

Both her hands were in his and she was smiling up into his face, a sudden ridiculous and overwhelming joy making her oblivious of everything and everybody save that he was there.

'Rodney! Oh, Rodney!'

She found herself whispering his name; and then, even as her lips echoed the smile on his and she wondered if they all could hear the quick beating of her heart, she remembered what she had to say to him. Still holding tightly to his hands, her fingers digging into his warningly, she said:

'I have told Father about Francis!' She saw the surprise in his face, and added quickly: 'I have told how he died aboard the *Santa Perpetua* in our fight with the Spanish galleons. I have told them all how brave Francis was and how proud we were of him.'

She saw Rodney's expression change and knew that he understood. She felt his fingers tighten on hers comfortingly, reassuringly, and then easily he turned to Sir Harry.

'I am sorry, Sir, that we had to bring you bad news as well as good.'

Sir Harry put a heavy hand on Rodney's shoulder.

'I am proud to have given my son in such a cause,' he said. 'We will speak further of it another time. We must not let our personal sadness dim the gladness you feel on your arrival here.'

Lizbeth drew a deep breath of relief, the awkward moment was passed over. Wine and fresh dishes were brought to the Banqueting Hall. It seemed to Lizbeth for a moment as she listened to Rodney talking to her father that they might once again be seated round the table in the after cabin.

But Phillida was there listening too. There was a faint colour in her cheeks and her lips were smiling as they had not smiled for a long time.

'She will learn to love him,' Lizbeth said to herself, and was startled by the pain she experienced at the thought.

Rodney was talking in the way she knew so well, gesticulating occasionally with his hands, but needing no gesture to underline the fire and purpose behind his words. Lizbeth, who had heard him so often, could see now the effect of his words on the other members of her family.

Sir Harry was leaning back in his chair, comfortably at his ease, yet attentive to everything that was said. Catherine, with her arms on the table, her chin cupped in in her hands, was watching Rodney's lips as he spoke, her eyes narrowed a little, her own mouth twisted enticingly; and Phillida was listening, too!

Lizbeth, watching her half-sister, saw that she was entranced by Rodney's stories. She was leaning forward a little in her chair, the exquisite poised grace of her neck and shoulders was never shown to greater advantage. Lizbeth knew suddenly that she could bear no more.

When Rodney left the room after dinner to pay for the men and horses who had brought him to Camfield from Plymouth, and who wished to start the journey back at dawn, Lizbeth seized her opportunity.

'I will leave for London early tomorrow morning,' she

said. 'It would be rude to linger now that Mister Hawk-hurst has returned.

She saw the relief on Sir Harry's face.

'Everything is in readiness,' Catherine said smoothly, and Lizbeth knew that she was glad to be rid of her.

She crept away then before Rodney came back. But as she crossed the Hall she met him face to face. Swiftly she looked around; there was no one within earshot. She laid her hand on his arm and spoke barely above a whisper:

'Francis is dead. I have no time to relate how and why he died, but tell Father . . . and the others . . . that he was brave and that you were . . . proud of him.' Her eyes besought him.

'I will do as you ask,' Rodney replied.

'Thank you! Oh, thank you.'

Her eyes, soft and grateful, met Rodney's and the words of gratitude died on her lips. She was so close to him that she could hear the quick intake of his breath. For a moment the Hall swam around her and was gone. They were alone—she and Rodney on the edge of the world, there was nothing and nobody else, only the two of them together.

Then like a thunderbolt Sir Harry's voice boomed out:

'Come back to the fire, Hawkhurst; God's mercy, but it is as cold as charity out here!'

Lizbeth looked over her shoulder. Her father was standing in the doorway of the Great Chamber, a glass of wine in his hand.

'I am coming, Sir,' Rodney replied. 'I was just speaking with Lizbeth about the voyage.'

'If the girl wants to talk, bring her back to the fire,' Sir Harry said testily.

But Lizbeth was already running up the stairs.

'Good night, Rodney.'

Her voice seemed to echo and re-echo round the high walls. If he answered, she did not hear him, and the door of her bedroom closed behind her.

She sat down at her dressing-table. He had gone back

to Phillida! She had half-expected that Phillida would come upstairs with her; but Phillida, who had been too weak to leave her bed but a few days before, was sitting listening to Rodney.

Lizbeth let Nanna undress her and take away her clothes, and she made a pretence of settling herself among the pillows; but she knew she would not sleep. Taking a book, she attempted to read; but two hours later, when she heard the others coming upstairs to bed, she realised that not one word of the pages she had turned had penetrated her consciousness.

Rodney was under the same roof. She had often thought of him lying in his bunk on the other side of the ship; and yet that he was here at Camfield, her own home, made him seem somehow closer than he had ever been before.

She thought of the hardships and the dangers they had shared together and wondered if, lying in luxury on the thick feather mattress in one of the fine, panelled guest chambers, he too, was thinking of her.

Then she remembered how Phillida had looked at him across the supper table, and she knew that she was only being foolish. Don Miguel might have called her lovely, but she had no beauty in comparison with the gold-and-white fairness of her half-sister.

Lizbeth blew out the candles, crept from her bed and, drawing back the curtains, sat in the window-seat to look out on the darkness of the night. She could hear the wind whistling round the house and the rain pattering sharply against the diamond-paned casement. She felt desperately sad and utterly alone.

Francis was gone, her mother was dead—there was no one left who really mattered to her. She would go away. Perhaps in service to the Queen she would find forgetfulness.

She heard the hours strike one by one and then she must have fallen asleep, for when she awoke she was cramped and cold and the night had passed. It was a grey, blustery day; and yet she was glad—there was nothing about it to remind her of the Caribbean sun.

Not long after eight o'clock, Lizbeth, having break-fasted in her room, came downstairs. Her horse and an escort of grooms and outriders were waiting for her outside the front door. Her luggage was piled up on a coach in which Nanna was also to travel to London.

Lizbeth had wanted to say good-bye to Phillida, but she was told that Phillida was asleep. Catherine also would make no appearance at this hour in the morning, Lizbeth knew, and she was glad that she would not have to say farewell to her stepmother.

Her father was up, as she had expected he would be. He kissed her boisterously, told her to behave herself, and put a heavy purse of money into her hand.

'When you need more, you have but to send for it,' he said.

'Thank you, Father.'

His generosity, she knew, was not for herself but for the position she would hold as Maid of Honour, which he took as a personal tribute to his own importance.

She said good-bye to the servants in the Hall and then the groom helped her to mount her favourite horse.

She looked very different from what she usually did when she rode at Camfield. There were no high boots and short breeches upon her today to scandalise the citizens of London. Her full-skirted riding habit was of green velvet and the plume which decorated her hat was canary yellow and reached almost to her shoulders.

She gathered up the reins in her gloved hand and even as she opened her lips to give the order to go, she saw someone come through the doorway of the house and walk towards her. She felt herself tingle and every vein and muscle in her body seemed to awake to a throbbing excitement.

'You are leaving, Lizbeth?'

She must have imagined the dismay in his voice.

'I am going to London. Father will tell you that I am to become Maid of Honour to Her Majesty.'

'I had no idea of this.'

233

Was it only astonishment in his expression? she wondered.

'I have not seen you alone,' he added. 'There is much we should discuss together.'

'I am afraid I must go.'

Lizbeth spoke quickly. She was afraid, desperately afraid, of losing her self-control as she looked down into his eyes. She wanted, more than she had wanted anything in the whole of her life before, to lean down and press her lips against his. She felt as though everything would be worth the risk, even the horror, indignation and scandal it would cause. She dared not look at him again.

'I must go,' she said, urging her horse forward. 'Everything is arranged.'

She was moving now—quicker and quicker.

'Lizbeth, I beg of you . . .'

His voice was lost in the clatter of hoofs. She knew without turning that he was still standing there in the drive, watching the cavalcade of servants following her at a jog-trot. It was agony not to turn round. She felt the sweat break out on her forehead in spite of the cold of the day.

There were the gates ahead; now he could no longer be looking at her—they were out of sight. She wanted to cry. She wanted to scream her love for him aloud so that all could hear. But she did none of these things; she just kept riding on down the twisting, narrow road, puddled and rutted, which would lead presently to the broader high road which led directly into London. . . .

Lizbeth had of course been to London on many occasions; but always the City which had been called 'the storehouse and mart of Europe' never ceased to thrill her. From the moment they came in sight of the old City wall, a relic of its battlemented past, she would feel excitement springing within her. Whatever the weather, it seemed to her that in winter, summer or spring London looked beautiful.

Its spires and roofs today were silver against a grey sky and the Thames was a deep molten silver on which were reflected hundreds of snowy-plumaged swans which were as much a part of the river's life as the great barges.

Lizbeth loved travelling by water, and indeed, everyone preferred the river, for it was much more pleasant and in many ways safer than travelling by road. But today she only had a glimpse of the Thames as they rode through the crowded streets. As usual, she was amused and delighted by the hubbub and the noise.

There were men and women crying hot apple-pies, live periwinkles and hot oat cakes. There was the sweep announcing himself with a lengthy call, and pretty girls selling oranges and lemons with a special song so that all should hear their clear musical notes arising from the general *mêlée* and come out to buy.

Lizbeth found she had forgotten the diversity of things there were to see and hear in London. Porters staggering and sweating under enormous burdens hurried past her. Grave-faced merchants bound for the Royal Exchange passed slowly by in their long, richly-furred robes and their fine gold chains; gallants resplendent in silks, satins and jewels made a glittering show as they swaggered past, envied by the countrymen in their russet jackets with blue cambric sleeves and buttons, their 'slop' breeches, green bonnets and hose of grey kersey.

Lizbeth rode along Cheapside—the Holborn highway, which was the most important road in all London. It was a broad, well-paved street, famous for all the gold and silver vessels displayed for sale in its shops.

Everyone who visited London was well aware that it was dangerous to linger in many of the less-famous thoroughfares. Dirty and over-crowded, there were numberless streets in which Elizabeth was trying to force the rule of 'one house—one family'. But even the Council was powerless against the network of narrow, badly-paved lanes, half-darkened by the overhanging fronts of the houses and rendered insanitary by the custom of their inhabitants of depositing their garbage outside the front door.

In the better parts of the City there were gardens to all the grand houses; and though they were now flowerless and leafless, Lizbeth knew that when the spring and summer came they would be filled with flowers, fruit and shady trees. But for the moment there was no need to miss the beauties of spring and summer when the colourful trays of pedlars were held high in their arms for Lizbeth's inspection as she rode through the crowds.

'Fine Seville oranges, fine lemons.'

'Hey ye any corns on your feet or toes?'

'What do ye lack? Do ye buy, Mistress. See what ye lack: pins, points, garters, Spanish gloves or silk ribbons.'

'Will ye buy any starch or clear complexion, Mistress?'

Lizbeth was laughing as she brushed the importunate pedlars aside and came at length to the quiet and dignity of the Palace of Whitehall.

For a moment she felt afraid as she looked at the great, sprawling grey building fronting on to the river, where waited the Queen's state barge.

She had a sudden longing for Camfield and the peace of her own bedroom looking out over the park and lakes, and then with a little mental shake of her shoulders she told herself she was being ridiculous. She had to forget Camfield and all it contained. This was a new and exciting life and what was there in it to make her afraid?

It was, however, difficult not to be overawed by the Palace, and long before she reached the apartments of the Maids of Honour Lizbeth found herself awed and astonished not once but a dozen times. Great galleries hung with pictures and fine tapestries took her breath away. The Tilt Yard and the Bowling Green were green oases seen from the diamond-paned casements opening out of a labyrinth of corridors, high chambers and fine staircases.

'I shall never find my way out of here,' Lizbeth thought breathlessly, and she felt for one mad moment as if she were imprisoned in some architectural maze from which she could never escape. And then, when she came to the Maids of Honours' apartments, she was entranced. From the windows she looked out over the Thames.

There were barges moving along the still water, some of them belonging to the great Livery Companies, or to the nobles whose houses lined the river between Westminster and the City. There were watermen plying for hire on the river, with every kind of cry; and among them moved the swans, quite unperturbed by the traffic around them, arching their white necks or dipping them low as if in search of hidden treasure.

Lizbeth clapped her hands together.

'Tis lovely,' she exclaimed, 'lovely!' and turned to see Nanna smiling at her.

'Of course it's lovely,' Nanna agreed stoutly. 'A palace fit for a Queen, and that's how it should be.'

Lizbeth laughed at that. It had been a great concession on Catherine's part to allow her to bring Nanna with her. She had suggested various other maids, but Lizbeth had been insistent, and after much argument Nanna had finally been permitted to accompany her.

'Come and look at London,' Lizbeth said, linking her arm through that of the old woman.

'I've got no time for sightseeing,' Nanna retored sternly. 'There's all the unpacking to do and the good Lord knows what else to be seen to.'

Lizbeth laughed out loud as Nanna hurried away to direct the porters who were carrying up the trunks.

Watching the barges, then, Lizbeth felt her mind drift away to Rodney. She could never be free of him for long, and now once again she could hear his voice calling her as she had fled away from him down the drive. Should she have waited? She asked herself that question; and even as she did so, she knew she had done the right thing. She had left him to Phillida.

Restlessly, because she could not sit and think of them together, she walked across the room. All over England girls of her own age would be envying her today—a new Maid of Honour to Her Majesty, a new face at Whitehall. She was to be revered, speculated about and envied.

It was hard to believe it was true that she was here in

237

the Palace and in a short while, perhaps in a few hours, she would be in the presence of the most important woman in the whole world—Elizabeth, to whom the whole world looked in admiration, in envy, and as far as her own subjects were concerned, in adoration. She, Lizbeth, was to serve her, wait on her and constantly to be in that splendid, awe-inspiring presence!

And then, as she thought of her good fortune, Lizbeth, looking out over the busy river with the walls of Whitehall encompassing her, knew that all this pomp and glory was wasted on her. For she wanted only the arms of one man around her for security, for splendour and glory the touch of his lips on hers.

14

Lizbeth quieted her horse which was restive with the cheers and cries of the crowd and the fluttering of handkerchiefs and flags.

The Strand and Fleet Street were decked in blue and there were ensigns and banners fluttering in the crisp air from every house along the route to St. Paul's Cathedral. It was Sunday, the 24th of November, and the Queen was going in state to celebrate the country's deliverance from Spain.

Her Majesty was seated in a chariot on which was set a throne supported by four pillars and surmounted by a lion and a dragon holding the arms of England. It was drawn by two milk-white steeds and attended by the pensioners and state footmen. At the head of the procession moved the heralds, gentlemen ushers and harbingers, followed by the Court Physicians, Judges, bishops and nobles, while just before the Queen's chariot walked the French Ambassador, her Counsellors and Chamberlain, and upon the flanks filed the Serjeant-at-Arms and halberdiers.

It was a wonderful sight, Lizbeth thought; and she felt that she could not look enough at the colour, beauty and richness of the great throng, which was unlike anything she had ever seen before.

Near to Her Majesty, leading the richly-caparisoned horse of state, rode the new Master of the Horse, the gay and gallant Earl of Essex; and the six Maids of Honour who followed cast many a glance in his direction. His young, bearded face, Lizbeth thought, was handsome enough; but for good looks she preferred Sir Walter Raleigh who, surrounded by his guardsmen, their halberds gilded and with handles set in rich velvet, seemed to watch the new favourite with a brooding resentment which no one pretended to misunderstand.

Lizbeth, in a robe of white satin embroidered with silver flowers, had thought herself finely garbed until she saw the gowns of the other Maids of Honour and the glittering splendour of the Queen herself.

She had grown used, in the few days she had been at Court, to expect Her Majesty to be resplendent; but today it appeared she surpassed all other occasions, and even the vivid Aldermen in their scarlet robes and the sparkling jewels of the Lord Mayor seemed but a pale reflection of her splendour.

At the gate at Temple Bar the procession was saluted with music by the City Waits. Here the Lord Mayor welcomed the Queen to the City and Chamber, and after going through the usual ceremony of the keys and swords, set the sceptre in her hand. When the procession passed on, the City Companies with their banners lined one side of the route; on the other were marshalled the lawyers and gentlemen of the Inns of Court.

'Mark the Courtiers,' Lizbeth heard Sir Francis Bacon say in a perfectly audible voice as they passed by him in his black robe. 'Those who bow first to the citizens are in debt; those who bow first to us are at law!'

At the great West Door of St. Paul's Cathedral, the Queen dismounted from her chariot throne, and while she was being received by the Bishop of London, the Dean and fifty other clergy in their fine embroidered vestments, the Maids of Honour also dismounted and arranged themselves in a procession behind the Queen.

The Marchioness of Winchester carried Her Majesty's train, and as she moved forward slowly, Lizbeth, looking up, saw that the banners and other trophies from the conquered Armada were hung in the Cathedral.

She meant to follow the service; but somehow after the cheering crowds that thronged the streets she found it

240

hard to listen to the choir chanting the Litany or to the Bishop of Salisbury's eloquent sermon. There was so much to see around her; and though she was ashamed of her lack of religious feeling, Lizbeth could not help watching the glittering, colourful congregation which seemed to have stepped straight from some pageant rather than to be real people being themselves.

She saw Lord Treasurer Burleigh, looking cautious and determined as was his wont, groaning with the gout, but wise in judgment and still capable of tremendous work. Her eyes flickered for a moment over Sir Francis Walsingham, a martyr to the stone, but his nature was as ardent and his grasp of affairs as cunning and brilliant as ever they had been. And then they came back nearer home to the Maids of Honour.

Lady Mary Howard audaciously was striving to catch the attention of the Earl of Essex. She had the merriest, prettiest and naughtiest face Lizbeth had ever seen; and though she had been such a short time at Whitehall, already she knew that Lady Mary was invariably in trouble with the Queen and that her attempts to flirt with the new favourite boded ill for her future.

And yet Lizbeth loved Lady Mary. She had been sitting alone, looking out at the river on that first afternoon after her arrival from Camfield, when Lady Mary peeped round the door and with what seemed to Lizbeth a cry of delight ran across the room to welcome her.

From that moment Lizbeth found it almost impossible to be sad or depressed. It was Lady Mary who told her what her duties were and made them sound so amusing that Lizbeth found herself laughing helplessly. It was a state she found herself in continually for the next forty-eight hours, for the Queen's Maids of Honour were a gay, irresponsible, noisy lot of young women who, it appeared, were continuously at war with the gentlemen of Her Majesty's Household.

They slept, Lizbeth found to her surprise, all together in a long room opening out of the room to which she had been shown on arrival and which was used as their private

241

sitting-room. When she expressed her surprise at their living as it were in a dormitory, Lady Mary had laughed.

'Her Majesty imagines that it keeps us out of mischief,' she said; but the look on her face told Lizbeth that Lady Mary at any rate found ways to circumvent the Queen's pious hope.

Lizbeth had her first experience that very evening of the bad reputation into which the Maids of Honour had got themselves. After they had retired for the night, they were chattering loudly together and two of the girls were showing Lizbeth the latest dances when the door opened and Sir Francis Knowles, a learned old soldier, marched into the room and berated them soundly. He was in déshabillé with a big book in his hand and a pair of spectacles on his nose, and it was impossible not to giggle as he marched up and down declaiming in Latin against their behaviour, which he said made it vain for him to attempt to sleep or study.

Some of the Maids of Honour who were half-undressed begged him to go away, but he swore he would not leave them in possession of their bedroom unless they permitted him to rest. It was only when they promised to be as quiet as possible that he finally retired.

There were always incidents of some sort happening, Lizbeth discovered, and it was not surprising that the Maids of Honour found plenty to make them laugh. They were, however, all desperately afraid of the Queen and Lizbeth could well understand it when she was brought into the Royal presence.

It was impossible to believe, when one looked at her, that the Queen was fifty-five years of age. With her great farthingale spread out about her, a bodice of blue and silver with an open throat, slashed and puffed sleeves sewn with pearls the size of birds' eggs, she looked not only regal but beautiful.

As Lizbeth curtsied low, everything she had heard and learned about the Queen seemed unimportant save this amazing air of dignity and attraction intermingled one with the other so that it was hard to know where the

Sovereign ended and the woman began.

For the first time Lizbeth could understand how the Queen's influence had extended and made itself felt over the whole world. She could realise why men were willing to strive and fight and die for Elizabeth of England, and why she was utterly and completely incomprehensible to the peoples of other nations.

Lizbeth, as she swept to the ground, remembered the throb in Rodney's voice as he spoke of Gloriana; and now she saw, as other people had seen before her, how the Queen, so intelligent, so effervescent, imperious and regal, intoxicated both the Court and the country, and guided the realm with the intensity of her own spirit.

No one but a woman could have done it, and no woman without superlative gifts.

Late that evening, as Lizbeth stood watching the dancing, Sir Christopher Hatton, the Lord Chancellor, came to her side and asked her how she had fared her first day at Court. This question took Lizbeth unawares and for a moment she could only stammer her reply.

'Tis all so amazing,' she said, 'and . . . and . . . the Queen. . . .'

Sir Christopher smiled.

'The Queen does fish for men's souls,' he said, 'and has so sweet a bait that no one can escape her net.'

Lizbeth had known what he meant, and in the days that followed she knew that her own soul had been caught in Elizabeth's net. The Queen's virtues were extolled whenever her name was spoken, but perhaps her Maids of Honour saw her in a different light from other people.

To them she was always letting impulse break through the regal formalities of the Court. She could be sweet and gentle and tender, although a second later she would be berating the same person with a fury and anger that was like a summer thunderstorm. Tears followed smiles and yet the smiles would come again as quickly as they had been extinguished.

Yet even when she was angry, Lizbeth thought, the Queen never lost her regal dignity. Today in white on the

243

gold throne she appeared like a goddess, and it was easy to understand why every man's heart, whether he was young as the Earl of Essex or as old as Sir Francis Walsingham, beat the faster because they were near her.

The Earl seemed to Lizbeth to swing between fiery vigour and sulky lassitude, and yet everyone at the Court admired him and the Queen seemed, when he was not there, to yearn for his fresh, gay youth.

All the Maids of Honour were in love with someone. Lady Mary Howard daringly with the young Earl, Elizabeth Throgmorton, whose blue eyes and gold hair reminded Lizbeth of Phillida, dreamed and yearned for Sir Walter Raleigh. There were others who fancied the haughty Earl of Southampton, the tall and graceful Sir Charles Blount, another of the Queen's favourites, or her god-son, Sir John Harrington.

'You will be in love with someone before you have been here a week,' Lady Mary threatened.

Lizbeth gave her no confidences, knowing that none of these young men, however fine, however distinguished, could compare in her own mind with Rodney. And it was impossible for her not to think of him almost every minute and every second of the twenty-four hours.

Ballads and music played during the Queen's banquets spoke always of love. When Her Majesty dined in private, she would listen to songs which invariably seemed to arouse the most tender emotion in those who heard them. Indeed, the whole place, old and grey as might be its walls, seemed a fitting setting for the splendid men and the lovely women who moved there, with Cupid loosing his arrows from behind every pillar.

The Company was rising now to leave the Cathedral. Lizbeth collected her wandering thoughts and took her place amongst the other Maids as they moved in procession slowly down the aisle. The Queen was to proceed to the Bishop of London's Palace to dine, after which they would return through the streets in the same order as before, but by the light of torches.

As they came from the Cathedral, people were shouting:

'God save Your Majesty.'

The Queen, smiling and waving to them, replied:

'God bless you all, my good people.'

There was a great roar at the sound of her words and then in a clear voice the Queen said:

'You may well have a greater Prince, but you shall never have a more loving Prince.'

There was a full-throated roar at this and suddenly Lizbeth found that her eyes were wet. The Queen always seemed to say the right thing at the right moment, she thought, and those words would be remembered for ever by everyone who had been present that day.

The banquet which followed was impressive, but as Lady Mary said with a little grimace:

'Once you've been to one banquet, you find that all the others are much of a muchness.'

There was music and a great deal of talk before finally they started on their homeward journey. Once again Lizbeth had trouble with her horse, for the torches blowing in the wind caused him to shy. Several times the other Maids of Honour told her to be more careful as she bumped into them.

At length they came to Whitehall, the Queen dismounted and her ladies followed her into the Palace. Lizbeth saw Sir Francis Walsingham detach himself from the other gentlemen of the household and step forward to greet someone who was standing waiting for them in the high entrance Hall.

She had one look, then felt her heart begin to throb madly. It was Rodney who stood there, Rodney more richly garbed than she had ever seen him, in velvet and lace, and his jewelled buttons flashed as he moved forward to be presented to the Queen; and now in a daze Lizbeth found herself following the rest of the Court to the Long Gallery where the Queen liked to sit in the evenings. When the candles were lit in the great silver sconces, the whole gallery seemed to sparkle and glitter as if it were bejewelled.

Lizbeth hardly dared to look at Rodney for fear her

eyes would betray her secret to him once and for all. But he was not looking for her; his eyes were on the Queen, and Her Majesty was being exceedingly gracious talking with him; and though Lizbeth could not hear what they said, she guessed that they spoke of his voyage and of the great cargo he had brought back with him. Then, as she watched, Rodney went down on one knee and placed a small casket in the Queen's hand. She accepted it from him and as she opened the lid and looked inside, Lizbeth knew what lay there.

It was pearls from the pearling lugger, she was certain of that, and she guessed now that Rodney had meant the Queen to have them from the very first moment they had been found beneath the floor-boards of the Captain's cabin. They were indeed a gift worthy of Gloriana. Then, as Lizbeth watched, standing a little to one side in the humblest position as became the youngest and least-important Maid of Honour, she heard the Queen tell Lord Burleigh to bring her a sword, and despite herself, Lizbeth drew a deep and audible breath of excitement.

Rodney knelt and the Queen laid the gold sword on his shoulder and bade him rise. It was with difficulty then that Lizbeth prevented herself from rushing forward and being the first to congratulate him, telling him how proud she was and how she had always known that her faith in him was justified. Instead, she must stand still, her hands clasped together so tightly that her knuckles showed white.

Sir Rodney Hawkhurst! She wanted to cry the words aloud, but at that moment she saw the Queen was retiring for the night and that she must follow in the wake of the Marchioness of Winchester and the Countess of Warwick who were already accompanying Her Majesty down the Gallery.

The gentlemen were standing aside and Lizbeth realised that she would have to pass close to Rodney and it would be impossible for him not to see her. His face was alight; she saw by his expression that he was thrilled with the honour that had been accorded him; then his eyes met hers and for a moment everything was forgotten. Lizbeth was not aware that she was still walking forward, she felt that for one moment there was nobody in the Long Gallery save herself and Rodney and that they reached out their arms to each other.

Then the moment passed and she found him bowing over her hand and she was curtseying to him.

'Meet me in the Great Hall as soon as you can,' he said in a voice so low that she could barely hear it. 'I must see you.'

She had no time to answer him—in fact she was far too frightened to say anything. Already she was behind the other Maids of Honour, and now she scurried after them, wondering if anyone could have overheard what Rodney said to her.

It was not going to be easy to meet him, she knew that, yet not for one moment did she think of disobeying his command. Somehow it must be managed, and she felt that the only thing to do was not to retire to the bedchamber with the others, but to hide herself so that they might think that the Queen had kept her or that she had been sent on an errand by one of the Ladies of the Bedchamber.

So she moved with the others towards the Queen's apartments where Her Majesty turned to bid them goodnight.

'It has been a great day,' the Queen said, 'and one we shall always remember. We must give thanks to God.'

'Yes, Ma'am.'

There was a little chorus of assent as the ladies sank in a low obeisance.

'A great day,' the Queen repeated, almost to herself. Then with a flash of mischief in her eyes she added, *'Dux femina facti.'*

There was a little ripple of laughter and Lizbeth, who knew the words meant 'It was done by a woman', remembered that they had been inscribed on some of the medals struck in commemoration of the victory over the Armada.

The Queen then withdrew into the inner room, followed by the Ladies of the Bedchamber.

As soon as she was out of sight, the Maids of Honour began to chatter and gossip among themselves and this was Lizbeth's opportunity. The corridor was full of shadows. She slipped behind a pillar and waited till the voices had almost died away, then sped towards the stairs.

The Yeomen of the Guard looked at her in surprise as she passed, but it was not their business to enquire what she was doing alone at this time of night; the grooms and pages in their broidered coats of Venice gold were yawning as they wandered away to their own quarters, tired after the long hours of duty.

Lizbeth was afraid she might meet some of the older Ladies-in-Waiting; but in this she was fortunate and she reached the Hall to find no one there save Rodney standing alone, his jewelled buttons sparkling in the firelight. Lizbeth ran to him impulsively. It was hard to remember at that moment to keep a rigid control upon herself, to think of Phillida, to know that she must not betray the secret of her own heart.

'Rodney, I am so proud.'

The words came unrestrainedly from her lips.

'I'm glad you were there,' he said. 'In truth, you should have shared it with me.'

He looked at her as he spoke and she felt there was some meaning in his voice which she did not understand. Then, hastily, as if he recalled something of importance to his mind, he said:

'Come, there is someone waiting to see you outside.'

'Outside?' Lizbeth echoed in astonishment.

Rodney nodded; then swinging his embroidered velvet cape from his shoulders he placed it on hers.

'Twill be cold,' he said, 'but you need not stay long.'

'But who is there?' Lizbeth asked.

If it had not been Rodney, she would have refused to go outside at this hour of night in her richest gown, with jewels around her neck and in her ears, which might attract the attention of footpads and robbers.

'Come, do not be afraid,' Rodney reassured her.

And now, his cloak warmly round her shoulders, she let him lead her past the sentries at the door. There were several horses standing in the courtyard and even in the dim light of the lanterns Lizbeth recognised a chestnut mare. She gave an exclamation which turned to a cry of sheer surprise as she saw who rode her; and then as she ran down the steps, Phillida dismounted and came to meet her.

'Phillida, what does this mean?'

Lizbeth's surprise was mingled with the sudden thought that Rodney and Phillida were married. That must be why they were here. They had ridden together from Camfield and there could be no other explanation of Phillida's presence; and then, as she felt herself grow cold, she knew that it came not from the clear frosted air, but from the sudden sinking of her spirits.

Phillida bent to kiss her and drew her aside so that they were out of earshot of the grooms and sentries.

'I had to see you, little Lizbeth,' she said, and as she spoke Lizbeth saw her face and knew that she was happy.

She tried to repress the pang of jealousy that shot through her as with lips suddenly dry she asked:

'You are married—you and Rodney?'

'No, indeed!' Phillida's response was quick and joyous. 'It is other news I have for you, Lizbeth, news so wonderful, so unexpected that even now I can hardly believe it is true.'

Lizbeth felt she had never seen her half-sister like this before, talking excitedly, with a flush on her cheeks that were usually so pale.

'Tell me,' Lizbeth pleaded, 'tell me quickly.'

'It is Rodney who has arranged everything for me,' Philida answered. 'I am leaving for France tonight. I go to Havre, to enter the Convent of *Notre Dame de Consolation.*'

'To a Convent?' Lizbeth found it hard to say the words.

'Yes, indeed, and Rodney has arranged everything for me.'

Phillida's eyes dropped in sudden embarrassment and Lizbeth knew, without being told, that Rodney had arranged not only to send her to France, but to give her the dowry which would ensure her entrance into the Convent.

'How has he managed this? Are you sure you will be accepted?' Lizbeth asked, bewildered; and Rodney answered the questions from behind her.

''Twas not as hard as it appears. She will be welcomed, I can stake my oath on it, for my sister is the Reverend Mother of the Convent to which she travels.'

'Your sister—and a Catholic!' Lizbeth ejaculated.

Rodney looked uncomfortable for the moment.

'Faith, I warrant 'tis not a thing a man would talk about unnecessarily,' he replied.

Lizbeth laughed at that. It was so funny that she should have been hiding the truth from Rodney about Phillida and he was keeping secret the fact that his sister was also a Catholic, and a Reverend Mother at that.

'My sister is much older than I am,' he said, as if somehow that made the situation better.

'I told Rodney the truth,' Phillida was saying contentedly, 'and then everything was easy. He promised to help me. How can I ever be grateful enough?'

'By coming away now, at once,' Rodney replied. 'We must not linger here. Lizbeth might get into trouble, and your ship sails on the dawn tide.'

'I will come at once,' Phillida answered.

She bent down and put her arms round Lizbeth.

'Good-bye, little sister,' she said, 'we may never meet again, but I am happy, remember that, always. I am happy.'

'That is what matters,' Lizbeth said; 'and oh, Phillida, I am so glad for you.'

Phillida's cheek was against hers; it was cool and soft, and she whispered very low so that only Lizbeth could hear:

250

'You love him, I know that; I saw it in your eyes the night that he arrived at Camfield. I shall pray that you will find happiness together.'

Lizbeth could not find words to answer her. She hugged her closely. Then Rodney swung Phillida up into the saddle and they were on the move, their horses' hoofs clattering over the cobbled yard.

It was only when they were gone that Lizbeth realised that she still wore Rodney's cloak about her shoulders. She went back into the Palace, took it off and held it gently in her hands, before with a sudden passion, she cradled it against her breast. It was his, a part of him, he had worn it. She pressed her lips against the soft material. She loved him and now miraculously he was free—but she was not certain that he would come to her.

She hid the cloak in a chest in her room and found that fortunately her absence had gone practically unnoticed. The Maids of Honour were talking too excitedly of what had happened during the day. Only Elizabeth Throgmorton was silent with a dreamy look in her soft blue eyes as she sat on her bed thinking of Sir Walter.

'I shall win my Lord Essex from the Queen, what do you wager me?' Lady Mary was asking, her face sparkling with mischief, as Lizbeth crossed the room.

'How can you dare say such a thing aloud?' one of the Maids of Honour asked. 'The Queen will send you to the Tower if you so much as look at him.'

'I shall do a great deal more than look,' Lady Mary threatened.

The others cried out at that, telling her she was crazed; but she only laughed at them and flung herself down on her bed, lying with her arms crossed behind her head.

'The Queen is old,' she announced. 'Do you realise that we shall grow old, too? Why should we waste our youth and our beauty and all the love which lies within our hearts?'

'You will not live to grow old if the Queen hears you,' someone threatened.

'I do not think that I care one way or another,' Lady

Mary replied. 'Old age is horrible! It will mean that we shall have to dye our hair; our teeth will decay and grow black; we shall feel all the pains of hell in our withered bodies. We shall have to rest—rest! when we might be dancing or riding or running hand in hand through the gardens with someone we love.'

'Be quiet. You make me depressed.'

It was Elizabeth Throgmorton who spoke for the first time, a look of fear on her lovely face as if she knew the years were passing by and she might never win the man she loved so dearly.

''Tis true,' Lady Mary replied stubbornly.

Lizbeth could listen to no more of their chatter. It was true, as Lady Mary had inferred, that the Queen's hair was dyed and her teeth black; yet she could inspire such men as Drake, Raleigh and Rodney to great deeds, to a devotion which was expressed in that they served her not only with their bodies and their minds, but with their very hearts and souls. What more could any woman ask? It was not youth that mattered; it was something greater and more important than the counting of years.

She did not sleep for a long time. When she awoke, it was only just dawn and a pale light was coming like a grey ghost through the sides of the curtains. The other Maids of Honour were all still asleep, and as she lay there and listened to their gentle breathing Lizbeth suddenly felt a yearning for the open air of the countryside, for the wind blowing up the valley at Camfield, for the frost lying white on the grass of the parkland.

She rose softly from her bed and slipping into the other room, sent the maid who was on duty in search of Nanna. The old woman came hurrying. Lizbeth commanded her riding habit and sent a message below that she required her horse immediately.

'You should not be going out as early as this,' Nanna said scoldingly. ''Tis all very well for you to indulge your fads and fancies at Camfield, but Her Majesty will not allow it at Whitehall.'

'I want to breathe,' Lizbeth said.

Grumbling and protesting Nanna brought her riding habit and plumed hat; and when at length she was ready, Lizbeth looked at the river through the window and saw that the early sun was dispersing the silver mists. It was cold, but there was an invigorating crispness in the air and the frost brought the colour to her cheeks as she guided her horse through the narrow streets until she reached the Park.

There was a beauty she did not expect in the leafless branches of the trees silhouetted against the pale sky. In the distance the Serpentine gleamed silver as the lake at Camfield might have done. There was the smell of autumn on the air, the aroma of rotting leaves and the faint acrid smoke of the woodcutter's fire.

Her horse was fresh and Lizbeth gave him his head. Soon she had left the groom far behind and was alone, forgetting convention and formality and everything except the joy of feeling herself move in one accord with the great animal on whose back she sat.

And then, as if this moment had been predestined from the beginning of their lives, as if everything they had thought and done led to this moment, she saw Rodney come riding towards her through the trees. The sunshine was on her face as she greeted him, not in words, but with a sudden glory in her eyes and the parting of her lips.

He reined in his horse beside hers. For a moment neither of them spoke. The animals, spirited though they were, seemed suddenly to grow quiet as if they were waiting for the drama to unfold and for the climax of the play to be reached.

'Lizbeth . . .' Rodney began, but as he looked into her eyes, he forgot what he was going to say. 'I love you . . .' he stammered. 'I adore you . . . I worship you, I did not realise until you left me. I did not know until my life was empty without you how much you meant and how little I could do without you.'

Lizbeth thought then as she listened that she must be dreaming. For one wild moment she believed she would wake up and find herself in bed, not at Camfield or at Whitehall, but aboard the *Santa Perpetua*. It was for this she had yearned for so long, aching to hear this note in Rodney's voice, to see this look in his eyes.

It was true! With a little incoherent murmur she put out her hand towards him. He drew the glove from her fingers and, turning her hand over in his, raised it to his lips and kissed the soft palm with lips which bespoke his passion without words.

She felt a quiver and a thrill go through her. She felt herself tremble. Suddenly the whole world was too dazzling, too golden to be borne.

'I love you,' Rodney said again, his voice low and deep with emotion.

Vaguely and like an echo she seemed to hear another voice saying the same thing, and then everything was forgotten in the knowledge that Rodney was here beside her and her love for him was welling up within her like a flood-tide which could not be denied.

His hold tightened on her hand, and now, skilful in horsemanship as in everything else, he moved close beside her so that he could reach out and put his arm round her waist. She felt him draw her near to him. Her face was upturned to his, her lips waiting to be surrendered.

Swiftly to her mind came the thought that this was the beginning. There was much ahead of them both, so many adventures, so many marvels, so much glory to be striven for and achieved. Then, masterfully and with a sudden passion that would not be denied, Rodney held her against his heart.

'You are mine,' he cried, 'and I will never let you go again.'

She looked up at him and it seemed to her as if every different facet of his character was there in his expression. She saw the reverence and adoration which he offered the Queen, the grim determination he showed to the Spaniards, the mercifulness he offered the ill-treated natives, the hatred of Don Miguel which had frightened her in its intensity, and a new and strange emotion which she did not recognise.

For a moment she thought it was courage—that shining, brilliant courage which was to her characteristic of everything Rodney thought and did, and then she knew it for an expression of love.

Rodney loved her, and everything he was and would be he laid at her feet. Lizbeth could hear the thumping of her heart, her whole being was a-thrill. Breathlessly she parted her lips, but before she could speak Rodney's mouth was on hers. She felt the world whirl round her—this was life, this was living, this was an adventure more poignant, more marvellous than any she had experienced before.

She knew then that Rodney's heart was hers for ever and for all time—but he was still dedicated to Gloriana. As Lizbeth thought of the Queen she felt one last fleeting pang of jealousy, then Rodney's voice, low, broken and deeply moved, whispered:

'My little love, my sweet, my beloved!'

She felt his lips drawing her very soul from her body and with a sob of sheer, untrammelled happiness, she surrendered herself unreservedly to her lover's kiss—her Elizabethan lover!

If you would like a complete list of Arrow books please send a postcard to P.O. Box 29, Douglas, Isle of Man, Great Britain.